## "So I am a already dama

"Don't ever let me hear you say that again."

At the thunder in his voice, Iantha jumped and stepped hastily back. His lordship did not move, but his voice softened. "Forgive me. I did not mean to shout. But I am serious, Iantha. Do not allow them the victory of seeing yourself that way. Do not allow *anyone* to do that to you."

Iantha stared down at her shoes. He was right, of course. "I try not to, but it is very hard."

"I'm sure it is." She sensed him reaching for her, then dropping his hand to his side. She didn't know whether to be glad or sorry that he hadn't touched her. Perhaps he didn't want to. She lifted her gaze to his. The expression in his eyes surprised her.

There was a *wanting* in them.

Could he possibly really *want* her?

\* \* \*

***A Scandalous Situation***
**Harlequin Historical #716—August 2004**

# PATRICIA FRANCES ROWELL

# A SCANDALOUS SITUATION

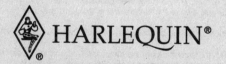

## HARLEQUIN®

TORONTO • NEW YORK • LONDON
AMSTERDAM • PARIS • SYDNEY • HAMBURG
STOCKHOLM • ATHENS • TOKYO • MILAN • MADRID
PRAGUE • WARSAW • BUDAPEST • AUCKLAND

ISBN 0-373-29316-X

A SCANDALOUS SITUATION

Copyright © 2004 by Patricia Frances Rowell

This edition published by arrangement with Harlequin Books S.A.

® and TM are trademarks of the publisher. Trademarks indicated with ® are registered in the United States Patent and Trademark Office, the Canadian Trade Marks Office and in other countries.

www.eHarlequin.com

**Printed in U.S.A.**

Please address questions and book requests to:
Harlequin Reader Service
U.S.: 3010 Walden Ave., P.O. Box 1325, Buffalo, NY 14269
Canadian: P.O. Box 609, Fort Erie, Ont. L2A 5X3

This book is for my talented sons—
Andrew Nathaniel, James Houghton and
John Adam Annand. We grew up together, didn't we, guys?

And for grandchildren Amber Niccole
(because I spelled her name wrong the last time) and
Aidan Thomas (because we didn't have him the last time).

And for Johnny—always my hero.

ACKNOWLEDGMENT
My thanks to Paul D. Ware, M.D., and Jean Cason, MSW,
who taught me how people recover from trauma,
and many other important life lessons.

# Prologue

*Just North of London, 1801*

I must be dying.

She could no longer feel the pain.

Then again, perhaps the agony had simply increased to the point of numbness as she lay on the frozen ground, drifting in and out of the blackness.

Death would be better.

They were still there. She heard them moving about.

And she smelled them. A strange smoke. The odor of nervous and excited men.

She fought to control a shudder.

She must not move, not even breathe.

Perhaps they would believe she *was* dead. Oh, God, please let them believe that! Let it be so. Then surely they would not do it again.

Against the background of her closed eyes distorted images swirled. Heads swathed in crimson masks. Eyes glittering through the eyeholes. Hot breath pouring through the mouth openings. Gleaming blades.

Pain. Pain everywhere.

Mask after mask after mask.

The blackness sought her. She reached for it, welcoming it. Suddenly a loud, braying laugh, the sound of a hand striking flesh and an angry, hissed whisper snatched it away.

"Quiet, fool!"

She held her breath. The creak of leather. Horses galloping away. Empty silence.

The smell of blood. The cold.

And blackness.

# Chapter One

*Cumberland, England, 1807*

Careful not to move, he sat astride his bay stallion with his hands in the air and concentrated on the pistol pointed at his heart. A pistol held in the steady, gloved hands of a lady. Not a large lady, true. Dainty, rather, and delicate. But a lady wearing a very determined expression.

He could probably disarm her. Probably. A sudden charge. A quick grab. It would work. Probably. Of course, he always stood the chance of getting either himself or his horse shot. Robert Armstrong was not a man who liked *probably*. Not with a pistol leveled at his chest. No, for the moment discretion definitely appeared to be the better part of valor. He did his best to sound soothing.

"Ma'am, I assure you I mean you no harm. If you do not allow me to get down and help you free your horse, the next mass of snow that slides down that mountain will bury not only your gig, but you and the horse as well."

As if to punctuate his words, a small cascade of frozen chunks tumbled down the hill and landed at the feet of the very determined pistol-pointing lady. She flung a quick glance upward, then steadied the pistol. "I fear you are correct. Your assistance would be most welcome. You may dismount."

Rob raised one sardonic eyebrow. "Much obliged to you."

Feeling not at all welcome, he swung himself down from his mount and waded through the deep snow to the overturned conveyance. The woman stepped away cautiously, keeping the pistol trained on his back. A spot between his shoulder blades began to itch. He shrugged uneasily. Surely she wouldn't shoot him in the back while he was extricating her from her predicament.

Would she?

Murmuring softly to the frantic cob, still harnessed to the gig trying desperately to keep his feet, Rob took hold of its bridle and surveyed the situation. The small snow-slide had knocked the carriage into the drifts on the far side of the road, turning it half on its side and all but engulfing it. The very determined lady could count herself fortunate indeed to have been thrown clear. The far shaft had broken free of the body of the gig, and the off-balance horse had stepped over it with a hind leg, thus jamming itself firmly between the splintered stub and the near shaft.

"Got yourself into the very devil of a scrape, haven't you, old fellow? We'd best get you out before you're much older, or I'm likely to find myself in the same case."

Rob studied the hillside above him with narrowed eyes. Not very high, but very steep and almost devoid of vegetation, the escarpment was crowned by a long, sheer rock precipice. The surprisingly mild day had softened the snow, causing the slide, but soon it would freeze solid once more. He could feel the temperature dropping. The rising wind blew sparkling flurries from the crest against a mounting backdrop of blue-gray clouds. Another storm. Matters were going from bad to worse.

At any moment the wind might trigger another small avalanche. Rob pulled the knife out of the top of his boot. At a sharp hiss of indrawn breath behind him, he looked over his shoulder.

"What are you doing?" The lady's already pale face had gone deathly white. The previously steady hands that held the pistol now trembled. Not a good sign.

Rob straightened and frowned. "Ma'am, please. Lower your weapon. I have no wish to end this misadventure with a bullet lodged in me. I must cut the straps loose from the shafts, and I have no time to waste dealing with frozen buckles."

"I…" She took a deep breath and stilled her shaking. The pistol wavered, finally pointed at the ground. "Yes, of course. Please proceed."

Rolling his eyes skyward, Rob went back to his task. What ailed the woman? Fear was writ in every tense line of her slender body, her clenched hands, her taut face. Surely he had done nothing to inspire it? Except… Yes, he had drawn his knife. Until that moment she had been merely wary, but now she looked terrified. Why?

Tabling that question for a more opportune moment, Rob turned back to the task of calming the small horse and delivering it from its entanglement. This he accomplished with a few efficient strokes of his blade. Pausing only long enough to sheath the knife and pick up the handle of a rectangular leather case that had spilled out of the gig, he led the badly limping cob toward its mistress.

"I'm afraid your horse has strained a tendon. He will not be able…"

A deep rumble and a faint vibration of the earth were all the warning he had. Rob dropped the reins of the cob and launched himself at the woman. Neither thinking nor pausing, he scooped her up across his shoulder and ran, his powerful legs slicing through the soft snow. The pistol went flying and discharged with a loud crack. Both horses galloped ahead of him, whinnying in fright. A wall of rocks, earth and half-frozen snow roared down the slope, picking up speed as it came. Rob doubled his effort, desperately traversing the hillside, trying to get them out of the main path of the slide.

Suddenly, he tripped, and both of them went sprawling.

He flung himself over the woman, trying to hold the leather case over his own head. A rock struck it and bounced away. Another. A clod of dirt and ice hit his shoulder and icy slush filled his boot and trickled inside his collar. Great God! Were they buried?

Time seemed to stretch interminably as the roaring mass came ever closer. Then, as suddenly as it had begun, the roar came to an abrupt halt. Near panic, Rob thrust himself upward. To his untold relief his head and upper body emerged into a startling silence. Carefully he sat up and looked around him.

And shuddered.

He lay just beyond the edge of a huge pile of debris that now filled a section of the shallow valley. The overturned gig could no longer be seen at all. The road disappeared under the heap of snow and dirt. Rob pulled his leg free of the mass and turned to the still-recumbent lady. "Ma'am, are you hurt?"

She lay as if frozen, her eyes tightly shut, her skin

completely devoid of color. For the first time Rob had the opportunity for a close look. She was younger than he had thought. The silvery hair peeping from under the hood of her ermine coat had misled him. She had the unlined face of a very young woman, no older, surely, than her mid-twenties. She didn't move.

"Miss? Miss!" Alarmed now by her pallor, he shook her shoulder gently. Had he knocked the breath out of her? "Miss, can you speak?"

Her eyelids fluttered and Rob found himself staring into eyes as deep a violet as the mountain sky. Their clarity took his breath away. And his voice. "Uh... Uh, miss..." He cleared his throat. "Are you injured?"

She took a long breath and swallowed. "No... No, I do not believe I am."

She struggled to sit and Rob quickly got to one knee and offered his hand. She regarded it gravely for a moment, then put her fingers in his and allowed herself to be pulled to her feet as he stood. She glanced about, looking bewildered. "What happened to my carriage?"

"I'm afraid it is now completely buried."

"And my pistol?"

Rob shrugged. Just as well to see the last of the pistol. "I have no idea." He stamped the snow from his boots and brushed it off his clothes, gazing around for the horses. "But I believe it is best that we make haste away from here."

"But where...?" The lady turned in a circle, searching the buried road. The strengthening wind molded her damp coat to her slight frame, and she shivered. A few flakes of fresh snow danced around her.

"My home is there, atop the cliff." Rob indicated, a little distance away, the outline of an old fortress against the growing clouds.

The lady's eyes widened. "The Eyrie? I thought it un-occupied."

"It has been for some years. I have just recently re-turned from India. I'm Robert Armstrong."

"Baron Duncan?"

"The same."

"I see. I…" She lifted her chin proudly. "I am Iantha Kethley." She did not offer her hand.

Nor did she smile.

Ah, well. Not exactly the reward the gallant rescuer of a beautiful maiden in distress might wish for. At least, she might be a beautiful maiden had she deigned to smile.

Whistling for his bay, he retrieved the cob from where it stood forlornly a few yards away and ran his hand expertly down its leg. "We will both have to use my horse. Your poor pony is considerably the worse for two narrow escapes. Let me mount first, and I will lift you up before me."

"Uh…" The fear flickered once more in those re-markable eyes. "No. That is… I prefer to ride behind you. I will mount first."

"But the road is very steep. You will likely slide off. It would be far safer—"

"I will ride behind." Her lifted chin took on a stub-born tilt.

Rob sighed. "As you wish. We have no time for ar-gument." He glanced at the lowering sky and got a face full of snow for his trouble. "Whatever we do, we'd best do it soon. That storm will be upon us in earnest very shortly."

As he was about to lift her, she stopped him again, backing away from him. "My paints." She pointed to the leather case. "I will carry them."

"Your paints?" Rob smothered a snort of exasperation. "Very well. As soon as you are seated." He caught her before she could make yet another objection, his broad hands all but encompassing her fragile waist. She seemed almost to float upward as he set her sideways behind the saddle. Handing up the case when she had settled herself, he gathered up the cob's reins and mounted his own horse awkwardly, swinging his foot over the animal's head. The bay sidled, signaling his annoyance at this unorthodox procedure.

Rob settled into the saddle, only to be jabbed between the shoulder blades by something sharp. Now what? Turning, he realized that his damsel in distress had placed the paint case between herself and his sturdy back and was trying to hold on to him around it. That was the outside of enough!

"Give me that!" He unceremoniously yanked the case out of her grasp and balanced it across the saddle in front of him with one hand. "Now hold on to me. We have no time for this nonsense."

Urging his mount across the escarpment below the towering cliff, Rob made for the old castle by the shortest route. The wind howled around them now, the snow blowing sideways, stinging their faces. More drifts were already forming across what was left of the road below them in the valley. It would be of no further use to them, but his path would take them directly to the trail that led up to his home. His bay might have made short work of the trip had not the lame cob held him back, but they should still safely reach shelter.

As the laboring horses struggled up a sharp incline, Rob heard a strangled squeak, and the small arms around his waist abruptly disappeared. The bay reared slightly as his load shifted. Rob steadied him and looked back in alarm to see his passenger sitting in the snow, legs stretched before her and her skirts above her knees, exposing white leather knee boots.

And another pistol strapped to the top of one boot.

Great heavens, the woman went about armed to the teeth!

To his relief she looked startled, but not stunned. She scrambled hastily to her feet and came to where Rob waited aboard his mount, nobly forbearing to say *I told you so.* She at least had the grace to appear chagrined, two rosy spots coloring her cheeks. He extended a hand. "Put your foot on top of mine and push as I lift you."

She obeyed this command without a word and, giving her the paint case to hold, Rob pulled her up into his arms and set her in front of him. His arm tightened around her waist as he dug his heels into the bay's sides. Immediately her whole body went stiff. He frowned, puzzled. What was wrong with her? It wasn't as though he were kidnapping her. He was rescuing her, for God's sake!

He pulled the horse in. "Miss Kethley." She did not respond. He couldn't see her face. She set it resolutely ahead, like a prisoner going bravely to meet her fate. He grasped her chin and turned her toward him. He gazed into her face, baffled.

"Miss Kethley, please tell me what I have done to offend you so." She shook her head, opened her mouth to speak, and closed it again. "Have I offered you any harm, any insult?"

She swallowed and shook her head. "N..." She moistened her lips and tried again. "N-no."

"Nor will I."

Rob shut his mouth grimly and set off up the mountain.

As they made their way up the slope, Iantha sat in the shelter of the baron's body and willed herself to think, to remain calm. She *would* control her fear. The man had done nothing to provoke it. He had done nothing but what was right and proper—gallant even. Yet when he had fallen across her, she had thought her heart would stop. Even the roar of the snowslide had been drowned out by the roaring inside her mind; the fear of being buried alive paled beside the fear engendered by the weight of his body on top of hers.

If only she could banish those hateful images from her mind, she would feel relieved that she no longer had to fight every moment to keep her seat. And with her rescuer's bulk blocking the wind and snow, the cold didn't bite into her as it had been doing. Even so, her fingers felt frozen to the handle of her paint case, and she could no longer feel her toes.

Sitting thus, she realized that his lordship was much taller than he had seemed when he'd stood some distance away. The breadth of his muscular shoulders had made him appear much shorter. He was a big man. Strong. Yet, she reminded herself, he had used his strength only to aid her. She must think about that. Use it to bridle her rebelling emotions.

Control. Control was her fortress.

She *would* maintain control.

Just when Iantha thought the cold and the wind blasting along the escarpment would go on forever, they encountered the road that ran between the valley and the castle. Several switchbacks later they found themselves in the enveloping silence and welcome warmth of a large stone stable. Iantha straightened her aching shoulders and looked about. A stockily built groom with grizzled hair was hurrying toward them.

"Me lord! You're home safe at last. Burnside and me

was just debating should we mount a search.'' He reached up, squinting at her, and took the paint case out of Iantha's stiff fingers. ''And who might we have here?''

Setting the case on the ground, he lifted his arms again, and Iantha slid off the saddle into them. He put her down, careful to keep a steadying hand on her arm. It was well that he did. Her half-frozen feet and legs threatened to fail her. She took hold of the saddle with her other hand.

''Have you ever known me not to show up intact, Feller?'' His lordship swung himself down easily, smiling at the groom.

''Nay, me lord, saving that time in Orissa. You wasn't by no means intact on that occasion.'' Feller grinned. ''I told Burnside, I did, 'Just you watch. He'll turn up like a bad penny, he will.' And here you are.''

''And here I am,'' agreed his lordship. ''This lady is Miss Kethley. As you can see, she and her cob suffered a mishap on the road.''

''That I do see.'' Feller turned to examine the sturdy horse, frowning. ''Poor old mate here is a mite bunged up.''

He released Iantha's arm, moving to her horse. As he did, Iantha felt her knees give way and clutched again at the saddle.

''Careful, now!'' Lord Duncan stepped quickly to throw a supporting arm around her waist. ''Are you faint?''

''No.'' Iantha shook her head. ''Just cold and stiff. I will be fine in a minute.''

''Perhaps.'' He scowled doubtfully. ''Shall I carry you?''

''No!'' The denial emerged much more sharply than she had intended. ''I mean…thank you. That isn't necessary.''

"Let me help you, then." His lordship still looked doubtful. "We need to get you to a fire. We'll go up through the old castle, to avoid the wind." He tightened his arm around her and guided her toward a door at the side of the stable.

Close. He was much too close.

Iantha shut her eyes, drew in a long breath and forbade herself to pull away. If she did that, she would surely find herself sitting on the ground. She could endure his proximity for a few minutes.

Control.

He led her through the stable door and up a flight of steep spiral steps. At the top they wound through a series of short passages with narrow doors, each facing a different direction.

"This is the portal to the original castle," he explained. "The turns were designed to keep out an invading force. This section was abandoned long ago, but we still use it to come up from the stable when we wish to avoid the weather." They emerged from an empty stone chamber through a newer door into a wide entry hall. Lord Duncan removed his shallow-crowned hat and knocked the snow off it against his leg, revealing a thick thatch of rich brown curls.

"Here is the new building." He grinned. "Relatively speaking. The old part was built in the fourteenth century, the *new* part in the early 1600s. It is considerably more comfortable than the original structure ever was, although it does have its share of eccentricities." He tugged at a bell rope. "Burnside! Burnside, where are you?"

Iantha winced at the sudden shout. His lordship's vocal vigor, however, was rewarded by the prompt appearance of a wiry man of middle years.

"Aye, me lord?" The newcomer stopped abruptly at

the sight of Iantha and looked questioningly at Lord Duncan.

"Miss Kethley was caught in the storm and will be staying with us. Please ask Thursby to go and make up a fire in the dowager's bedchamber and fetch Miss Kethley some hot water."

"Oh. Aye, me lord, right away. There be a fire in the library now if Miss Kethley would like to…"

"Ah, very good." His lordship turned to Iantha. "May I help you with your coat?"

"Thank you." Iantha allowed him to remove the garment, using the opportunity to step away from his supporting arm. As the hood came off, she braced herself. But surely he was too much the gentleman to comment on her silvery hair.

And, of course, he was.

After assisting Lord Duncan off with his greatcoat, Burnside departed as quickly as he had come, taking the wet wraps with him. His lordship opened the door to a comfortable room off the entryway. Books lined the walls, and more books and scrolls lay in piles and in crates. Some of them displayed covers of soft leather with exotic art, but a few had no covers at all.

"Forgive my disorder. I am in the process of integrating my own collection with my father's library." He set a chair near the fireplace and ushered her to it.

"I have found many interesting volumes in the East, some of them very old. I have been studying the various languages in order to read the texts." He pulled up a chair for himself and sat, extending capable-looking hands to the fire.

Iantha clasped her own hands together in her lap and cleared her throat. "Lord Duncan, I feel I should say…

Please forgive me if I have seemed ungrateful for your help. I found the situation very…very disturbing.''

His lordship raised one eyebrow. "Apparently."

"I *am* appreciative. Truly I am." She looked into his face—which displayed a hint of a wry smile and a twinkle in his coffee-brown eyes. A very good-natured response, indeed, to what she'd put him through. "What I would have done had you not arrived when you did, I don't know. I had not realized that there was so much snow in the fells—and certainly not that another storm was brewing."

He nodded. "A deceptively mild day. I succumbed to the temptation to get outside myself. Very unusual to have so much snow this early in the year."

Iantha mustered a smile. "And I am *very* sorry to impose on you."

"Not a bit in the world, Miss Kethley. My only concern is for your comfort. This is a very awkward situation for you. I regret that I do not even have a housekeeper, let alone a maid, to assist you at present. I returned somewhat earlier than my agent expected, and he has not yet assembled a permanent staff. Fortunately, he had already ordered a thorough cleaning, so at least you will not be choked with dust, and there is food aplenty stored in the cellars." He turned as the door opened. "Yes, Burnside?"

"I thought the lady might be the better for a cup of tea." Burnside edged through the door and awkwardly set a large tray with teapot and cups on a table.

"Very well thought of. Thank you." Lord Duncan swiveled to face his henchman, grinning. "And what is offered for dinner? I'm expecting at least three courses."

Burnside winked at a very startled Iantha. "Me lord is only funning. He knows that from me he gets plain fare—

good hearty north country cooking with a few Indian tricks added in.'' He bowed to his employer, heading to the door. ''The fire is made upstairs, me lord, and hot water on the hob when Miss Kethley is ready.''

''Thank you. We will wait a bit until the room warms.'' Burnside departed and his lordship turned back to Iantha. ''Burnside's cooking is plain, as he said, but quite good. At least you won't starve.'' His lordship eyed the tea tray askance. ''Would you do me the favor of pouring, Miss Kethley? I'd very likely make a mull of it.''

What a strange establishment! Feeling a bit bewildered, Iantha picked up the pot. ''I'd be happy to. Milk?''

''No, thank you.''

She passed him the cup and poured one for herself. As they were treating the situation as a social occasion, and conversation was the inevitable accompaniment to tea, Iantha made a strong effort to marshal her thoughts. ''How long did you live in India, my lord?''

''Thirteen years.''

''With the East India Company?''

''No, I went as a private merchant. The Armstrong fortunes had fallen on hard times, and my father felt even going into trade justified by the circumstances.''

''I see.'' Iantha pondered this information as she sipped the warming tea. An unusual step for a nobleman, but better, no doubt, than genteel poverty. ''Did you not care for it there?''

''Oh, aye. It suited me very well. So much to see, to hear, to smell and touch.'' He smiled at her over his cup, eyes crinkling at the corners. He really had a very engaging smile. ''The Orient is a veritable feast for the senses. New foods, new textures, bright colors. More new

experiences every day than the English mind can con-
ceive.''

''But you came home.''

He stared into the fire for a heartbeat before looking
at her. ''One always wants to come home.''

Finding nothing to add to that, Iantha sipped in silence.
Lord Duncan drew a deep breath. ''There were other reasons, also.'' He paused, then went on, leaving Iantha with
the impression that he had left something unsaid. ''For
one, profit has become too dependent on the opium trade
with China. The East India Company holds the monopoly
on cultivation only in Bengal, but I could not stomach
selling it in any event. If you could but see the poor
devils... Er, excuse my language, but enslavement to
opium is indeed a damnable condition.'' He set down his
cup and stood. ''But I can bore on forever about India.
Have you finished your tea? I'll escort you upstairs.''

Iantha followed his example, and after only a second's
hesitation, took the arm he offered, walking as far from
his side as the arrangement allowed. His other hand
closed over the sleeve of her dress. ''I fear your gown is
still wet. You will need a change of clothes.''

Iantha glanced down at the muddied hem of her white
wool dress. ''That would be a great relief, but I don't see
how it can be accomplished.''

''I believe there are some clothes in the bedchamber
we are preparing for you, but they belonged to my grandmother.'' He looked down at her and grinned as they
made their way up two broad flights of stairs. ''She was
quite the fashionable lady in her day, but alas, that time
is a long way in the past. She was also very thrifty—kept
everything. You should find something clean and dry, but
you will hardly be a model of mode.''

For the first time since the heap of snow had inundated

her vehicle, Iantha chuckled, but then the full realization of her situation dawned. At all appearances she would be here for an extended stay.

Great God in heaven! How would she survive it? How could she tolerate a whole household of men—strangers—for so much time?

Control. She must rely on her control, her intellect.

# Chapter Two

After a prolonged struggle with the buttons up the back of her bodice, Iantha finally slipped out of the soiled dress with a sigh. Gratefully dipping a cloth into the warm water, she smoothed it over her arms, face and neck, relaxing the tense muscles. What a comfort to her chilled skin and somewhat battered body! A full, hot bath would have been heaven, but she could hardly request one under the circumstances. Lord Duncan had been more than courteous, and she did not want to create a problem for his small staff.

Or find herself completely naked in a house full of men. The bedchamber to which his lordship had conducted her, decorated in feminine pastels and smelling of old wood, had but two doors, both provided with working keys. After a quick peek into the adjoining sitting room, Iantha firmly locked both, imposing strict control on her uneasiness.

Her petticoats had fared no better than her gown, and she let them fall to the floor with it. Her tightly fitted boots presented more of a problem, but after a brief tussle, she got them and her stockings off. Never again would she take the services of a maid for granted. In fact, she would make it a point to give Molly a nice gift when she got home.

If she ever got home. The briefest glance at the window revealed nothing but blinding snow and the wind crying at the casement. They were extremely fortunate to have made the shelter of the stable when they had.

Calming her panic with a deep breath, Iantha opened the wardrobe and concentrated on its contents. It did, indeed, contain a welter of silks and satins. She pulled out a gown of pale blue brocade with falls of white lace and spread it out on the bed. Truly lovely. But of a style that required a large hoop. That wouldn't do. She would never be able to get into it by herself, let alone manage hoops.

Iantha replaced it and drew out a soft lavender silk that would reflect her eyes and complement her delicate features and fair skin. Much better. The fitted bodice laced up the front, so she could fasten it herself, and the square neckline did not reveal as much bosom as current dinner gowns. Further search revealed enough petticoats to hold the full skirt out sufficiently so that she would not trip. Luckily, the former Lady Duncan seemed to have been a bit shorter than Iantha.

She donned the gown and replaced the hidden pistol under her skirts. A short session with the comb found on the old-fashioned dresser got the snarls out of her shining hair, and she arranged it simply, with her own silver combs holding part of it high on her head. The rest fell in soft curls. At least when it had lost its color, it had not lost its curl.

Feeling rather as she had as a child playing dress-up in her own grandmother's clothes, Iantha opened the door and peered into the corridor. Seeing no one about, she set off down the hall in the direction she thought she had come with Lord Duncan. She had almost decided that she had come the wrong way when she turned a corner she did not remember and almost collided with the most astounding apparition.

Iantha gasped and jerked back.

The apparition did likewise.

And then it bowed.

"Forgive me, madam. I have startled you. I am Vijaya Sabara."

Iantha found herself staring at a slender man of medium height, his head wrapped in an elaborate silk turban, and a neat black beard covering olive cheeks and chin. A huge sapphire fixed to his headdress dangled in the middle of his forehead. And his clothing... She could only gaze in wonder. So colorful. So rich. So...

So *barbaric.*

"I...uh... How—how do you do?" So utterly inept! The man would think her a fool. Iantha flushed.

"Very well, thank you." His brow wrinkled in puzzlement. "I did not know we had a lady in residence."

"Lord Duncan rescued me from the storm. I am Iantha Kethley. Can you direct me to the dining room?"

"Ah. Please allow me to guide you. You are going in quite the wrong direction." The apparition did not offer his arm, but with a sweep of his hand indicated that she should retrace her steps. She turned and accompanied him back the way she had come. What a sight the two of them must make, she in her antique dress, he in his soft, jewel-adorned silks. Like guests at a masquerade.

Iantha's head spun. She seemed to be losing her grip on reality, rather like the heroine in a penny dreadful. She felt the storm had swept her away from her own time and place to...to what? Would she next encounter a specter with its head under one arm?

Heaven forfend!

A sigh of relief escaped her as she beheld the stalwart frame of Lord Duncan coming up the staircase. At least he looked English and familiar and ordinary in buckskin trousers and a neat coat stretched across broad shoulders. Reality settled once more into place.

"There you are, Miss Kethley. I was just coming to escort you to dinner. One can easily lose one's way in this great pile." Just as he started to offer his arm, Iantha placed a hand on the banister, pretending not to notice.

"Yes. I had done just that." She smiled. "I seem to require much rescuing today."

His lordship grinned. "Our pleasure. I see you have met my friend Prince Vijaya. He has come from India to England with me to learn more about our country on behalf of his father, who is a maharaja in the district of Orissa."

At the door of a small dining parlor the Indian bowed again. "Your servant, Miss Kethley. If you will excuse me?"

With no further explanation he disappeared down the corridor. Iantha looked questioningly at his lordship.

"Vijaya prefers to eat alone." Rob ushered her into the room and held a chair for her, then sat across from her. "Many Indians regard eating as something that should be done in private. Considering the table manners of some of our best people, one can see their point."

A smile softened her delicate face. He had been correct in his earlier assessment. His distressed damsel *was* beautiful when she smiled. Extremely so. And the old-fashioned dress seemed to suit her. "That gown is very becoming to you. You make me think of the younger portraits of my grandmother with her powdered hair."

Her smile faded, and she looked down at her folded hands.

Hmm. Obviously he had erred. The lady must be sensitive about her hair. "Forgive me. I seem to have been less than tactful, but I think your hair is lovely. Do you dislike it?"

The lady wrinkled her dainty nose, but looked him in the eye. "One hardly wishes to appear so old at the age of four-and-twenty."

"Old?" A bark of laugher escaped him. "My dear Miss Kethley, you could not look old if—" He broke off and shook his head. "Not under any circumstances whatsoever. You are much too beautiful."

"Now you are flattering me." She cocked her head and raised her eyebrows, but the smile hovered around the corners of her mouth.

Rob grinned. "Do you perceive me as a man who is skilled in flattery?"

She considered him thoughtfully. "No," she said at last. "No, you seem rather to be a man given to plain speaking."

"That I am, a plain man, and I am plainly stating that I find you unusually striking. May I serve you a glass of wine?"

"Thank you." She nodded her acceptance of the wine, if not the compliment, but a small frown replaced her smile. "I know the storm is raging, but... Is there no way to get a message to Hill House, to my parents? They will be frantic with worry. I did not even tell them...."

"That you were going out? I wondered who allowed you to come up here alone." Rob's own smile faded. "I'm sorry, but I cannot set out into that blizzard. I would be dead in an hour."

"Oh, no! I do not ask that. I only hoped..." She sighed. "I was being foolish. Forgive me."

Rob started to reach across the table to clasp her hand, but just as the impulse struck, the slender hand slipped from the table into her lap. Hmm. It had not escaped his attention that when he had placed his hand on her back to guide her to her chair, she had quietly stepped away after the briefest contact. Nor had she taken his arm coming down the stairs. Apparently his rescued damsel remained a bit wary of her rescuer. And under the circumstances... Well, perhaps time and better acquaintance would cure that.

"Nay, not foolish—understandably concerned." He poured himself a tankard of ale from a pitcher. "It is certainly a very bad situation, but I see no way to remedy it tonight—and possibly not tomorrow. So you reside with your parents? Since you answer to 'miss,' I collect that you are not married?"

"No. I am not." She took an infinitesimal sip of wine. Little danger of this cautious lady becoming fuddled by strong drink. "I live with my family. My father is Viscount Rosley. I have two younger brothers and a sister still at home. I also have an older sister, who has married Lord Rochland, and an older brother in the cavalry."

"A hopeful family, indeed. Do you often drive out alone?"

"Yes, frequently."

"And your parents do not object?"

A slightly impish smile brightened her serious face. Charming. "I did not say they do not object. But they understand...." She sobered. "There are times when I simply must be by myself. And I cannot bear to stay inside for long periods. So I take my paints and come into the fells and find something spacious and uplifting to paint. I had been driving for about an hour when the mishap occurred. I intended to paint the Eyrie in the snow.''

''Ah. Now I understand the paint case. So painting is your favorite pastime?''

''Yes. And I sometimes write a bit of poetry...and other things.''

At that moment Burnside appeared with a large tray. He set it carefully on the sideboard and began awkwardly to place dishes on the table. ''You'll have to excuse me, miss. I ain't no dab hand at this. We've been eating in the kitchen till the butler shows his front.''

''Oh, my. I *am* sorry to be putting you to so much trouble. I would have been happy to eat in the kitchen.''

''No lady is going to eat in the kitchen in my house,'' Rob interjected firmly. ''It is well enough for a rough fellow such as myself, but for you... No.''

''Rough? Not at all. In fact, you have been the epitome of a gentleman.'' Blushing a little, the lady laughed. A quiet, pleasant laugh. ''In spite of a rather inauspicious meeting.''

''I must admit I have never before been introduced to a lady at pistol point. A novel experience.'' He grinned. ''The experience has induced me to be on my best behavior, but that is bound to wear off.''

But not too rapidly, considering the second pistol she probably still wore under her petticoats. The pistol notwithstanding, he saw something sad in the lady's twilight eyes. Something that made him want to gather her into his strong arms and comfort her. To shelter her.

But not tonight.

Considering the pistol.

He lifted the cover from a platter, revealing large rolls

stuffed with sausage. "May I serve you some of Burn-side's excellent fare? And some stewed apples?"

"Yes, thank you. What is that in the tureen? It smells very interesting." She leaned forward and took a deep breath.

"Lamb curry." He lifted the cover. The aroma of meat and spices filled the room. "I am not sure you will care for it. It is very highly seasoned, I warn you." He spooned some rice onto her plate and added a very small dollop of the curry. "I suggest you approach it carefully." He ladled a large serving onto his own plate.

She picked up her fork and took an appropriately dainty nibble. "Mmm. It is very good... Oh, my." She gasped and reached for her wine.

Rob hastily clasped her hand, stopping her from sipping. "The wine will only increase the effect of the peppers. Better you should have a bit of roll."

She nodded and quickly followed this advice. "My goodness." She wiped a tear from the corner of her eye. "I have never tasted peppers so hot. But the dish has a delightful flavor. Perhaps it is an acquired taste."

"One must certainly become accustomed to it." Rob laughed. "Are you all right now?" He took a large bite of his own serving.

"Oh, yes. I was just taken by surprise." She tried another minute morsel. A brave lady.

"Perhaps Burnside can mix some curry powder for you with less pepper. I don't want my first guest to go away with a blistered mouth."

"Nor do I." She quickly took another bite of bread and very precisely blotted her lips with her napkin. "I believe that is enough for now, but I *would* like to try it again sometime—perhaps with less pepper."

"You seem surprisingly adventurous. You look so...so fragile."

She stared pensively at the fire. "Perhaps I would like adventure. Fragility can become very tiresome."

Rob pondered that response for a moment. The lady was definitely involved in an adventure now, one from which she would not emerge unscathed. "Miss Kethley, I am afraid that this particular adventure is going to be very damaging to your reputation. I think we should discuss—"

She turned her clear violet gaze on him. "Lord Duncan, I assure you that damage to my reputation is not a problem at all."

And try as he might, he could not persuade her to say one more word on the subject.

The storm rampaged through the night and into the morning, and although Iantha had a pleasant conversation with Lord Duncan over breakfast and spent some time with him in the library examining his books, she became aware of a growing tension in herself. The need to get away. To get out of the place.

To put some distance between herself and his lordship's overwhelmingly masculine presence.

He had done nothing—nothing at all—to cause her alarm. He observed every courtesy. He took pains to provide her every comfort. He did not touch her. Yet he seemed to fill up the room with his big body and his big voice. And...and with something else. A robust energy emanated from him, taking form in his ready grin and his hearty laughter. His enthusiasm for his library. His wholehearted enjoyment of life.

Try as she might, she could not shut his lordship out. She did so very successfully with most people. Her barriers, built of intellectual conversation and control of her emotions, were well constructed and well maintained. She kept even people whom she liked outside of them. But with Lord Duncan... Even while discussing old Hindu manuscripts and his study of the various languages in which he engaged with Vijaya, she found herself more aware of the man than of the subject.

She needed to go home.

Shortly after they had eaten a light nuncheon, the wind died and the clouds rolled themselves up behind the mountains, leaving a blinding brightness in their wake. Iantha peered out a window.

"At last! Now I can return to my parents and relieve you of an unwanted guest, Lord Duncan."

His lordship strolled to join her at the casement. "Never unwanted, Miss Kethley."

Iantha smiled. "You are very gallant, my lord, but at the very best, I am an uninvited guest. Will you provide me with a horse? I fear I cannot leave the same way I arrived."

"I fear you cannot leave at all, Miss Kethley. At least, not for a while. Nay, wait." When she would have protested, he held up a restraining hand. "Just because the storm has abated does not mean the roads are open."

"But I must get home. My poor parents—"

"I am sure they are extremely worried. But that will not clear the drifts. After a blizzard of this magnitude, they will be frozen in place."

Iantha's heart dropped to her slippers. She *must* go. He couldn't make her stay. He wouldn't. She drew herself up and bestowed a frosty glance on his lordship. "Nonetheless, I must attempt it. May I make use of a horse or not?"

His lordship snorted. "Something tells me that if I refuse, you will set out walking. Very well, Miss Kethley. Please get your coat and meet me in the entrance hall.''

Iantha raced up the stairs and struggled back into her own clothes and fur coat. In a very few minutes she rejoined Lord Duncan in the hall. He had donned his greatcoat and hat. Without a word he led her back into the old part of the castle.

But instead of continuing down to the stables, he turned and started up a spiral staircase of worn stone. Iantha stopped, scowling, and gazed up the aged steps. "My lord, where are you going?"

He returned her scowl. "To the battlements, Miss Kethley.''

Panic began in Iantha's breast. "No! I am not going to the battlements. I am going home. With you or without you!''

Before she could dart through the old castle's portal, he jumped down the last few steps and seized her arm. "Miss Kethley, you try my patience. If you are determined to leave, at least first look at the situation you face. Then if you still believe you can travel, I will accompany you.''

He turned and towed the unwilling Iantha up the first few stairs. After several steps she yanked her arm out of his grasp, glaring at him. "Very well. If you insist, I will go up.''

His lordship said nothing, but moved aside, gesturing for her to precede him. The old castle was bitterly cold. Iantha wished she might thrust her gloved hands into the pockets of her heavy coat, but had to use them to hold up her skirts. Her nose threatened to drip. She could only sniff as unobtrusively as possible. Finally they reached a heavy wooden door. Lord Duncan reached past her and pulled it open.

Iantha stepped out into a dazzling landscape. When her eyes had adjusted from the dark of the old keep, she gazed about her at a sparkling fairyland. Against the dark clouds, snow covered all but the highest wind-scoured peaks. From many of them, where springs near the summit had frozen in their leap into the valley, diamond cascades of ice glistened. Everywhere the sun struck the hills at an angle, rainbows sprang up.

Iantha stood transfixed.

Lord Duncan stood beside her silently, apparently captive to the beauty of the sight himself. Together they began to walk the battlements, where the parapets had shielded the path from snow, pausing occasionally to appreciate a particularly breathtaking view. When they had traversed three sides of the castle, they stopped at the foot of another stone staircase. Less than three feet wide, it rose in dizzying flight from the battlements to the top of the tallest tower. Neither handrail nor barricade protected the climber. The drop fell sheer into the valley. Today snow and ice festooned the steps.

Iantha moved toward them. "Oh, look! How beautiful. What is up there?"

His lordship seemed a bit alarmed. "Only the lookout tower. But please do not attempt the stairs, Miss Kethley. They are not safe at any time, let alone when covered in ice."

"Yes, I can see that, but perhaps one day I may climb them. I have a very good head for heights."

"Which is more than I do. I could not permit it."

"Very well." Iantha shrugged and gazed around her, brows puckered. "But where is the road?"

"Where, indeed?" His lordship turned in a full circle. "If I am not mistaken, it lies just below us there." He pointed.

Iantha squinted down the hillside. "Where? I do not see it."

"Neither do I. But if you believe you can find it, it will be my honor to escort you home." His lordship folded his arms across his chest, looking insufferably smug. There was no kinder word for it; he looked *smug*.

Iantha bristled at this display of male arrogance. "Well, I won't know until I look, will I?"

"Nay. You won't." His expression softened, and he laid a hand on her shoulder. "Miss Kethley, I sympathize with your desire to relieve your family's anxiety and your desire to remove yourself from a situation that can be nothing other than uncomfortable for you, but you can see for yourself—it would be the height of folly to try to set out today."

Tears threatened to shatter Iantha's firm control on her emotions. She willed them away, concentrating on the problem at hand. She would *not* succumb to a womanly excess of sensibility. She must think, rely on her intelligence. Stepping back from his comforting hand, she nodded. "You are correct, of course. Forgive me."

His voice sounded gentle and kind. "Perhaps tomorrow, if it is warmer."

Iantha nodded and took several sustaining breaths, gazing around her once more. "I believe, my lord, if you do not object, I would like to bring my paints up here and attempt to capture this remarkable scene."

"I don't object, precisely, but I fear you would freeze."

Glancing around her, Iantha spied a small guardroom. "I could sit in the doorway there, out of the wind. I am warmly dressed. With your permission?"

Lord Duncan sighed. "If I cannot dissuade you. Come, I will show you a way directly from the old castle to the floor where your bedchamber is found. Your paint case is there, I believe.''

''Thank you.''

Iantha followed him partway down the stairs and through a connecting door. Several more turns brought her back to the door they sought. It took only a few minutes to locate what she wanted, and follow his lordship back to the older building. He left her there, and she hastened to find just the prospect she wanted to paint.

Quickly lost in her work, she started when a red-haired young man she had not seen before appeared at her elbow. He bowed politely. ''Good day, miss. I'm Thursby. His lordship asked me to make you a fire in the guardroom.''

Suiting the action to the word, he dumped coal and tinder into a brazier stored in the room, and pulled a rickety stool from the shadows and dusted it, setting it behind Iantha. Lost in the magic of the setting, trying fervently to transfer it to her paper, Iantha never heard him go.

She worked on through the afternoon, pausing to warm her hands at the brazier only when her fingers became too cold to hold her brush, or to melt another small cup of snow for the watercolors. Or when the colors froze in her brush.

Heedless, she worked on.

Her spirits soared like the mountains surrounding her, like the towering clouds. Space and air. Light and shadow. They liberated her as nothing else could. The walls fell away. No longer was she a prisoner in a strange place, nor a prisoner of her own emotions. As the light began to fail, she worked doggedly, hoping to get as much recorded as she could. To finish, she would have to rely on the pictures in her mind. On the enchantment stored in her heart.

She was striving to catch the effect of the last rays of light when Lord Duncan appeared before her, arms folded across his chest. She looked up, startled. He moved very quietly for so solid a man.

"Will you stay here all night, Miss Kethley?"

"Only a little longer. I need to use the last of the sunlight...."

He reached out and plucked the brush from her numb fingers and rinsed it in the crystalizing cup of water. Before Iantha could protest, he laid it in her case and pitched the water over the parapet. "I have come up several times these past three hours, but you seemed so absorbed in your painting, I had not the heart to stop you. But now it is getting colder, and I *must* call a halt. You will become ill. You have even taken off your glove." He took her bare hand in both of his, scowling in disapproval.

"It is very difficult to paint with a glove on. Indeed, I don't remember when—" Automatically Iantha tugged on the hand, but he did not let her go. Then the warmth of his strong grasp became so welcome, she did not want him to. She began to shiver. "I d-did not realize how c-cold I was getting." Her teeth rattled against one another. "I b-became so immersed in the p-painting...."

His lordship pulled her to her feet. "The only thing you need to be immersed in at the moment is a tub of warm water. I fear you may have frostbitten fingers—or toes. Can you feel your feet?"

Iantha wiggled her toes. "A little. I don't think they are frostbitten."

"Come then. I will send Thursby to fetch your paints. I left Burnside filling a bath for you." He took her elbow and steadied her steps down the rough stairs.

She could feel his energy coursing through her arm and into her fingertips.

She simply could not shield herself from him.

## Chapter Three

She floated down the stairs, a wraith made solid by the desire of the beholder. Rob almost held his breath for fear that she would disappear. Did her feet even touch the floor? She had chosen another of his grandmother's gowns, this one a deep sky-blue. A shawl of silver lace lay across her shoulders, and silver slippers peeped from under her skirt. Around her neck, completing the ethereal effect, lay a fine silver chain with moonstones depending from it.

In spite of his better judgment, even knowing she would evade him, he extended a hand to help her down the last step. She allowed him to assist her, then gently reclaimed her hand.

"Good evening, my lord."

"Your servant, Miss Kethley." Rob bowed, continuing to regard her appreciatively. "You quite take my breath away. Have you gotten completely warm?"

"Most of me has. I hope you don't mind my making free with your grandmama's wardrobe. Her things are so beautiful. I found this necklace in a chest on the dresser." She smiled up into his eyes. "I am quite enjoying my masquerade."

Rob was obliged to take a deep breath. God, she was lovely. "Of course. Whatever is there is at your disposal. Come into the library for a moment. I had Thursby bring your painting there."

He held the door for her, and she glided past him, stopping before the easel, her head tilted, a critical expression on her face. At last she sighed. "One never quite achieves the aura that nature bestows. Of course, it is not completely finished."

Rob shook his head, smiling wryly. "I suppose that is the hazard of being a talented artist. They are never finished, are they? I find your painting exquisite."

"Do you really?" Her face brightened.

"Indeed, I do. The delicate detail…like that snow piled on the twisted tree, or the subtle colors of the ice cascades against the dark clouds. I see those things in nature, but I would not know how to recreate them on paper."

She nodded seriously. "You have an appreciative eye. You have described the very challenge. Do you think the background too dark?"

Rob considered gravely. "Nay, it sets off the detail."

"Yes, I think so. I do like the effect, although I usually use light, airy colors. I am a great admirer of Anne Vallayer-Coster, but I find her backgrounds too dark. Do you know her work?"

"I'm not familiar with it, but I have heard her name. She was Marie Antoinette's painter, wasn't she?" Rob moved a chair nearer the fire, and his guest sat.

"Yes, painter to the court, and one of only four women admitted to the French Royal Academy of Painting and Sculpture." Miss Kethley sighed. "She is in eclipse since the advent of the revolution, but she was fortunate to have her genius recognized. It is so difficult for women."

Wondering if her own talent had been belittled, Rob nodded sympathetically. "I fear that is so."

"And not only in art—in writing, also. Many female writers use men's names in order to have their work published. And female dancers are reduced to..." She blushed. "To such a low status that... Well..."

Rob took pity on her embarrassment. "That they are little better than prostitutes," he finished for her. "You are right. It is not fair at all."

Still blushing, she smiled. "Plain speaking can be very useful."

"I have always found it so." He grinned. "But here is Burnside attempting to announce dinner."

Over another excellent repast of ham with Cumberland sauce, Iantha studied her host. Again, he did not wear evening clothes, but remained at his ease in buckskins, with a simple cravat tucked into an unadorned waistcoat. A plain man, as he had said. But quite handsome for all that, with a square face and a strong, cleft chin. The fire struck reddish lights in his rich brown curls, and lines from laughter seemed always to crinkle his dark eyes. A very likable man.

Just...just a little overpowering.

He had *done* nothing to create that impression. He just *was*. Very broad, very strong, very physical. Perhaps that quality accounted for her feeling overpowered. She could not ignore it. Not that he stood too close or touched her more than courtesy required—except when she had been a bit... Well, perhaps a bit difficult. Even then he had been only slightly impatient and concerned for her welfare. But he exuded... What? Power. Yes, he exuded a subdued, but confident, power.

But he was speaking. "I'm sorry, my lord. I was not attending. You were saying?"

"I suggested that you try a bit more curry. Burnside made this especially for you—chicken, I believe, this time." He ladled a portion for her over rice studded with almonds.

"Why, thank you. How kind of him." And of his lordship. His kindness grew more apparent each hour she knew him. "Ooh. It is quite delicious. Just the right amount of pepper, but so exotic. English food is so dull and predictable. I have never tasted anything like this."

"No, the ingredients are not usually found in England. I had them shipped back ahead of me." As he spoke a few discordant strains of music drifted up from the lower reaches of the castle. "Aha! Feller is tuning up his fiddle. Perhaps we can persuade you to join us for a little entertainment after we have eaten."

"Why...why that sounds delightful." At least it did at first. She enjoyed music. But then again, as she thought further, Iantha realized she'd be the only woman among several men.... *That* did not sound so delightful.

Just as she opened her mouth to make an excuse, his lordship took the decision out of her hands, declaring a fait accompli. "Very good. We'll gather in the library shortly. Feller plays only folk tunes, but they are lively and will relieve for all of us the boredom of being snowbound."

Rob waited a moment to see if see she would demure in spite of his intervention. She looked a bit distressed, but went back to her chicken curry without saying anything else. The fact that she ate with a good appetite pleased him. He could not abide women who picked at their food.

Because she was so delicate of body, he had expected her perhaps to be too thin, but when her ruffles fell back, he could see that her arms were only slender, not bony at all. He wondered about the rest of her, but dared not stare at her body. Hiding behind the act of cutting his ham, he risked a glance at her breasts. Full, round, well shaped. Nice.

Yes, very nice, indeed.

This elusive lady intrigued him. Like the wraith she resembled, he felt that he could see her, but not *feel* her. Her emotions emerged for only moments at time; she allowed the small touches of courtesy only until they had accomplished their purpose. Then she subtly moved away, never rudely or abruptly.

Very politely.

Very firmly.

His determination to breach her barricades, to discover what lay behind that reserved exterior, deepened. At first he'd believed she simply distrusted him, but now he thought the matter more complex. Surely he had proved himself trustworthy now. Perhaps with a little time and patience he could win through her reserve.

He did, after all, have an excellent reason to do so.

With dinner complete, the small company assembled in the library, bringing with them a pitcher of ale. Only one. Rob had decreed sobriety as the order of the evening. He could trust his men to behave themselves, but nonetheless, he would not take a chance of offending Miss Kethley. Or of frightening her. She was too wary by half as it was.

The party consisted of all the current residents of the castle—Burnside, Feller with his fiddle, the young, red-headed Thursby and of course, Lord Duncan and Iantha. And, unexpectedly, Prince Vijaya. He appeared quietly as they were gathering and pulled a chair close the fire.

Thursby had brought with him a tea tray, which he set on a table between Iantha and the Indian.

Iantha had not spoken with Vijaya since the night before. His dress was no less resplendent than it had been on that occasion, consisting of a soft satin shirt and trousers, with an open robe over all. They glittered with rich embroidery worked with jewels. The sapphire resting against his forehead called attention to eyes astonishingly blue in the dark face.

The air of unreality again began to grow in Iantha, and the tension of confinement. And yet, she chided herself, what could constitute a more intriguing adventure than to listen to border folk music in the company of three sturdy north countrymen, an English border lord and an eastern prince? She studied the scene, recording every detail in her mind's eye to transfer to paper at her first opportunity.

As the only woman present, apparently the duty of pouring tea remained hers. "Who will drink tea?"

She glanced around the room as, one by one, all the men but Vijaya declined in favor of ale. After pouring two cups and passing one to the prince, Iantha leaned back and sipped her own. Remarkable. She rolled the unfamiliar flavor over her tongue. Smoky and exotic. If only she might include the flavor in her painting!

Feller drew his bow across the strings, and after two exploratory chords, launched into a familiar tune. At the end of a second tune, Iantha reached for another cup of tea.

"Do you enjoy the tea, madam? It is my own blend."

Iantha regarded the Indian with surprise. He had been so quiet she had almost forgotten him. "I like it very much, your highness. Thank you for sharing it with me."

"My pleasure. It is herbal in nature, designed to relax

one. As I do not drink alcohol, I find it useful.'' He extended his own cup, and Iantha took it and refilled it.

At her other side Lord Duncan sipped his ale and kept time with a toe tapping against the carpet. He smiled at her, but addressed his factotum. ''Come, Burnside, give us a jig.''

''I don't know, me lord.'' The man grinned with an obviously spurious show of reluctance. ''It's been a while since I danced for a lady.''

''Oh, please do, Burnside.'' Iantha leaned forward in her chair. ''I would love to see a jig performed.'' The adventure improved by the minute. What a story to tell her baby sister! And perhaps also… Yes, she must make notes tomorrow.

Burnside grinned and, setting his tankard aside, got to his feet. ''Well. I guess I could do it for *you,* Miss Kethley. But someone has got to keep time.''

His lordship laughed. ''We will all furnish that. Get to it.''

Feller stuck up the tune, and Burnside set his lean frame in motion, defying gravity with his agility. Lord Duncan and Thursby began to clap, and Iantha could not resist joining them. Music moved her as very little could do, but most of the musical occasions she attended were all too dignified in nature to clap time. She laughed aloud at Burnside's antics, and even the reserved Vijaya rapped rhythmic fingers against the table, smiling.

The music rose to a rousing finish, and Burnside bowed to his appreciative audience, wiping sweat from his brow. He nodded at his employer. ''Your turn, me lord.''

''Mine?'' His lordship took a long draft of ale. ''I can't keep up with you.''

"Ha! That will be the day. But no need to. I'm plumb used up." Burnside fanned his face with his hand.

"Well, if Miss Kethley will take into account my advanced years..." Lord Duncan set his ale on the floor by his chair and stepped to the center of the room, his thumbs hooked into his belt and his foot already beating a cadence.

He proved to be amazingly light on his feet. Iantha would never have thought so large a man could move so fast. As the speed of the music increased, his booted feet almost blurred, and the muscles of his thighs rippled beneath the tight buckskin trousers. The rest of them clapped harder and harder. At last, on a resounding chord, he flung up his hands and shouted, coming to a complete stop.

Iantha began to applaud. Surely he must be the only peer of the English realm who would dance with such abandon. He bowed to her and took a seat beside her, breathing hard. "Thank you, Miss Kethley. Your approval makes my efforts worthwhile."

"Your advanced years, indeed! I have never seen anyone dance like that, my lord. Where did you learn?"

"Here, of course, before I left for India. I used to love to go to the village dances."

"Similar dances exist among the older tribes of my country." Vijaya surprised Iantha by speaking. "But I have never learned them."

"A pity." His lordship took a restorative swallow of ale. "We would have had you up to demonstrate."

Vijaya simply shook his head and smiled.

"Then we shall have to fall back on Thursby. I'm told you do an excellent sword dance, Thursby."

The youth's fair-skinned face flamed. "Tolerable, me lord."

"Then by all means, let us see it. We will forgive you your Scots forebears."

"And I'll forgive you your English ones, me lord."

Amidst hoots of laughter and approval from the party, Lord Duncan went to the wall and removed two very old swords. He laid them in a cross in the middle of the floor.

"Perhaps in these close quarters we should dispense with the sword exercises. When you are ready, Thursby."

Still blushing, young Thursby walked to the swords, and Feller started a Highland tune. The group watched in breathless attention as the young man's feet flew around, between and over the blades, missing by a hairbreadth, but never touching them. He finished in good order, and this time everyone applauded in earnest.

"Thursby has joined us since we returned from India," his lordship explained.

"But Feller and Burnside went with you?"

"Aye. They have been with me since I was a lad." He turned the full force of his smile on her. "It is your turn. Will you honor me with a country dance?"

Alarm filled Iantha. "Oh! Oh, no. I couldn't. I have not danced since…in several years."

"But there are only us country fellows here tonight. A misstep will never be recognized."

Iantha shook her head firmly. "No, my lord. I couldn't."

His lordship sighed loudly. "Now what's to be done? Will you force me to dance with Burnside?"

In spite of the moment of panic, a laugh burst from Iantha. "I have no doubt that you will do it, my lord."

Shaking his head sadly, Lord Duncan rose and bowed to his henchman. With a simper, Burnside curtsied. A whoop of laughter burst from Thursby, and Iantha giggled. Even Vijaya chuckled. Feller began a Cumberland reel and the two men set about the steps of the dance, much tripping and tangling of feet contradicting their previous adroit performance. After several minutes Burnside made an awkward turn and sprawled on the floor.

He got up, rubbing his injured member, and grinning, appealed to Iantha. "Miss Kethley, you just naturally got to do it. I ain't cut out for to do this part."

Iantha's eyebrows rose. "What a fudge! Burnside, I fear the truth is not in you."

"He makes a poor partner, I must attest." His lordship knelt on one knee before Iantha's chair. "Come, Miss Kethley. Rescue me from this humiliation."

She could not help laughing aloud. "Like master, like man! My lord, you are as sly as he is."

He extended a hand. Before she had time to think, Iantha placed hers in it and found herself drawn to her feet. "But, my lord." The protest escaped even as he led her to the floor. "We cannot do a Ninepins Reel with only one couple."

"We will improvise, Miss Kethley." And improvise they did. It proved to be a most original version of the reel. Lord Duncan guided Iantha from position to position with no more than the lightest clasp of his fingertips on hers. Caught up in the laughter and buffoonery, she discovered that she had relaxed and was truly enjoying the first set she had danced in six years.

Not until the last strains of the music sounded did he catch her around the waist for a final spin. By then she had lost her breath from laughing, and he released her so quickly that she barely glimpsed the triumphant gleam in his eye.

The moment she awakened the next morning, Iantha sprang out of bed and ran to the window. To her great relief the sun poured through the casement, and she saw not a cloud in the sky. She hastened to the breakfast table to find Lord Duncan finishing off a generous serving of beef and eggs.

He quickly stood and held a chair for her to be seated, displaying his infectious grin. "Be of good cheer, Miss Kethley. Later this morning I intend to investigate the condition of the road. If I think it safe to proceed, this afternoon we will escort you to your anxious family."

"Oh, thank you, my lord. They must be beside themselves with worry. I would be very grateful to you for their sake."

*And for my own.* This morning his lordship's masculine energy seemed to flow from him in waves. Even as he relaxed over morning coffee, it set an unfamiliar sympathetic vibration rippling through Iantha as never before. Try as she might, she could not wall him out. Perhaps the camaraderie of the evening before accounted for the increased difficulty. She had relinquished her control, and she could not regret it, but...

His lordship had undeniably breached her walls. He had made her laugh. Genuinely laugh. She had even *danced* with him. But now...

Now she felt vulnerable again.

Afraid.

She finished a scone and hastily excused herself.

Rob tapped politely on the bedchamber door and mustered his patience for what seemed an unnecessarily long wait. At last his guest opened the door a crack and peered cautiously around it. Rob sighed. His evasive lady had once again fled. He had cherished hope that the relaxation of the previous evening would have a more permanent effect. Ah, well. He pushed lightly on the door, and she stepped back enough to allow him into the room.

At least his news should please her. "I believe that we may attempt the journey, Miss Kethley, if we go on horseback. I will take Feller and Thursby with us to help break the way and assist should we encounter any difficulties. Burnside and Vijaya can hold the keep."

A relieved smile brightened her face. "Thank you, Lord Duncan. I am more indebted to you than I can ever repay."

Rob studied her for a heartbeat. If she recognized what the inescapable consequence of this situation must be, she gave no sign of it. "No repayment is needed, Miss Kethley. I am happy to be of service to you. However, conditions are likely to become difficult. Can you manage one of my horses, or would you prefer to ride with me?"

She didn't hesitate a moment. "I will ride alone."

"As you wish." What other answer had he expected? He just hoped she did not overestimate her strength and skill.

They did not make the trip easily. Although the sun had softened the snow enough for the horses to push through, it required several hours of hard going for both men and beasts to cover the distance his charge had driven in an hour two days before. In places they were obliged to leave the drifted roadway completely and take to the boggy, windswept hillside, jumping the small freshets of melting snow. When at last the tired party trotted up the drive of Hill House, all of them showed signs of wear, but Miss Kethley still sat her saddle with a stiff spine. No, she was not nearly as fragile as she looked.

They had not yet reached the door when a tumult of

people and voices spilled out of the house to sur-
round them.

"Miss Iantha!"

"Annie, Annie!"

"Oh, my dear! Iantha."

Rob had no opportunity to help Miss Kethley from her
mount. A dozen hands reached for her before he had his
feet on the ground. A tall, slender youth sporting extremely high collar points lifted her down and enveloped
her in a bear hug, oblivious to the damage to his elabo-
rately tied cravat, while a younger boy hovered nearby.
She kissed the cheek of one and tousled the blond curls
of the other as she stepped back. "Thank you, Thomas.
Don't look so solemn, Nathaniel. I am quite well."

At that moment a small whirlwind of ribbons and petticoats launched herself into Miss Kethley's arms. "Oh,
Annie! Where have you been? We have been so worried.
I prayed and prayed...." Great tears coursed down the
pink cheeks.

Her sister enfolded the girl in a quick hug and then set
her away and wiped at the tears running down the young
cheeks. "Do not cry, Valeria. I had an accident, but Lord
Duncan saved me from the storm." She turned to the
lady of middle years with hair as silver as her own.
"Now do not *you* start to cry, Mama."

The older woman satisfied herself with a brief embrace
and released her daughter, wiping a tear from her own
violet eyes. "I am just so relieved, Iantha. I have been
quite distraught."

Miss Kethley turned to Rob. "May I present Lord
Duncan, Mama? My parents, Lord Duncan—Lord and
Lady Rosley."

"Your servant, ma'am." Rob bowed to the lady and,
shifting to face the tall, thin older man who had just come

up leaning on a cane, bowed a second time. "Lord Rosley, your servant, sir."

"Duncan." His lordship nodded, his eyes narrowed, but immediately swiveled toward his daughter. "Iantha, is everything well with you?"

"Quite well, Papa. A small snowslide struck the gig and almost buried it in the drifts. A shaft broke, and poor Toby was hurt. Lord Duncan arrived to extricate us just as the storm broke. We were fortunate to have been near his home at the Eyrie. I am unhurt—only very sorry for the anxiety I have caused you."

"Humph. As you should be, minx." Lord Rosley sniffed, cleared his throat and pinched her cheek. "Well, let us not stand here in the cold. All of you come in. You cannot return tonight."

"Thank you, my lord." Rob handed his reins to Feller who, followed by Thursby, led the horses away in the direction indicated by the Hill House grooms.

Rob followed his host. "If I may, Lord Rosley, I would like very much to have a word with you in private."

His lordship favored him with another hard stare.

"Yes, I should think you would."

Her mother took one look at her bedraggled state and hustled Iantha up the stairs to her bedchamber. Having gently, but firmly, evicted young Valeria with a promise to let her sit with Iantha later while she changed clothes, she turned to her older daughter.

"Are you truly all right? You have not been harmed in any way, or frightened?"

Iantha smiled reassuringly. "No, Mama. Truly, I have not. Of course, I was frightened, to be in such a situation...." She paused and took a deep breath. The fear she had felt two days before had begun to fade. Thank God. "But Lord Duncan proved a very kind gentleman—a gentleman in every way."

Her mother sank down on the bed with a relieved sigh. "Oh, I am so glad. I couldn't bear for you to have been hurt again—or even threatened."

"Nothing of that sort occurred, Mama." Iantha sat beside her. "I was never in any danger of harm except for the snowslides." *And my own difficult emotions.* Iantha patted her mother's hand.

"Snow*slides.*" Lady Rosley raised her eyebrows. "Never tell me there was more than one!" Her hands flew to her heart.

Oh, dear. She had said too much. Iantha quickly shook her head. "No…well, yes, Mama, but Lord Duncan plucked me out of the way of the second one."

"It seems we have much to thank him for." Her mother looked at Iantha with narrowed eyes.

"Yes." Iantha studied her hands. An uncomfortable thought had occurred to her. "Mama… What do you think he and Papa are discussing?"

"Why, dear, Lord Duncan is asking your father for your hand in marriage, of course."

## Chapter Four

Rob followed Lord Rosley into his library, uncomfortably aware of the latter's suspicious manner, but not overly concerned. Of course the Viscount was worried about what had happened to his daughter over the last two days—and would be more worried when he discovered that she had been the only woman in the house. But Rob knew exactly how to make allaying the older man's fears a simple matter.

He had given it a great deal of thought in the last day or two. As a gentleman who had carried a young, unmarried lady into a compromising situation, he would be expected to offer for her. And that certainly was to be preferred to finding himself facing one of her male relatives across pistols at dawn. But was he ready to do that? Did he want to marry this particular lady? Or might that prove a disaster for both of them?

On balance, he decided that it would not. He felt a need for a companion. A great many marriages were contracted on no acquaintance at all. And he found Miss Kethley a very interesting companion—talented, intelligent, beautiful. He was a bit troubled about her habit—apparently a very persistent habit—of wandering about the fells alone. But perhaps if he provided her with some of the adventure she craved, she would tolerate him as an escort.

And he had given a great deal of thought to the fact that she seemed to avoid being touched. A wife with such an aversion might make for a rather chilly bed. *Not* something with which he wanted to saddle himself for the rest of his life. He hoped he wasn't thinking like a cockscomb to believe that he could overcome that prejudice. Rob smiled to himself. After all, he *had* succeeded in getting her to dance with him. Surely he could succeed in…

He just hadn't wanted to marry again yet.

But Lord Rosley was speaking. "Take that chair, Duncan." His lordship eased himself into a similar chair and carefully lifted one slippered foot onto a low stool. "May I offer you some Madeira? I'll ask you to serve yourself." He winced. "Damned gout!"

"Thank you. May I serve you some as well?" Rob went to the desk and lifted the decanter. Was that a growl issuing from his prospective father-in-law?

"Might as well. The curst quacks say it aggravates the curst gout, but I can't see that it makes a curst bit of difference to leave it off."

Rob poured two glasses. Hmm. Not a propitious moment to be attempting to mollify a distrustful father. A man suffering the agony of gout was not likely to be amenable to reason. But then again, neither was he likely to call one out into a snowy dawn.

Rob handed a glass to his lordship and returned to his chair. Time to resort to plain speaking. "My lord, please allow me to reassure you as to your daughter's welfare. On my honor, she took no hurt at my hands. Nor was she injured in the snowslides. She must have had bruises, but she did not complain of them."

"No, she wouldn't." Lord Rosley shifted his limb on the footstool and grimaced. "In her way she is a very strong young lady."

"I noticed that." *Especially while she was pointing a pistol in my direction.* "Her appearance is deceptive. One would not think…"

"There are many things about Iantha that one would not think." Her father stared thoughtfully into the fire for a moment.

"The thing is…" Rob cleared his throat uneasily. This was the tricky part. "I believe that the most difficult circumstance of the situation for her was that I have only just returned from India and have not even a housekeeper to act as my hostess. Of course, we showed her every courtesy, but she seemed very distressed."

"I can imagine." Rosley sipped his wine, giving Rob a calculating glance over the rim of his glass. "Then you are not married?"

"No, sir. I am a widower." There it was. The marriage hint. Rob drew a deep breath. "I would, however, be honored to make Miss Kethley my wife."

"As you should be." His lordship stared at him silently for several heartbeats.

*Now what exactly did he mean by that?* Rob sipped his own wine and awaited a further response. It was not forthcoming. He frowned. "I realize, of course, that my title is not the equal of yours and that I have engaged in trade for the last few years, but I can keep your daughter in comfort. I feel certain you would want my man of business to call upon yours to assure yourself of that fact."

Lord Rosley waved a dismissive hand. "No, no. You misunderstand me. I daresay you can keep her, not only in comfort, but in luxury. Rumor has it that you are coming home a very wealthy man—a nabob, in fact. And your family has carried your title longer than mine has been in possession of ours. I have no objection to a man's engaging in honest trade. All of us invest in various enterprises. Don't know why we quibble at trade.''

He turned to gaze again into the fire. Rob waited. At last his lordship sighed and looked at Rob. "I meant only that any man should be honored to have Iantha for a wife. She is a fine young woman.'' He moved his foot again, using both hands this time. "And I am comforted by your willingness to act as a gentleman and do the proper thing. I would be extremely happy to see her married to a man of your caliber.''

"But…?" Rob raised his eyebrows.

"But there is a circumstance you should know. I will understand, of course, if you wish to withdraw your offer.''

Rob's eyebrows climbed higher. "I'm listening.''

Rosley nodded, then continued with the air of a man speaking between clenched teeth. "When Iantha was eighteen, she was attacked by a gang of…'' His fist struck the arm of his chair. "I know no word foul enough for them. But not to wrap it up in clean linen—she was raped by several masked men. She does not even know how many.''

"My God!" Rob's lips drew back in a snarl. "The… You are correct. No word filthy enough for them exists. No wonder she cannot endure the touch of a man.''

"Nor of anyone else. She even draws back from her mother when she seeks to comfort her. She shows physical affection only to her younger sister and brothers, but even with Thomas, since he is becoming a man…'' Lord Rosley shook his head sadly.

For a moment Rob sat stunned by the enormity of the

incident. That explained the proliferation of pistols. How had such a slight lady even survived? His own fist came down on his chair arm as a dark fury welled up in him. Had he but five minutes alone with each of those bastards…!

But he would not have that.

Rob took a long breath and let the anger flow out of him. "How did this happen?"

Rosley took a fortifying sip of wine. "It was the fall before she was to come out in the spring season. My oldest daughter, Andrea, was expecting a baby, and of course, Lady Rosley intended to go to her. But as bad luck would have it, Valeria and Nathaniel were both taken ill with the measles and needed her care. Complications developed. The children were very sick."

He paused in his tale, deep feeling marking his face. "Iantha had already had the measles, so was in no danger of communicating them to Andrea, who had not. She wanted to see the child and London—get a feel for town before her come-out. So I consented to her going to help her sister. I would have accompanied her, of course, but I have never had the damn measles, either. Still haven't had them. To be safe, I sent her in our own coach with a coachman, a footman and two armed outriders. And her old nurse as her chaperon."

He stopped again, his voice choked with emotion. Rob waited silently and respectfully. After a time his lordship again took up the story. "They shot all four men from ambush and tied them to the wheels of the coach. One of them died. The nurse they killed out of hand."

Now he ceased speaking altogether, bowed his head and covered his eyes with one hand. Rob's heart ached with sympathy, and he wiped a tear from his own eye.

"Lord Rosley, I can only imagine what you feel, but I believe I have some idea. I lost my daughter to illness."

"Then perhaps you *can* comprehend." The older man lifted his head. "To be laid by the heels here while those devils tormented my sweet Iantha... A day does not pass that I am not consumed by guilt." He closed his eyes, his jaw tight.

What a horror for a father! Rob well understood the guilt, too, and the helplessness of not being able to save his child. It always seemed that there should have been *something* he could have done. He gave Lord Rosley a moment to compose himself, and then asked, "The authorities have never apprehended these villains?"

Lord Rosley shook his head. "Strangely, they have not. I hired Bow Street to pursue the matter, but they made no progress at all, even though they tell me that several similar incidents occurred at different places around the country that same year. I suspect the detectives' lack of success has to do with the fact that the gang had all the accoutrements of—" he sneered and spat the word out "—*gentlemen.* They are not the ordinary rascals with whom Bow Street usually deals."

"The runners are limited in whom they can question."

"Exactly. Iantha has since received threatening and gloating letters couched in the vilest language. Thank God that she did not completely understand the words and thus brought them to me."

Rob's brows drew together as anger rose again in him. "What! Does she still receive them?"

"I'm not sure. I suspect she does and destroys them because they distress her mother and me. I have sent the ones that came into my hands to the runners, but they cannot trace them."

It seemed the horror had no end. Now Rob understood

the sadness in the lady's eyes. Not only the sanctity of her body, but her security and, indeed, her whole future had been ripped from her just as the bud of her womanhood was opening. How had she endured it at all? What unbelievable strength! His desire to comfort her, to shield her, grew. He could not bring his family back, but he *could* protect this gallant, injured wraith.

"Have I your permission to speak to her?"

"Of course, if you still wish to." Rosley shook his head sadly. "But she won't have you."

Iantha gazed at Lady Rosley in the dresser mirror while she lovingly arranged her hair. Iantha knew that her mother performed that service as a way of being near her. "But Mama…I can't. You *know* I can't. I could not stand it, and it wouldn't be fair to Lord Duncan."

"Please, Iantha. Do not refuse the offer without giving it a chance. I would so like to see you established in your own home. You are too fine a woman to dwindle into an aunt, and you know that—" Lady Rosley broke off and glanced at her youngest daughter, who sat on a footstool, leaning against Iantha.

"That I will never have another opportunity." Iantha stroked her little sister's hair. "I suspect that I will not have this opportunity, either, Mama. Papa is bound to have told him."

"Told him what?" Valeria looked up at her mother. "What are you two talking about?"

"Nothing that would interest you, dearest. But look, you have a spot on your dress." Lady Rosley patted the girl's shoulder. "Go and ask Miss Harrington to help you change, and you and Nathaniel may sit in the drawing room with us before dinner and visit with Lord Duncan."

Valeria skipped out of the room. When the door had

closed behind the child, her mother directed her attention to Iantha. "Of course your father will tell Lord Duncan about your...situation. It would hardly be honorable not to do so."

Iantha grimaced. "No, one cannot honorably deal in damaged goods without revealing their defects."

"Oh, Iantha, darling!" Lady Rosley dropped to the footstool vacated by Valeria and clasped one of Iantha's hands, gazing intently into her face. "Don't say that! Please don't. You are not d-damaged goods. You are not! You are good and sweet and..." Tears welled in her eyes.

"I'm sorry, Mama. That was unkind of me. I did not intend to wound you so." Iantha tightened her jaw and willed her own tears to remain unshed. "But we both know how men feel about this...*situation.*"

Her mother patted her hand. "I do know, dear. But I have a very good feeling about Lord Duncan. He seems...different somehow. I do not believe he will fail you."

"But I would fail him." Iantha shook her head. "Even if I were willing to trap him into marriage with the excuse of the last two days—which I am not, Mama!—I would not be able to perform the duties of a wife. You know I could not."

Lady Rosley sighed. "Iantha. What can I say to you? I *do* understand your hesitation. But, dear..." She paused for a moment, apparently choosing her words. "But, dear, the *duties of a wife,* as you called them, need not be unpleasant. In fact..." To Iantha's astonishment, her mother's face turned deep rose to the roots of her silver hair. "In fact, the marriage bed can be a great source of pleasure and comfort to...to both parties." She gazed

earnestly into her daughter's face. "I would like for you
have that comfort for yourself."

What a great effort that admission had cost her reserved mother. Iantha smiled at her fondly. "Thank you,
Mama. I will speak with him."

*In the unlikely event that I have that opportunity.*


Rob sat in the drawing room listening to Thomas, resplendent in an elaborate cravat and a shockingly puce
waistcoat, explain how it was that he had been sent down
from Oxford until after Christmas. "It was a silly prank.
I can't think how I allowed myself to become involved."

Rob nodded, suppressing a smile. How mature the
young man sounded. Now. After the damage was done.
"I myself found it discouragingly easy to become involved in silly pranks. Some sillier than others." The
smile crept up the corners of his mouth. "Some very
silly, indeed. I'm afraid I accounted for a large number
of my father's gray hairs."

"Well, yes, I suppose I have done my share for Papa.
But I have apologized, and Papa says that my allowance
will resume next quarter day, so that my pockets will not
be quite to let when I go back." The boy sighed.

"No doubt a mistake on my part," drawled Lord Rosley. "I am, in all likelihood, funding more mischief."

"Oh, no, Papa. I have promised not to get sent down
again before summer. Honor of a Kethley. Besides…"
The look the young assume when they believe they have
been unfairly used invaded his face. "I have not done so
nearly so often as John did."

"God be praised."

At Lord Rosley's dry rejoinder, Rob's ready laughter
escaped him in a loud burst. "I see that rearing sons is
a challenging undertaking."

At that moment the ladies entered, and all three gentlemen got to their feet, Lord Rosley with some effort.
He subsided gratefully into his chair as soon as his wife
and daughter had been seated. A few steps behind them,
the schoolroom party arrived under escort of Valeria's
governess. Rob came to his feet again and made a bow
as Lord Rosley presented his youngest progeny.

"Your most obedient servant, Miss Valeria. Nathaniel." Rob shook the boy's hand and solemnly kissed the
girl's petite fingers, smiling at the ensuing blush. "Would
you like to sit here?" He pulled a chair forward and
placed it beside his own. Not to be outdone in honor,
Nathaniel quickly drew his own seat near.

Rob studied the young lady perched demurely at his
side, her eyes fixed shyly on the hands in her lap. Her
honey-blond hair contrasted sharply with Laki's long
black curls, but the long thick lashes rested on her cheek
just as his own little girl's had done.

Rob missed his little daughter. How old would Laki
have been by now? No need to calculate. He knew to the
day. Only seven. The familiar lump rose in his throat.
Five years was much too short a life.

While her mother conversed with Thomas and her father tried in vain to achieve a comfortable position for
his afflicted foot, Iantha watched Lord Duncan quietly
from her place across the room. First he engaged Nathaniel in a lively discussion of hunting. A very manly
conversation, indeed.

One that Thomas could not resist joining, but his lordship gave the same grave attention to Nat's opinion of
Peel's hounds as he did that of his big brother. Iantha
smiled as her youngest brother swelled almost visibly
with increasing importance. Lord Duncan certainly knew
how to make a friend of *him!*

Then, by some means or other, he drew Valeria into the conversation. From her giggles and blushes and a few overheard words, Iantha deduced that the subject now had to do with prospective beaux. Even a few scornful comments from Nathaniel did not seem to dim the girl's pleasure. Unmistakable signs of incipient hero-worship blossomed on both the youngsters' faces. Yes, his lordship could definitely win children.

But she detected no sign that he felt any differently about damaged goods than any other man.

The dinner party quickly took on the air of a quiet celebration for the return of the lost. Even Lord Rosley managed a quip or two. His lady beamed at all of them. Rob did his jovial best, but his gaze persisted in traveling to Miss Kethley, who smiled silently and bestowed her attention on her food, presenting little clue to her thoughts. The interesting companion with whom he had dined at the Eyrie had retreated behind her wall of mannerly restraint.

What made him think she would entertain an offer from him? Perhaps he would be better advised to let the matter drop. But if he did that, she would certainly believe that he had changed his mind because of her misfortune. He despised that sort of thinking. He would never hold against her something over which she had no control. Men who were themselves the worst sort of rake seemed always the first to condemn women.

Rob did not intend to count himself in their number.

But her father had said she would not have him.

Well, they would see about *that.*

At last Lady Rosley rose from the table, and she and Miss Kethley turned to leave the room. Rob stood and cleared his throat. "If Lord Rosley and Thomas will forgive me for not sharing their port, I would like to have a few words with Miss Kethley, if I may."

"To be sure." His lordship nodded. "The sawbones says I can't drink port now, in any event, and Thomas will be the better for tea. We will join Lady Rosley." He struggled to his feet, reaching for his cane.

Rob offered Miss Kethley his arm, and she, with her usual hesitation, took it and directed him to a small parlor adjacent to the dining room. He could feel tension radiating from her body through her slender arm. He patted her hand comfortingly, but did not speak until they were ensconced before a cozy fire.

He would have preferred to share the sofa with her for this occasion, but she moved immediately to the chairs flanking the fireplace. Rob pulled the chairs closer together—near enough to face her across a much shorter distance. Deciding against taking her hand, he leaned forward with his forearms on his knees.

"Miss Kethley, I feel sure you know what I wish to discuss with you."

She held up a hand, palm outward, her expression serious. "Please, Lord Duncan. There is no need for this conversation. I appreciate your willingness to act as a gentleman, but I would not ensnare you simply because you had the ill fortune to save me from a storm. I have told you—my reputation is not at stake." She glanced at the fire, then down at her hands. "And I...I am sure my father told you..."

"About the terrible outrage you endured? Aye, he told me. And I have no desire to further the injustice done to you afterward."

She raised her eyes to his. "What do you mean?"

"That I see no justice whatever in denying you the

home and family you deserve simply because a set of blackguards chose to work their perverted will on you.''

''Plain speaking, indeed, my lord.''

''And why not? Their actions confer no shame on you.''

Iantha again retreated into staring at the fire. ''Mama also says that. But as you are well aware, Lord Duncan, most of the world does not share that opinion.''

''Most of the world be damned! Will you allow yourself to be held prisoner in the wilds of Cumberland by narrow minds?'' A frown drew his lordship's dark eyebrows together.

''I am not a prisoner, my lord. I go into society occasionally—to small neighborhood affairs. And Mama entertains. My parents have urged me to visit London, but... I... I do not want to go. Word of the incident spread like wildfire through the ton. Everyone knows. And beside that, it is very difficult for me to be with a large group of people.'' How could she make him understand?

The suffocating.

The bodies brushing against hers.

The constant struggle against panic. Iantha shuddered.

And of course, there were the hushed whispers and the occasional snicker. And the looks of sympathy. Suddenly the anger began to rise. She fought it back until she could say, quite evenly, ''I do not require your pity, Lord Duncan.''

''And I, therefore, do not offer it.''

He looked her steadily in the eyes.

''Then why are you so insistent on making this proposal?''

He sighed and leaned back in the chair. ''I am not sure. A large part of it is that I *hate* injustice. I have an ardent desire to correct it. But..." He grinned suddenly. "I believe that a larger part of my determination stems from the fact that I have recently made the acquaintance of a most fascinating female. One who is not only lovely, but who is intelligent and talented and adventurous. I have a strong need for adventure myself—and for someone to share it with me."

"But you returned from your great adventure in India. Did you tire of it?"

Lord Duncan sobered. "No. No, I finally realized that part of my life is over." He took a turn at gazing into the fire. Iantha waited for him to gather his thoughts. "You see, I married there—a lovely Indian lady. She died two years ago."

"You are still grieving."

"In a way I suppose I am. I will certainly never forget her. But more than that, I am lonely. I miss them...." He rubbed his cheek thoughtfully. "I also lost my little girl to the same fever." His voice wavered. "The Indian climate is the very devil for fevers." He cleared his throat and surreptitiously dabbed at the corner of his eye. "It is for my daughter that I still grieve."

Iantha pushed back a wave of sadness. "I'm so very sorry. Losing a child must be terrible."

"Aye, it's that." He took a long breath. "And since they died, I have encountered no other lady who took my interest. Until you pointed that pistol at me." His grin returned.

In spite of herself, Iantha blushed. "I *do* apologize. It is just that—that..."

"You have no intention of repeating your earlier experience."

"Exactly." She looked up, startled. "Yet I simply cannot stay within doors all the time. Nor can I abide being followed around by a groom—always cautioning me and hurrying me. Besides, I had four men with me before. The gang shot them all. Had I had a number of pistols in the coach, the story might have been different.''

If nothing else, she might have shot herself.

A decided improvement over what had actually happened.

The skin between Lord Duncan's eyebrows once again pulled into a frown. ''I cannot hear the incident mentioned without wanting to do those fellows a severe injury.''

''I appreciate your indignation on my behalf.'' Iantha leaned forward. ''But don't you see, Lord Duncan? It is not only my body they hurt. My spirit is wounded. I may never again be whole.''

He leaned toward her in turn, this time taking her hand. ''I would like to heal that hurt. I would very much like to see you whole.''

Could that ever be? Iantha started to withdraw her hand, then subdued the impulse. If only he knew how much effort it cost her. His nearness stirred tremors deep inside her, profound, disturbing. Confusing.

''I might never be able to give you another daughter. I'm afraid I could never be a true wife to you.''

''I know that it would be very difficult for you, but it would not be necessary at first. I believe that together we can slowly overcome this dreadful fear.'' He smiled. ''After all, Miss Kethley, learning to make love is one of life's greatest adventures. Share it with me. Let me help you. Step by step, touch by touch. Starting with allowing me to kiss your hand.'' He lifted her fingers and brushed his lips across them, then returned the hand to her own keeping.

She rubbed the spot that his mouth had touched. A

home. Perhaps children. Children were the only humans with whom she now felt at ease. How comforting it would be to have her own.

And someone to share adventures with.

Life's greatest adventure. Was it still possible?

"Might we first have a long engagement?"

"As long as you need."

"You are indeed willing to make so great an effort?"

"Aye."

Iantha's mouth firmed. "Then I can but equal it."

# Chapter Five

The spirit at breakfast was even more celebratory than that of the previous evening. Mama was jubilant—very quietly and discreetly, of course, only her sparkling eyes betraying her. Papa looked as if the weight of the world had been removed from his back. Lord Duncan seemed excessively pleased with himself.

Iantha fought for control.

What had she done? Even at her own family's table his presence flooded her with unaccustomed sensations, tightening every muscle in her body. And then he would say something that made her laugh in spite of herself. And turn his warm smile on her. And she would forget for a moment. Perhaps he was correct in believing that he could help her become whole. One thing was certain— she would never again have the opportunity he offered.

She would make the attempt. With every fiber of her being, she would do her best to put the past behind her— to become the woman she had once hoped to be. Lest the terror again sweep over her, Iantha forced herself to think about the conversation at hand.

Her mother was speaking. "I believe we should announce the betrothal at Christmas. That is such a lovely time for a joyous occasion, and people love to come to the country for the holiday. I shall begin making a list at once. We must have all our acquaintances. But of course, Iantha, dear, if you would prefer—''

Iantha shook her head. She had much rather put off any announcing until she felt more sure that she had made the correct decision. But her mother's face positively glowed with anticipation. ''Perhaps a small party, Mama. I...'' Lady Rosley's face dimmed. Iantha could not bear to disappoint her. ''But I will defer to your judgment. You will know best what to do.''

''I believe Christmas is a first-rate idea, Lady Rosley.'' Lord Duncan set down his fork. ''But may I suggest a slight alteration to the plan? There is something I have been wanting to do, and I would welcome your help with it.''

Lady Rosley raised her eyebrows. ''Why of course, if I can assist you with anything...''

''The thing is, I would like to make my return to England more widely known. I have been thinking of having a house party at Christmas myself to reopen the Eyrie. I'm sure my aunt, Lady Dalston, would be willing to act as my hostess, but she is rather elderly, and I need help with the guest list and other arrangements. Those matters are beyond my ken.'' He gave the lady the full effect of his winning smile. ''If you would be willing, as a favor to me, to allow me to host the affair and help me with it, Lord Rosley might make the announcement then.''

Very delicately handled. Now why did his lordship *really* want to host the party? Iantha aimed a questioning glance in his direction, but he contrived not to see it.

''Having an affair to announce your return is well thought of.'' Lord Rosley considered as he added cream to his coffee. "I'm sure you will wish to continue to pursue your business interests. You will want to renew acquaintance with certain influential people."

"Exactly. What do you say, Lady Rosley? Do you think we can make the Eyrie sufficiently festive for such an occasion?"

The gleam of challenge appeared in Lady Rosley's eye. "I'm sure we can, my lord, although I have not visited there in many years. It has been kept up?"

"Yes, ma'am, by my agent. But it could use a lady's hand."

Her ladyship warmed to the subject. "Christmas in a castle. Oh, yes. We must use evergreen garlands, of course, lots of them, and have musicians who can perform suitable music—carols and lays and—"

"And plenty of dances." Lord Duncan winked at Iantha.

The decision had been removed from her hands. Great heaven! How could she tolerate so many people for so long a time?

The answer to both her recent questions was forthcoming as she walked Lord Duncan to the door. The rest of the family diplomatically took themselves elsewhere so that they could speak privately. He turned to her with a smile. "Have I been inexcusably managing? Do you wish me at Jericho?"

Iantha shook her head resignedly, but returned the smile. "I can see that it will require forcible measures for me to assert my will in the future."

"Not at all." He started to reach for her hand, then aborted the gesture. "If you dislike my arranging a great deal, I will immediately withdraw it."

"I…I am a bit apprehensive about dealing with a large crowd for several days."

"I know." A hint of sadness tinged his smile. "But I want you to have an opportunity to spend some time in your future home. And I believe we will do well to confront the gossips at the outset."

"To begin as we mean to go on?"

"Precisely. I am confident that no one would dare be insulting to you in my house, but if they express so much as a single innuendo, I will feel free to deal with them as I see fit. I could not do that in your parents' home."

"I see." What a fierce protector she had acquired!

"We must contrive to give you the privacy you need. I want you to be able to withdraw when you feel pressed. You would not do that if you felt obliged to help your mother in her home."

"No," Iantha admitted. "I would not. You are very thoughtful, Lord Duncan."

"I intend to keep my promise to you, Miss Kethley. We will achieve your liberation one small bit at a time. You will not be required to brave a baptism of fire. But tell me…"

"Yes?"

"Now that we are betrothed, may I have the use of your given name?"

Startled, Iantha laughed. "I hadn't thought of that. Of course, if you like."

"I like. And I would like even more for you to call me Rob." Without giving her time to respond, or to think, he leaned down and bestowed a quick kiss on her cheek.

And walked away whistling.

The invitations to the house party were duly inscribed and sent, inviting the guests to arrive the day before

Christmas Eve and stay for a week if they could. A week! Iantha shuddered at the thought. And yet she felt an excitement she had not felt in years, made up of equal parts anticipation and anxiety.

What had she agreed to? Marriage? A husband, his bed? Could she endure it? His lordship believed that she could gradually overcome her fear. Was her mind and her rigid discipline enough to get her through that challenge? She wanted it to be.

Curse those devils! She wanted a normal life! Not this half existence of confinement, shame and fear. And if Robert Armstrong had the courage to offer her marriage, she would spend every ounce of her own to make that marriage a success.

Somewhere she must find the strength.

Today she traveled to visit her new home in the company of her parents, to discuss arrangements for the Christmas announcement party. How different this trip seemed from her fateful one two weeks ago. Today the sun shone brightly, and the snow remained only in shaded spots. Released from their winter prison, small cataracts of snowmelt tumbled joyously from the crest of every hill, joining the stream that cut through the floor of the narrow valley.

Last time, she had driven alone in the open air. Now weeks later she rode confined in a coach with Mama and Papa. Dear though her parents were to her, Iantha longed for her paints and the solitude and fresh air of her gig. That useful equipage had been retrieved from the snowbank, but despite many promises, had yet to be repaired.

She glanced at her father and smiled. Papa was being sly. She doubted very much that the little carriage would be returned to service before her nuptials—whenever those were to be. At that point, her safety would become Lord Duncan's concern, and Papa would heave a sigh of relief.

The coach made a sharp turn and started up the winding road to the Eyrie. In due time they pulled up in a courtyard under the ramparts of the old keep. At one time the enclosure had been the bailey, but now the walls lay in disarray. Emerging from the carriage, Iantha could see the roofs of the stable at a lower level.

And Lord Duncan standing in the door. Rob, she reminded herself. She must remember to call him Rob. At the sight of them he descended the few steps and strode forward to help her down from the carriage. Behind him hovered a figure she had not seen before, a figure bearing all the earmarks of a butler. Apparently the new staff had arrived.

"Welcome! Welcome to the Eyrie. Lady Rosley. My lord. I trust your gout is improved?"

Lord Rosley trust out a hand, and Rob shook it. "A bit better, thank God. At least I can get a boot on."

Rob turned back toward her. "Iantha."

Detecting a different quality in his voice as he spoke her name, Iantha glanced into his face and experienced a shock. His intense, dark gaze reflected the feeling in his voice. Her breath caught in her throat, and it was with great control that she prevented herself from retreating into the coach. "Th-thank you, my lord."

A large, warm hand grasped hers. She stepped to the cobbles and carefully took the arm he extended, giving her attention to the management of her skirts rather than looking at his face. Having not seen him since their betrothal, she had allowed his image to fade, providing a fog of safety. Now the full force of his energy again pummeled her, creating a storm of conflicting feelings.

The four of them climbed to the door amid trivial comments on the road and the possibility of more snow. In the entry hall their wraps were collected by the butler, with the assistance of two footmen. Yes, a new order had definitely been established at the Eyrie.

As her fiancé ushered them up the stairs, Iantha found herself missing the friendly, informal air that had accompanied her last visit—even with the disturbing sensations it had engendered. Becoming steadily more aware of the stone walls surrounding her, Iantha thought that, although fortresses were built for safety, they also made excellent traps. She carefully controlled a shudder and straightened her shoulders. No, she would never allow herself to be trapped again.

But all images of traps evaporated as she followed Lord Duncan and her mother into the spacious drawing room done in shades of cream, blue and lavender. The room, situated at the rear of the house, perched on the back edge of the great stone cliff on which the Eyrie rested. A rank of tall windows marched across the far wall, revealing a view of tier after tier of mountains.

"How wonderful!" Iantha hastened to stand before the central window, devouring the expanse of hill and sky.

The rest of the party joined her, Lord Duncan coming to stand beside her. "I knew you would like this room. It was in holland covers during your last visit."

"It's breathtaking."

"Aye, it is." Something in his voice caused Iantha to look up at him. He was gazing not at the view, but at her.

She flushed and turned back to the rest of the room. She rarely received compliments from a man unless insulting innuendo was written clear upon his face. In fact, most men avoided her. She saw no such thing in Lord

Duncan, and of course, he had already declared honorable intentions. But still… The implications of the expression on his face unnerved her.

Directly opposite her, a large framed painting over the white marble fireplace caught her eye. "Why, that's the painting I did while we were snowbound! I had forgotten about it."

"Aye, do you like it there?" Rob strolled toward the fire, and the rest of the group assembled beside him.

"Oh, Iantha, dearest. I do believe that is one of your best." Her mother patted her arm. Iantha was careful not to step away. It hurt Mama so when she did that.

"Yes, yes. Very nice." Lord Rosley peered through his quizzing glass. "But, as I have told you many times, minx, lovely as it is, no one will take your work seriously until you start working in oils. Watercolors are all very well for young misses, but they will never garner critical acclaim."

"Yes, Papa, I know. But I feel that my talent is best suited to the more delicate, translucent shades." Iantha let the frequently repeated advice roll off with only a small twinge of annoyance. Papa meant well.

A tiny frown puckered Rob's brow. "I have had heard that watercolors are much more demanding than oils. Have you more at home?"

Iantha laughed. "You could say that. I have a roomful of them."

"Would you allow me to hang more in this room? Those colors seem to be just the thing for it." Lord Duncan—would she ever learn to call him Rob?—placed a large hand at the small of her back. His heat seeped through her gown, and she stiffened. She might have pulled away, but suddenly remembered her decision to learn to accept his touch.

Consciously relaxing, Iantha took in a long breath. "Oh, no, my work is not suitable to—"

"That is a perfect idea, Lord Duncan." Mama interrupted Iantha's disclaimer. "Really, Iantha dearest, your talent should be displayed, especially on this occasion. It is not as though you sing or play the harp at parties, as some young ladies do."

"Thank goodness." Lord Duncan made a wry face, then at a sharp glance from his spouse, he hastened to add, "Most of them do it very badly." And then, with a noble effort at diplomacy, he stated, "We have nothing to blush for in Iantha's work."

"Why, thank you, Papa, for such high praise." Iantha responded dryly.

Her fiancé's eyes twinkled. "May I have some then?"

"Well, yes, if you want them."

"I do." His lordship smiled. "You won't disappoint me, will you?"

The smile had an uncomfortable affect on Iantha. In spite of a determination to do so, she no longer felt exasperated at Lord Duncan's high-handed ways. He was being kind, after all.

"No. When I say I will do a thing, you may be sure that I will do it."

He captured her hand and kissed her fingers, an impish expression in his eyes. "I am very glad to hear that."

He meant more than he had said, she could tell, but for the life of her, Iantha could not decide what it was.

A week later the day before Christmas Eve arrived cold and blustery, but though clouds persisted, no sign of snow appeared. The Kethley clan had traveled to the Eyrie the previous evening. As it was Christmas, the party had been planned for families. The younger Keth-leys were thrilled to be included in such a grand affair.

Valeria and Nathaniel looked forward to the company of several of their particular friends who were invited along with their parents, and numerous amusements were planned to fill the time of the schoolroom set. Trying to look unimpressed, Thomas was to have the pleasure of joining his first party as an adult, and was pretending a lofty disinterest in the assortment of young ladies whom he knew to be on the guest list.

Rob strolled into the breakfast parlor that morning to discover Lord Rosley already at table. His future father-in-law nodded a greeting while buttering a scone. "Morning, Duncan. Glad to see another early riser. Are you ready for the invasion?"

Rob chuckled. "That I am. Like any good general pre-paring for an onslaught, I have provided myself with sufficient officers to carry out my plans without my having to worry about the details. I intend to enjoy myself."

And he intended to have enough free time to mount a more important campaign. This would likely be his best opportunity to begin the seducing of his bride-to-be. That was likely to present a long and arduous challenge. Rob had to ask himself again why he had offered to take on such a difficult task. But every time he asked that question, the image of a gentle and innocent girl being cruelly abused leapt into his mind. Followed by one of that girl's courageous and lonely battle to find a place in a world that had no place for her.

Before he had filled his plate, the chance to begin pre-sented itself. Iantha floated into the room in a cloud of rose-colored muslin. He hurried to escort her to the buffet, gently guiding her with his hand on her elbow. He felt the tension in her increase the moment he touched her. Yes, this would be a long process.

Turning her slightly toward him, he looked questioningly into her upturned face, but did not remove his hand. He saw determination flood her eyes. By Jupiter, she *was* a brave little thing. Smiling, he squeezed her arm slightly.

She took a deep breath and, returning the smile tentatively, held her ground. "Good morning, my lord."

Rob nodded in approval and released her. "I hope you were comfortable last night?"

"Oh, certainly. I am becoming very fond of your grandmother's room. I almost feel that I know her." Iantha served herself, and he held her chair as she sat. He let his hand barely brush her shoulder as he returned to his seat.

"Have you seen the adjacent sitting room? I want you to make use of it at any time—any time at all." Again he looked directly into her eyes.

She smiled at him. "Thank you, Rob."

Slowly, hesitantly, she reached out and touched his hand with one finger—as light and fleeting as a butterfly's caress.

Satisfaction flooded Rob. Long though it might prove to be, he was going to win this battle.

As the day wore on, guests began to arrive. And the clouds continued to build. The last visitors appeared just as it began to snow, this occurrence eliciting whoops of joy from the younger contingent tucked away above the stairs. A white Christmas!

Rob's aunt, Lady Dalston, who proved to be a plump, happy elf of a woman, presided over the affair with the ease of decades as a hostess. As dinner neared, the drawing room filled to capacity with the adults of the party.

Iantha delayed her arrival as long as she could, but at last Mama appeared at her bedchamber door and insisted that no more adjustments to Iantha's appearance were necessary. As she approached the drawing room, Iantha took a deep breath and closed her eyes, as if preparing to dive into the sea.

The sea would be easier.

"Ah, there you are." Rob's deep voice sounded at her elbow. Iantha started and opened her eyes. He offered her his arm, and for once, she gratefully accepted its support. He patted her hand. "Come now. You will be fine. You are missing all the compliments on your paintings."

As he escorted her into the room, it seemed to Iantha that the hum of conversation halted for a heartbeat. But perhaps that was her imagination. She *was* sensitive to the reaction of others to her…*situation*. Still, she could see that the presence of her paintings in Lord Duncan's home, added to her presence on his arm, had started eyebrows rising speculatively.

Many of the guests were neighbors Iantha had known all her life. Most of them were kind to her—if she overlooked the occasional pitying glance. But there were several people from London whom she did not recognize. Rob set about remedying that situation immediately.

Approaching a stout, red-faced gentleman with thinning white hair, Rob turned to Iantha. "Miss Kethley, may I present my associate, Mr. Welwyn? Mr. Welwyn represents the firm with whom I bank and invest."

"How do you do?" Iantha could not quite bring herself to extend her hand.

Apparently it was not necessary. Mr. Welwyn bowed. "Your servant, Miss Kethley. Honored to know you." He gazed around the room. "Have you met my assistant,

Stephen Wycomb? The young rascal is here somewhere.''

''I haven't had that pleasure.'' Iantha managed a smile
in spite of the stiffening of her muscles.

''We will find him eventually.'' Rob nodded at his
banker and led Iantha past him to a group of younger
people, several of them neighbors. ''I think you know
these young ladies.''

Iantha nodded. ''Of course. Good evening, Miss Carlisle, Miss Clifton. Hello, Meg. It is nice to see you.''
The daughters of the Kethley's neighbors returned her
greeting, the expressions on their faces varying from
friendliness to curiosity to uncertainty. Only Meg Farlam
extended her hand. Iantha clasped it briefly, smiled again
and turned to the gentlemen who were being introduced
to her.

''Miss Kethley, allow me to present my cousin, Samuel Broughton. Sam also serves as my agent. And do you
know Horace Raunds? He assists his father, Lord Alton,
in the Home Office.''

The fair-haired young diplomat identified himself by
bowing, a warm expression on his pleasant face. Iantha
thought that, in spite of his smile, his eyes held a certain
sadness. She nodded, her neck aching, and produced another smile.

''And this is a fellow repatriate.'' Rob indicated a gentleman with brown hair, a world-weary expression dim-
ming his piercing blue eyes. He looked to be several
years older than Raunds. ''Lord Sebergham spent ten
years in the West Indies—the other side of the world
from where I spent my last decade.''

''Your most obedient servant, Miss Kethley.'' Sebergham bowed.

''Lord Sebergham.'' Iantha found one more smile.

Rob nodded to the two remaining men. "And this is Lord Kendal and Cosby Carrock, whom I believe you know."

"Yes, certainly." With the greatest effort Iantha prevented herself from wrinkling her nose. She knew both the local gentlemen, but she had never liked either of them. They bowed, and she nodded. Carrock was about her age, and nice enough looking, with shining blond hair and an angular face. But ever since the attack he always seemed to her to be smirking. Tonight was no exception. And Kendal… Kendal had a way of looking at all women with speculation in his face.

"If you will excuse us…" Rob deftly moved her away and found her a seat in a window alcove. "I see that this is enough introducing. You are taut as a harp string." He snagged a glass of champagne from a tray carried by a passing footman and pressed it into her hand. "I'll stand here and intercept traffic while you sip that."

Iantha gratefully accepted the wine and turned her shoulder to the room in favor of the view of moonlit mountains beyond the window. Suiting his action to the word, Rob engaged several nearby guests in conversation, his broad shoulders forming a highly effective barricade. Happily, there was to be no party after dinner. If she could get through the meal, she would be able to retreat.

Thank heaven.

*He twirled his champagne glass idly as his gaze followed the slender, silver-haired figure's progress around the room. So the bitch played the fine lady, did she? In spite of her sullied condition, like all the titled gentry's women, she still exuded arrogance and superiority from every pore. They all thought they were so untouchable,*

*so safe from the crude attentions of the opposite sex,
especially the lower members of society. He controlled a
sneer.*

*Perhaps he could yet arrange to bring her down from
that lofty perch.*

*Giving her another lesson should prove highly amus-
ing, in any event.*

## Chapter Six

"Annie, Annie!" The following morning the door of Iantha's sitting room burst open, and Valeria and Nathaniel dashed in. "We are all going out to make snowmen. Come and help us."

She looked up from the notes she was making. "Good morning, loves. Close the door behind you, please, Nat. Now…what is this about snowmen?"

"Everyone is going out to make them. Come on…get your coat."

Iantha frowned. "I don't know, Valeria. I'm not sure that is a suitable activity for a lady at a house party."

"But it's Christmas Eve. Lots of grown-ups are going out. Thomas and Miss Farlam are already outside."

Smiling at this definition of *grown-up,* Iantha shook her head. "But they are very young grown-ups. I'm not sure that I—"

"Aw, please, Annie." Nathaniel put on his most persuasive expression. "You build the *best* snowmen of anyone."

"Hmm. So you believe flattery will sway me, Nat?" She couldn't help but chuckle.

"Yes. I mean, it's true." Her brother shrugged.

Valeria tried another tack. "Lord Duncan is going."

Iantha pondered that information. Did that make her more or less interested in the project? On the one hand, she did enjoy his company. On the other, however, she would need to deal with the effect of his strong masculine energy on her and with the likelihood of his courtly touch. But perhaps that was becoming a bit less of a trial. Last night his arm had been welcome support and his energy an effective screen between her and the crowded room.

It was really not an inappropriate pastime at a house party.

And most of the adult guests would remain near the warmth of the fire. She would have an opportunity to enjoy the children.

And Iantha loved to build snowmen.

Half an hour later Iantha found herself putting the finishing touches on their snowwoman, while her younger siblings wandered off to inspect the handiwork of several others. They had only been gone a few minutes when the two of them came running back.

"Iantha! Valeria and Lord Duncan and I are challenging you to a snowball fight!"

"Now wait!" She turned to smile at them. "Three against one is not fair at all."

"No, but you can choose a team, too. You will be captain of one, and Lord Duncan will lead the other."

"I believe I can readily deduce who initiated this plan." Her eyes twinkled as Rob approached.

"Guilty as charged, ma'am." His ready grin irresistibly brought an answering one from Iantha.

"You will have me playing the complete hoyden."

Rob appeared to give this idea careful consideration,

his head to one side, his expression grave. After a moment he shook his head. "I find it quite impossible to characterize you as a hoyden. You will not say no to this very mild adventure, will you?"

Iantha favored him with a stern look. "I can see that you will forever fling that dare at me whenever I hesitate to fly into whatever scheme you are promoting."

His grin did not diminish. "Very likely. Choose your team."

"Then I must have Thomas. Tom! Come here, I need you and Meg."

Rob turned to Meg. "No, no! I must have Miss Farlam. Will you assist me, ma'am?"

The pert redhead nodded, laughing. "You'd best look to yourself, Tom."

"Then I must have Henry and Sarah," Iantha declared. Two youngsters of an age with Nat and Valeria ran up to stand behind her. Soon all the younger fry had been divided between the two forces.

As Lord Rosley appeared on the steps, Rob called to him. "Here, sir, will you judge the winners of the battle?"

"Happy to." His lordship smiled down at his offspring and their friends. "You have two minutes to gather your ammunition. Then I will give the signal to start." With due ceremony he pulled a gold watch out of his pocket.

For the next two minutes, snow flew in all directions as the combatants scrambled to supply themselves with snowballs, and Lord Rosley studied his watch. Then...

"Now!" shouted his lordship, laughing heartily as the snow began to fly with more purpose.

A chaotic few minutes ensued. Suddenly Rob shouted an order, and with loud battle cries, his side charged Iantha's. Her team responded valiantly, and soon the action degenerated into a melee where every hand was raised against its neighbor, pelting friend and foe alike.

Without warning, as Iantha hurled a missile toward Rob's rapidly approaching figure, she stepped on a patch of ice and began to topple. He made a grab for her, but the ice was no kinder to him than it had been to her. He, too, slipped, and both of them slammed into Iantha's luckless snow maiden. All three went down in a pile of white.

As she fell, Iantha felt Rob's arms close around her. Somehow he twisted so that she landed on top of him, both of them disappearing into the drift.

"Hold! Hold your fire!" Lord Rosley ordered. "The war is over. Both the leaders are down, so clearly it is a tie."

Groans, laughter and protests answered this decision, all parties simultaneously gasping for breath. Iantha sat up and quickly moved off of Rob. He followed suit, brushing snow from his face. Behind them could be heard a bevy of nursemaids, calling their charges in for hot chocolate and cakes and a general warming. Whooping with glee, the younger crowd quickly disappeared into the castle, leaving Rob and Iantha sitting in the snow.

They looked at one another and began to laugh. Long-suppressed mirth bubbled up in Iantha, and she laughed so hard that tears ran down her face. Rob was also wiping his eyes.

Suddenly, something in Iantha broke free.

The laughter changed, and a sob choked its way out of her throat. Horrified, she did her best to stifle it, but she could not. Sob followed sob.

"Iantha! What's wrong?" Rob leaned toward her solicitously. "Why are you crying?"

"I—I d-don't know," she managed to sniffle. "I *never*

cry. I haven't cried since..." She stumbled to a stop, fishing in her pocket for a handkerchief. She *must* regain control. Gulping long breaths, Iantha willed herself to stop crying and blew her nose.

"Since you were assaulted?"

She nodded. "I will *not* behave like a watering pot." Another sob threatened to emerge. She clamped down on it and forbade it to come out.

Rob was looking at her thoughtfully. "You have never wept for what was done to you—for what you lost?"

"No." She raised her chin and firmed her mouth. "What good would it do? I am much better off when I keep a firm rein on my emotions. I simply dropped my guard in the exuberance of the snow fight. I will be more careful."

"So the bastards also stole from you your ability to grieve or to enjoy yourself intensely."

She looked back at him, considering. "I suppose you might say that. Though why I should start crying when I was having such a good time, I'm sure I don't know."

He gently brushed the freezing drops away from her cheek. "It is my experience that when one's soul is full of anguish, laughter and tears lie very close together."

Rob damned the scoundrels with every curse he had garnered in his well-traveled life. By the time Iantha had retired to her room, she was completely composed—on the outside. But today's incident showed clearly how much torment she stored inside. He had been correct in believing that she would enjoy a romp in the snow with the youngsters and that it might loosen the rigidity with which she conducted herself. He had not realized how much was held at bay behind the fortress.

He should have known.

His own experience should have told him that.

Had he taken on an impossible task? Rob refused to think so. The fact that Iantha's barriers had failed for a few heartbeats encouraged him. She *could* laugh and cry. But it was unlikely that any progress would be achieved with so many others about. She would be too embarrassed if another tearful episode occurred. Now she would surely lock all her emotions up behind a heavy dungeon door.

A dungeon in which she had imprisoned herself.

Rob needed a new plan.

Late in the afternoon the party guests and most of the staff assembled in the entry of the castle for the lighting of the yule log. Rob had ordered a huge tree trunk hauled up the mountain, and it now rested in the enormous fireplace. Earlier in the day the younger children had all had a hand in decorating it with holly and mistletoe.

The gathering waxed a bit louder and more boisterous than the previous evening, this fact being attributable largely to the fact that several of the gentlemen had been liberally availing themselves of Rob's excellent cellar as they whiled away the afternoon playing cards. And it was Christmas Eve. But in spite of their exuberance, all maintained a decorum suitable to the presence of ladies and children.

A moment of silence prevailed as Rob took a torch from Burnside and approached the fireplace. This was shattered by a piercing wail from the youngest log decorator when he realized that his handiwork was about to go up in flames. Happily, his nurse had the presence of mind to mollify the distressed artist with a large tea cake.

Amid the general laughter, Rob applied the torch to

the kindling, then turned back to his guests. "Merry Christmas, everyone! And welcome to the Eyrie."

A cheer went up. Cups of hot chocolate and eggnog were passed around and conversation resumed. Iantha sipped sparingly from her drink. Considering the disaster following the snowball war, she had best be very careful not to drink too much. If she ever let her restraint slip, there was no saying what she might do. She watched Rob pass among his guests, laughing and joking with them. Would she never feel that ease again, that ability to just live and enjoy life?

Six years.

Six long, bitter, agonizing years.

Would she ever be free?

As she watched him, Rob angled in the direction of a group of gentlemen whose discussion had gotten a bit loud. Iantha felt quite sure that his lordship would not tolerate an unruly affair, and that he had every capability of maintaining order in his house. Even from her vantage point in a corner, she could sense his quiet power flowing around him as he joined the circle.

The plump banker, Welwyn, and a tall gray-haired man with impressive side-whiskers looked to be the center of the group. They were surrounded by several of the younger men Iantha had met the night before. She recognized the young diplomat, Horace Raunds, and from a family resemblance, deduced that the whiskered gentleman was his father, Lord Alton of the Home Office. By process of elimination, the slender, dark, hawk-faced young man she didn't know must be Mr. Welwyn's assistant, Stephen Wycomb. Certainly no resemblance there. And apparently little agreement of opinion.

"I say, Duncan." Lord Alton rounded on Rob as he approached the group. "Add your weight to what Welwyn and I are trying to explain to these youngsters. Napoleon is a threat to the civilized world.''

"Come now, Father. Hardly that." Horace spoke earnestly, ticking his points off on his fingers. "Look at what he has accomplished on the Continent. He has brought order out of utter chaos. He has stabilized the currency. His Napoleonic code has made sense of the old French common law after years of injustice. Hardly a threat to civilized life. He—''

"All very well, of course, Raunds," the banker interrupted. "But what of his Continental Plan? His design to exclude England from the European market? The effect would be devastating to our balance of trade."

"And in addition to that, England would lose her ability to control Europe through our financial largesse," Lord Alton insisted. "That is all Bonaparte needs to garner enough support to invade us."

His son looked disgusted. "Simply buying friendship. It never succeeds in the long run."

Alton shook his head. "Ah, but it *does* succeed, Horace! And British customs and morals are far better suited to managing the affairs of the world than those of the French."

Rob sighed inwardly. How was it that the English seemed to be blissfully and ignorantly unable to see past their own point of view, despite the wealth of culture and information available in other parts of the world? He opened his mouth to speak, but before he could comment, the younger Raunds spoke again.

"How can you say that, Father, when we have a king who is mad as a mayfly and an heir little better?"

"Now there you have a point!" Stephen Wycomb, the younger banker, spoke up, a sneer on his sharp face. "George and Prinny are as strange a pair as you may find. And the money they and the royal dukes spend...! Were it not for the funds we receive from our colonies, they would have bankrupted us long ago.''

This point Rob could appreciate. He nodded. ''That is certainly true, Wycomb. And we will not be able to keep raping our colonies forever. We have already lost America, and we will one day lose India.''

''Nonsense!'' Lord Alton looked appalled. ''The Indians can hardly be expected to rule themselves. They are little better than pagan savages. We must—'' He stopped his tirade abruptly as Vijaya, who was leaning against the wall a short distance away, straightened, his jeweled clothing creating a ripple of light, and turned his brilliant blue gaze toward the speaker.

''Hear, hear!'' All the gentlemen looked in the direction of the new voice. Cosby Carrock approached the group, his faltering footsteps testifying to the amount of spirits he had consumed in the course of the afternoon. ''Alton has the right of it. Can't have bloody heathens in control. Why should they have all those jewels and the gold and the opium?'' Vijaya stiffened and took a step forward, and Carrock looked pointedly first at him, then at Rob. ''And how any English gentleman can bring one of them here and expose our women to— Damnation!'' He broke off his tirade to mop at the wine he had just spilled down his waistcoat.

Out of the corner of his eye, Rob saw Vijaya take another step toward them. Rob moved to put himself between his friend and Carrock. From different parts of the room, Samuel Broughton and Lord Sebergham were converging on what appeared to be a growing trouble spot. Lord Alton seemed to be looking for a way to make an embarrassed retreat.

Rob fixed Carrock with an authoritative eye. "That will be enough, Cosby. Take a damper. You're foxed."

Vijaya paused a few feet away. Sam Broughton stopped beside him, while Sebergham made for Cosby Carrock.

The baron took Cosby's arm. "You need a fresh glass and a fresh waistcoat, Carrock. Come, I'll go with you."

"But…" Carrock pulled back. "Haven't had my say yet."

"You've had it." Rod nodded grimly at Sebergham, who leveled an icy stare at his charge and tightened his grip.

Carrock glared sullenly at his host for a moment. Rob didn't move, but returned the stare implacably. Carrock yanked his arm away from the baron and stumbled toward the stairs. Sebergham followed him out. A gust of air seemed to sweep through the room as the crowd exhaled held breaths.

Rob glanced around to see Sam and Vijaya strolling toward the opposite door before letting his own breath out. Damn Carrock, the drunken young lout! Rob wasn't naive enough to believe that Vijaya would be universally accepted in England, but he had hoped his first foray into society might be a bit more comfortable. But he knew Vijaya.

He would hold his own.

And so would Rob's bride to be.

Nothing more was seen of Cosby Carrock for the rest of the evening, and of course, Vijaya did not appear at the table for dinner. He later joined them in the drawing room and conversed quietly with Sam and Mr. Farlam.

Iantha stayed with the party long enough to drink a cup of tea and then quietly excused herself and retired to her own sitting room. What a relief! She stood for a while looking out at the moonlit snow, drinking in the silence, then took out her notes and began to write. She was still writing when a soft knock sounded at her door.

Iantha shivered. When had the room gotten so cold? Pulling a shawl around her shoulders, she went to the door. "Who's there?"

"Rob. May I come in?"

Iantha hesitated. She wasn't quite ready to give up her solitude. Still, he was doing everything in his power to make her stay enjoyable. She owed him some consideration. Turning the key in the lock, she opened the door a crack. Rob pushed it wider and stepped into the room. He wrapped his arms around himself and scowled.

"It's freezing in here! Why didn't you ring for someone to make up the fire?" He knelt beside the hearth and poked the embers, then added a couple of logs.

"Thank you. I became so engrossed in my work, I didn't even notice the cold." Iantha tugged the shawl tighter around her.

"One day I shall find you a frozen corpse in some out of the way place." Standing, Rob dusted off his hands and smiled at Iantha. "You are not ready for bed. What have you been doing so long?"

"I was writing." She glanced at the mantel clock. "My goodness! I had no idea it was so late. No wonder the fire died down."

"What are you writing? May I see it?"

"Oh, no!" Iantha moved to block his view of the desk. "I… It is not ready to be seen."

Rob smiled down at her. "Then, by all means, I will not look. Most of the guests have gone to bed, but there is a Christmas celebration afoot in the servants' hall. Would you like to go down with me and meet everyone?

I have gifts to distribute. You might help me if you are
not too tired.''

"No, I am not tired.'' Iantha thought for a moment.
"I believe I will join you. If I am to be mistress here
one day, I should meet them all.''

"I think so.'' Rob offered her his arm. After only the
briefest hesitation, Iantha took it, and they strolled
through the hall and down several flights of stairs. The
servants' hall was bright with a fire in the huge hearth,
and garlands draped the mantel. Feller was tuning his
fiddle, and tankards of ale were being passed around.
Iantha drew back at the sight of the crowded room, but
Rob patted her hand reassuringly and led her through the
door.

"Welcome! Welcome, me lord…Miss Kethley. Come
in.'' Burnside hastened toward them.

Iantha smiled at the familiar face. "Hello, Burnside.
How have you been?''

"Fine as silk, Miss Kethley. And good it is to see you
again.'' He pulled a chair toward her. "Do sit.''

"Not yet.'' Rob placed a detaining hand on her shoulder. "We have a task to do first.'' He lifted one of several
large baskets that were lined up against the wall. Brightly
wrapped gifts were heaped in it to the point of spilling
out. Rob began to call out names, handing the gifts to
Iantha. She gave the package to the person who stepped
forward, repeating the name and wishing him or her a
merry Christmas. A very good way to learn everyone on
her staff, she reflected.

At first Iantha felt awkward, but the faces all were
smiling or shy, never judgmental nor pitying. It occurred
to her that the women of the servant class were often
abused by more highly placed men, and the blame frequently fell on the woman.

Had any of these smiling girls, in their previous employment, ever been accosted in that manner? Iantha had heard of several such cases, but had never given it the thought it deserved. Now she understood their predicament. The idea gave her a feeling of camraderie with them, and she relaxed even more, startled as she realized how much more comfortable she was with them than with her own peers.

When the gifts had all been distributed, the furniture was pushed back against the wall and Feller struck up a tune. Sets were formed for country dances, and Iantha was treated to seeing several more jigs. When everyone urged Rob to jig, Iantha found herself joining in, laughing as he pulled off his coat and took the floor.

She found herself enjoying his robust vigor and the sight of his muscles moving under his clothes. Something in her warmed.

At last the sets formed for a ninepins reel. Rob extended his hand. "Come, Miss Kethley, we now have the opportunity to perform the reel correctly."

Before she could demur, he drew her to her feet and into the set. Soon she found herself passed merrily from position to position amid much stamping and clapping. The music got faster, and she raced to match it, catching Rob's hand each time the steps brought them together. The dance ended with a great cheer and his arm around her waist.

Iantha retreated to her seat, fanning herself with her hand, but before she could sit down, Rob drew her to the door, shouting Christmas wishes to his staff. She laughed and waved, calling her own farewells, as he guided her out the exit.

They ran laughing up the first flight of stairs. At the top they paused to catch their breath, and before Iantha knew what he was about, Rob clasped her in his arms and pulled her close. His warm mouth came down on hers. For a moment Iantha couldn't move. And then, before she knew what she wanted to do, he released her and stood smiling down at her.

"You enjoyed yourself." It was more a statement than a question.

"I...uh... Yes, indeed, I did." She stood looking up at him, a bit stunned. He had kissed her. Actually kissed her!

For the first time in her life.

It had all happened so fast that she hadn't time to react at all or to feel afraid. So what had she felt? Certainly it had not been unpleasant, but...

Rob returned her gaze soberly for a moment. Then he lowered his lips to hers again, this time more deliberately. Now he did not hold her tightly, but rather merely rested his hands on her arms. Iantha stiffened, but did not pull away. She felt his breath on her lips, smelled the smoky scent that surrounded him. For a moment she held her breath. Then she closed her eyes.

His mouth touched hers softly, very gently. She could hear him breathing. Feel his hands tightening on her arms. Even as she became aware of each sensation, he released her and stepped back.

"Well." He took a deep breath and wiped a hand over his face. "I did not intend that, but it proved very enjoyable indeed. Thank you." He smiled, a question in his eyes.

"I... Yes. That was very...very nice."

He must have heard the hesitation in her voice, for he responded to it. "But it is enough for now?"

Iantha nodded thoughtfully. "Yes... Yes, I believe so."

"Very well." He turned and guided her up the stairs. "Enough is as good as a feast."

Had that been progress or a reverse? Rob wasn't at all sure. As twice before, his bride-to-be had relaxed in a moment of fun and physical activity, only to retreat even further the following morning. At breakfast she had been her former polite, withdrawn self, subtly moving away at the slightest touch.

She *had* let him kiss her. Twice. But she had been stiff as a poker the second time, which had been a distinct disappointment to a stiffening portion of his own anatomy. At this rate he might succeed eventually in getting her into his bed, but not as a willing partner. She would be, rather, a compliant wife who simply tolerated him.

The devil with that!

He hungered for her touch, her response, for her to desire him. Somehow he must find a way to release her emotions from the prison in which she so firmly kept them. Otherwise he would find himself, for the rest of his life, caged in his own prison of loneliness.

In spite of himself his thoughts drifted back to Shakti's earthy warmth. His first wife had joined him with a beautiful natural enthusiasm that always left him weak with satisfaction. Strange how the physical exchange created that sense of acceptance and affection. Was he being foolish to think he could have that with this injured wraith?

The more he was with her, the more he wanted it. She kindled feelings in him that he had not had in two years. Of course, the first was the wish to protect her, to use his brawny body to shelter her from further undeserved harm and unhappiness. But a more physical desire grew stronger in him every day. For a brief moment last night he had relished the delicate feel of her, the tininess of her waist, the softness of full, high breasts. No two women could possibly be more different than his Iantha and his Shakti. Both were desirable in their own way.

And Iantha was in this world with him.

Most of the ladies were retiring for an afternoon rest in preparation for the ball Christmas night—the ball at which her father would announce her engagement to Lord Duncan. Iantha shivered as she climbed the stairs. Her betrothal was becoming a reality. She moved hourly toward a man and a marriage bed that she might not be able to endure. What *was* she to do?

Perhaps she should cry off now, Iantha thought, but she resisted the idea. She didn't want to take advantage of his lordship, entrapping him in a cold bed, but neither was she quite ready to admit defeat. He was so kind, so understanding. If she relinquished this opportunity, she would never have another chance at the family and home she wanted. And on a hopeful note, she had weathered her first kisses none too ill. Of course, the first one had happened so fast she hardly knew that it had happened at all.

But then there was the second one.

The one she'd had time to think about. Thank God he had not held her as tightly as he had during the first one— as some of them had when… No! She would not allow herself to think of them, of her bruised, cut lips… No! Iantha stopped her thoughts again. She must never allow herself to be drawn back to that day.

Besides, Lord Duncan's kiss had been nothing like what happened before. He felt different and he smelled different and he touched her with such gentleness. She might become accustomed to him. Yes, there was an excellent chance. She must rely on her intellect, not let herself think about...

Control. She would exert control.

Lost in her thoughts, Iantha looked up, startled when she perceived a figure lounging at the top of the staircase. "Oh! Good afternoon, Lord Kendal. I did not see you there."

Kendal straightened and bowed. "I have been waiting for you. I heard you bidding the ladies goodbye and felt sure you were coming up to your room."

Oh, dear. A most disquieting situation. Iantha searched for an unmistakable dismissal. "Yes. I am very tired, and I have the headache. If you will excuse me..."

She walked around him, but he turned to accompany her. Iantha could feel every muscle in her body growing tight. He placed a hand on her neck and rubbed. "I know an excellent cure for the headache. If you will allow me, it would be my pleasure to serve you."

Serve her! As though she were a mare and he a stallion? Surely that was not what he meant. She pulled away from his hand and turned to glare at him. "That will not be necessary, I thank you."

He quickly captured her fingers. "Come now, Miss Kethley, we both know you are no innocent schoolroom miss. I am sure I could be of service to you." He turned her hand over and kissed the palm.

Damn him! He was not the first man to think that her experience somehow conferred a need on her that only a man could satisfy. She jerked her hand away, stepping back against the wall. "Sir! You forget yourself! Please allow me to pass."

"Yes, Kendal. You also forget me." Both Kendal and Iantha jumped and turned toward Rob, who was approaching down the corridor. "I am not accustomed to allowing ladies to suffer unwanted attention in my home." He stopped a few steps away, holding Kendal's gaze with his own.

Kendal stepped away from Iantha, but did not withdraw. "Perhaps you should ask the lady *her* preferences before you interfere."

"I know this lady's preference. I suggest you move on."

Kendal continued to glare and did not move on. Rob shrugged. "There is a nasty storm brewing, Kendal. You wouldn't want to find yourself out in it."

The other man narrowed his eyes in speculation, then bowed, a knowing smirk on his face. "Of course. I always respect a lady's *preference*."

He whirled and went back down the stairs. Rob turned to Iantha. "I'm sorry you had to endure that. May I walk you to your sitting room?"

"Thank you." She drew herself up, and cursing the blush she knew must be coloring her face, started down the hall, careful not to touch his lordship. Why must he see that episode? The very thought of what had just happened made her feel dirty. She didn't want anyone to know that some men saw her the way Kendal did. And he had strained the precious control she was depending on to deal with Lord Duncan.

Rob was watching her closely as he opened the door of her parlor. As soon as he had closed it behind them, he turned to face her. "Why are you embarrassed? You are not responsible for Kendal's behavior."

Iantha walked to the window and stood looking out at the blowing snow. She could almost wish that Rob *had* put Kendal out into it. She felt Rob's presence as he moved to stand behind her. Without turning around she said, "He makes me feel soiled."

"You aren't, you know." His voice was gentle.

"You and Mama keep telling me that. But other people—people like Lord Kendal—clearly think I am. How anyone can think that what I experienced made me *want* to repeat it I cannot imagine."

"Men such as he would like to think that *all* women find them irresistible." Iantha could hear the smile in Rob's voice. She turned toward him, and he sobered. "But Kendal is cautious in whom he approaches."

"So he chooses me—already damaged goods."

"Don't ever let me hear you say that again!"

At the thunder in his voice, Iantha jumped and stepped hastily back. His lordship did not move, but his voice softened. "Forgive me. I did not meant to shout. But I am serious, Iantha. Do not allow them the victory of your seeing yourself that way. Do not allow the likes of Kendal to make you view yourself in that light. Do not allow *anyone* to do that to you."

Iantha stared down at her shoes. He was right, of course. "I try not to, but it is very hard."

"I'm sure it is." She sensed him reaching for her, then dropping his hand to his side. She didn't know whether to be glad or sorry that he had not touched her. Perhaps he didn't want to. She lifted her gaze to his. The expression in his eyes surprised her.

There was a *wanting* in them.

Could he possibly really want her?

# Chapter Seven

Rob looked down into Iantha's upturned face. Her violet eyes were clear and deep and questioning. Something in him wanted desperately to step into them and soar with her into the mountain sky. To seek the highest pinnacle. To wrap her in his arms and make her no longer a wraith. To make her real.

But not today.

No, this was hardly an auspicious moment to indulge that lofty dream. Rob shook himself and came back to the reality of situation. He smiled ruefully. "Let us consign Lord Kendal and his ilk to the devil. This is Christmas." He reached into his coat pocket and withdrew a small, wrapped parcel. "I have something for you."

Iantha's face brightened. "A gift for me? How kind of you." She signaled that they should sit on the sofa in front of the fire and led the way. When they were comfortably settled, he handed her the package and watched her pull the ribbon and paper off, relieved and pleased when the happiest smile he had yet seen on her face appeared.

"An Anne Vallayer-Coster miniature! I would know

her work anywhere. How marvelous! I would not have thought you could find anything by her in Cumberland.''

Rob grinned. ''I didn't. Sam went to London last week. I threatened him and told him not to dare come back without one. I had hoped for something larger, but this was all he could find on short notice.''

Iantha smiled. ''This is perfect. I will set it on my bed table in a place of honor. But you are going to laugh. I have something for you, also.''

''Why am I going to laugh at that?'' Rob watched the graceful sway of her hips as she walked to the desk and returned with a slightly larger package.

''Open it and you will see.''

Rob made short work of the wrappings, uncovering a folder of heavy marbleized paper. Opening it carefully, he revealed a small painting of a waterfall in full spate, done in strong glowing colors. Mounted on the opposite side of the cover was a short poem, written in a delicate script.

And chuckle he did. ''Another painting. Well, they do say great minds run together.''

''Do you like it? I did the watercolor about a year ago when I went with my father to Crag Force. It… Somehow it seemed to suit you, so I added the poem.''

Rob cleared his throat and read aloud.

''Crag Force
O rush of water bright,
The very earth is cloven by thy might.
My poor senses thy thunder overwhelms,
Dizzied as in faerie's realm.
Captive held is my enraptured gaze.
It is my soul the ransom pays.

Dare I rest here in this hour,
Or will I crumble, shattered by thy power?
  "Iantha Elizabeth Kethley"


Rob slowly lowered the folder to his lap and, with one
finger, wiped a tear from the corner of his eye. He turned
to meet her anxious eyes. "That is beautiful. You wrote
it for me? I... No one ever gave me such a gift before.
I am touched and flattered more than I can say."

He reached out and stroked her face lightly with his big
hand, relieved when she did not move away. Rob wondered
if she realized the significance of her own words.

*"...will I crumble, shattered by thy power?"*

God! She was so afraid, and he couldn't even enclose
her in his arms to comfort her.

He would not, he vowed, be the cause of her crumbling.

Rob shut his eyes for a moment in a prayer for wisdom.


She had never really been to a ball. Had she made her
come-out, no doubt it would have become a routine experience by now. Iantha should have been excited, but
somehow her anxiety kept the excitement away. Tonight
the world would come to understand that Lord Duncan
planned to take the very questionable Miss Kethley to
wife. Every person in the room would be thinking about
what had happened to her, wondering what in the world
his lordship was thinking, what his true motivation might
be. And those who had heard the story of her sojourn in
his house would be speculating even further.

Heaven help her.

At least she looked reasonably well. Through the mirror she watched Molly put the finishing touches on her

hair. Her locks echoed the low-cut, silver ball gown and slender necklace. As Rob had said, she did look a bit like the powdered ladies of the last century. The effect was pleasant enough. She would not put her newly acquired fiancé to the blush.

A soft knock fell on the door. Iantha turned in that direction while Molly went to open it, pausing to pick up something lying on the floor in front of it. Rob, resplendent in formal attire, stepped in.

He was smiling his infectious smile. "Are you ready for the momentous occasion? I'll escort you down."

"I suppose I am." Iantha rose and walked to meet him, a reluctant smile coaxed out by his. "Perhaps when this is over, I shall be able to relax." She turned to her maid. "Thank you, Molly. That will be all."

Molly curtsied, handed her the object she had just retrieved from the floor, and went out the door. The object proved to be a folded note. Iantha unfolded the paper and glanced at the message. Her heart sank, and she could feel the blood draining from her face. She whirled around and started for the fire.

Rob intercepted her in two long strides. "Not so fast. What is that? You are white as the snow."

Iantha's mouth dried up, and she tried in vain to find words to answer him. How could she describe the vile thing? Rob didn't wait for an explanation, but took the letter from her and scanned it. As he read, his eyebrows drew closer and closer together until he finally let out a roar.

"Damnation!" He started toward the fire himself, took a step and halted, turning back to Iantha, his expression dark. "If anything deserves to be cast in the flames, this atrocity certainly does. But I think we should make a push to discover who sent it. We might be able to identify the writer by his hand.''

Rob stuffed it into his pocket and reached out to clasp Iantha's arms. She continued to look down at her hands, shame taking her breath.

"How many of these bloody abominations have you received?''

Iantha shrugged. "I have no idea. I have gotten at least one a month for the last six years.''

"And you have hidden them from your parents?''

"After they became upset. Now I...I just burn the letters.''

"Dear heaven! Were they all like this one?''

"Yes...well, the language was the same. I can't even understand much of it. Some are like this one, calling me vile names, reminding me of my condition and accusing me of a haughtiness to which I have no right. Others...'' Oh, God, the others. How could she even think of the others?

Iantha drew in a long breath. Control. She reached for her control. "Some recount the...the event in great detail and tell me how much they enjoyed it. They—they...'' Her composure was slipping. "They tell me that they will do it again s-soon.'' In spite of her determination, Iantha dropped her head into her hands.

The sound that issued from her prospective bridegroom sounded more like the growl of a beast than the utterance of a man. His arms closed around her, and to her surprise, he was trembling. She could hear him gulping air, trying to contain his rage. Somehow the extent of his anger comforted her. For a moment its energy shielded her.

Several heartbeats later he released her, and she looked up into his face. "Why? Why are they doing this to me?''

"Because they are evil and cruel and desire power.

They know how much their actions hurt you. It makes them feel powerful to stalk you, to remind you of it, to frighten you again. Damnation! And I invited one of them into your presence.''

''Oh, dear God! They are here! Someone is here, in this house. One of the men who did that to me is *right here!*'' A wave of rising hysteria threatened to choke her. She gasped for a sustaining breath and gritted her teeth. Control.

Rob's arm tightened around her shoulders. He stood silent for a long moment, his eyes narrowed. Finally he shook his head. ''Perhaps. But not necessarily. This letter does not mention the specific event. The writer may just be someone who is angry with you.''

''Lord Kendal?'' Iantha pulled away and begin to pace the floor.

''Hmm. That might fit with this afternoon's incident. But I have the impression that his intelligence is not sufficiently lacking for him to do anything so obvious. Is there someone else you have refused?''

''No one who is here. No…wait. Long before the attack occurred, I slapped Cosby Carrock's face, but that was just a boyish—''

''No.'' Rob held up one finger. ''That sort of behavior cannot be excused as boyish folly. I think I know you well enough to be convinced that you would not have struck him if you could have dismissed him politely.''

''Well, yes. He was extremely insistent and has since leered at me at every opportunity. I've known him all my life, but I have never liked him. He was a cruel child.''

''And, perhaps, a cruel young man.''

''I would think so. His taunting of Vijaya…'' Iantha nodded and came to a stop in front of Rob, eyes narrowed in thought. ''You may be correct. I have been thinking that all the notes came from those who participated in the assault, but some of them may be from malicious gossips—perhaps even women.''

''I doubt that a woman wrote that note, considering the language.'' Rob shook his head. ''But we do have a pair we may suspect. I will make it my business to see a sample of their handwriting. As drunk as Cosby was yesterday while he was gambling, someone very likely holds his vowels. I'll think of some way to see them. Kendal is too good a gambler for that.''

Rob opened the door and held out his arm, smiling. ''Now. I want my bride-to-be to put all judgmental persons out of her mind and march downstairs with her head held high like the strong soldier she is. We will rout this cowardly foe with a show of force.''

Iantha could not quite smile, but nodded, straightened her shoulders and placed her arm on his.

Control.


There was an audible murmur as Lord Rosley finished his announcement and lifted his glass in a toast to Iantha and Rob. It rose louder and a scattering of applause was heard as the meaning sank in and the guests began to crowd around them to offer felicitations. Iantha fought the urge to back away, pasting a smile on her face and responding with what she hoped was appropriate warmth. What thoughts were concealed behind those pleasant faces? Were the guests shocked? Disapproving?

Or actually happy for her?

She might as well take the well-wishes at face value. She would soon be Lady Duncan, an honored member of the community, no longer a disgraced single female living with her family. She would play the part. Not that anyone present would ever forget what had happened to her.

She certainly would not.

A moment of panic clutched her when she realized that she and Rob would be expected to lead out the first dance. She had danced nowhere but the servants' hall for the last six years. The staff's friendly acceptance of her had made it easy, but in this assembly everyone would be looking at her, remembering.

And wondering if Lord Duncan was out of his mind.

She placed her trembling hand in his and glanced up into his face. He appeared as happy as a bridegroom should. Iantha drew in a breath and tried to answer his smile.

And Rob winked at her.

Suddenly her tension released like a dam breaking. Iantha laughed aloud, and his lordship led her down the floor. For the first time she felt as though she had a companion with whom to face the world. What a heady relief!

From that point the evening progressed much better. Iantha danced with several partners, avoided several others and began to enjoy herself. Still, after hours of mingling with so many people she felt the need to withdraw for a moment. It would not do for the honoree of the ball to disappear for long, so she stepped into a curtained window embrasure and looked out into the night. As Rob had said earlier, a fierce storm was raging. It gave her a comfortable, cozy feeling to watch the windblown snow safely shut out of the house.

Suddenly, her peace was shattered by the sound of a raucous, drunken laugh. Iantha froze. She closed her eyes and was suddenly again lying on frozen ground, numb with pain, her heart pounding in her ears, tears frozen on her face. She had heard that laugh that night. Surely there were not two people in all the world who sounded that much like a braying donkey.

Oh, dear God. Was he standing a few feet away from her?

She tried to make herself move, to peep out of the curtain and discover the identity of the laughter.

She couldn't do it. Fear threatened to choke her.

How long Iantha stood immobile she didn't know. Finally her mind begin to work again. She must look. Perhaps she could at last identify one of her attackers. Sternly fighting the terror, she peered cautiously around the curtain. All she could see was the throng of dancers and clumps of people loudly conversing.

Where was Rob? She must tell Rob! Iantha darted out of the enclosure, gazing wildly about. Someone spoke to her, but she brushed past, almost running. Where was he? Where *was* he?

"Iantha!"

She stifled a shriek as someone grasped her arm.

"Iantha, stop. It is I."

Rob! She covered her face with both hands, trying to find enough control to speak. After several breaths she blurted out, "He's here!"

"Who?" Rob sent a searching gaze around the room.

"I don't know. I heard him laugh. He laughed the way he did the night they..." She couldn't go on.

Several people had stopped to listen, puzzled expressions gradually clearing when they realized what she meant. They, too, began to look around the room.

"You didn't see him?" Rob clasped her arms and looked into her face.

She shook her head. "I had stepped into the window for a moment."

"Then all we can do is hope he laughs again. Can you stay with me and listen for him? Can you do it?"

"I...I will try." Iantha straightened. "Yes. I will do it."

And she had done it, little though it had availed them. Iantha's courage was amazing, Rob thought. She had calmed herself, and they had strolled around the room together until the guests began to yawn and drift away toward their respective bedchambers.

But they heard no distinctive laugh.

The only disturbance occurred when Carrock once more made a drunken fool of himself and was once more escorted up to bed, this time by Wycomb. Lord Sebergham had made it plain that he had done that duty once and did not desire to do so again.

As Rob untied his cravat in preparation for bed, he reflected that he now had a growing list of persons whom he hoped never to see again. Carrock and Kendal would for damn sure never again be invited into his home.

Carrock was a nuisance, and Rob despised Kendal's sort, but his feelings toward the vicious letter writer and the noisy laugher were distinctly predatory. He would hunt them down if it was the last thing he ever did! Were they one and the same? If he had just one more clue, a hint of who the cad who'd laughed was, then perhaps he could determine if the man was, in fact, one of Iantha's attackers.

And if he was, heaven help him!

Suddenly, the unmistakable crack of a pistol shot reverberated through the stone corridors.

Flinging behind him the shirt he had just pulled off, Rob charged out of his bedchamber and raced in the direction from which he thought the sound had come. All down the hallway people were poking their heads out of their doors, a few of the men emerging in various degrees of dishabille, and everyone asking everyone else who had fired the shot. A quick survey pinpointed a door still tightly shut, midway down the corridor.

Rob approached the door and tried the handle. It didn't budge. He rattled it with an authoritative knock. There was no response. He turned to the watchers. "Whose room is this?"

A mutter of voices and a process of elimination ensued. Finally Horace Raunds spoke up. "It must be Carrock's room."

"Yes, it is. I brought him up here earlier this evening." Stephen Wycomb, tying the belt of his robe, rounded the corner from an adjoining wing in time to confirm this opinion.

"Do you have the key?" Rob shook the door again.

"No. Cosby had it. I had to unlock the door for him, but I returned the key to him."

"Did you hear him lock it?"

Wycomb shrugged. "I don't remember. I don't think so."

"Maybe he is just sleeping it off." Rob banged on the door with increasing vigor.

An anxious voice at Rob's elbow interrupted him. "Lord Duncan, excuse me." Rob looked down into the face of a short, slightly built man with graying hair. "I believe my son would have awakened by now with all this noise. Is there another key to the room?"

"I'm sure there is, Lord Kilbride, but my housekeeper probably has it." Rob glanced at the faces surrounding him, finally spotting a henchman in the back of the crowd. "Thursby, please go fetch Mrs. Lamonby and tell her to bring her keys."

The footman departed at a run for the back stairs. Various of the guests returned to their rooms to don shirts or dressing gowns. Rob did not. He wanted to be sure no one else tried to get into the locked chamber. Gradually the group of men in the hall grew larger, the women contenting themselves with peering out from their respective rooms.

After a short wait Thursby came back with Mrs. Lamonby. The housekeeper was wrapped in a flannel robe, her graying hair in a long braid. In her hand she carried a large ring of keys. Rob stepped back and indicated the door with a nod. He waited impatiently while she sorted through the keys, peering nearsightedly at various markings. At length she selected one, tried it and discarded it. Her second choice proved more successful, and Rob heard the click of the lock opening. He stepped forward and gestured for Mrs. Lamonby to move away.

She did so, and Rob turned the handle and opened the door a crack. He cautiously looked through it, then, with an oath, pushed the door open and dashed into the room. A small crowd of men surged in after him, stopping near the door at the sight that confronted them. Lord Alton placed a comforting hand on Lord Kilbride's shoulder.

Cosby Carrock lay facedown in a pool of blood. Rob knelt beside him and searched for a pulse. Finding none, he rolled Carrock onto his back. A large hole gaped in his bare chest. Rob glanced around for the pistol. He didn't find that, either. He got to his feet.

"Please. Everyone stay back. Does anyone see the pistol?" Presumably, everyone looked about, but no one answered. Rob stood. "We need to clear the room. If all of you would wait outside…" The shuffle of feet indicated a retreat. Rob waited until no one but himself was left in the room, then closed and locked the door, wrinkling his nose at the smell of death that pervaded the chamber.

Where was the damn pistol? From all appearances Carrock had shot himself in a locked room. But he hadn't done it without a weapon. And with that wound, he hadn't done anything at all after he was shot, let alone hide the gun.

Rob made a thorough search for the pistol. He discovered no weapon anywhere that Carrock might have flung it, even had he been able. The conclusion was inescapable. Cosby Carrock had not shot himself.

Rob had a murderer in his house.

# Chapter Eight

"But what happened to the damn pistol?" Rob was pacing back and forth in front of the fireplace in Iantha's sitting room. He had gone there immediately after re-locking Carrock's room. He wanted to be sure she was not frightened. And somehow, of late, discussing things with her had begun to feel natural. "The door was locked from the inside. I saw the key and removed it. So who locked it from the inside earlier, and where are they?"

"Cosby might have locked it himself." Iantha's brow puckered in thought.

"True. But he did not do it after he was shot, nor did he shoot himself with a nonexistent pistol. Someone was in that room with him, and that someone shot him. But how did they get out?" Rob stopped in front of Iantha and scowled.

"I don't know, my lord. Is there possibly a hidden way out?"

Rob pondered that question. "No, I'm pretty sure there isn't. Sam and I used to explore for such things when we were boys. We found one in the master bedchamber that comes out on a narrow track on the face of the cliff behind the castle, and one in the corridor that comes out in the kitchen. It was probably used by the servants in former times. We looked and looked for others, but didn't find them.''

"Maybe we should search again."

"Aye, I will do so tomorrow."

"Why don't we look now?"

"We? Now?" Rob turned toward her. "There is a dead body in the room now."

"True. But you covered it, didn't you?"

"The room stinks."

"I believe I could withstand that for the sake of a bit of adventure."

Rob grinned. "Ah, so that's how it is, is it? It's a pretty grim adventure, but probably safe enough. You're sure you want to accompany me?"

An impish smile lit her face. "You promised me adventure."

"So I did. Very well, let's go and look."


Iantha pulled her dressing gown more closely around herself and frowned. What good was an adventure that didn't prove to have a secret passage, after all? Her gaze traveled to the grotesque shape under the bloodstained sheet in the middle of the floor. Had Cosby Carrock written her the latest horrid letter? Was he possibly the source of that dreadful laugh? She had never heard him laugh that way, but of course, that wasn't surprising. She had avoided him throughout most of their acquaintance, especially when he was drunk. Iantha stared at the sheet.

She didn't know whether to pity Cosby or to gloat.

She turned to Rob. "Well, since it seems that I am not going to have the adventure of exploring a hidden passage, what should we do next?"

He shrugged. "We need to develop another theory. How *did* the rascal get out of this room?"

"He might have hidden, but that still doesn't answer the puzzle…unless…" She stared for a heartbeat at the closed door. Suddenly, she was certain. "Unless he was behind the door. Did you look there when you entered the room?"

"Nay, I did not. I was too alarmed when I saw Carrock. I made straight for him." Rob walked to the door and opened it, his eyes narrowed in thought. "Come, stand behind it for a moment."

Iantha obligingly stepped around the panel. Rob went out into the hall and turned to face the door. "I can't see you at all." He came a few steps into the room. "No, I still can't see you. I think you are on the track here. The whole crowd came into the room behind me. All the killer would have had to do was emerge from concealment and mingle with the others. Damnation! He was there all along!"

"He must have a very cool head." Iantha came to stand beside Rob.

"Indeed he must. And also a very good understanding of how the guests would react. He must have already had on his dressing gown. There was nothing to set him apart. Damn his eyes!" Rob's brows drew together in frustration.

"Yes, that must have been how he did it. But *why* did he do it? Cosby was annoying, but I would have thought him inept and therefore relatively harmless."

Rob's frown increased. "Perhaps he was too inept. The murderer feared he would reveal something." He thought for another moment. "A number of people saw your reaction to that guffaw. They also saw us patrolling the room, trying to identify the rogue."

"And someone who knew who the laugher was real- ized that I had recognized his voice *and* knew why it frightened me." The chill in Iantha was growing. "That would mean that Cosby *was* one of them."

Rob moved a little closer to her. "Aye. That is one likely explanation."

Iantha turned in a circle as if she might see through the walls. "If that is so, then there is another of them here."

"Yes, it means that, and that he is willing to kill to keep his identity secret."

"Oh, Rob."

Iantha took one step toward him, and he gathered her into his arms.

It also meant that Iantha might be in increased danger. The bastards continued to threaten her in those hateful letters. If they thought she might have other clues as to who they were, no doubt they would take steps to silence her. Rob glanced at his future father-in-law. His grave countenance suggested that he, too, had recognized the threat.

They sat in the library the morning after the shooting, awaiting the arrival of Lord Alton, the next guest on their list. Thank heaven Lord Rosley was the magistrate for the district. Last night's storm had ensured that no one would be able to get in or out of the castle for at least another day. They would have time to investigate the shooting.

Rob and Rosley came to their feet as Lord Alton en- tered. Obviously, his lordship was not best pleased. His eyebrows were almost meeting in the middle, and his side-whiskers bristled aggressively. He started speaking even while settling himself in the chair Rob indicated.

"See here, Duncan, what are you going to do about this outrage?"

So Alton realized the significance of the absent pistol. Rob kept his expression and his voice mild. "I am going to investigate it, and I hope bring a murderer to justice."

"What the devil is there to investigate?" Alton leaned forward in his chair. "Everyone knows who did it. We all saw how angry your Indian friend was at Carrock. I suspect I shall be next, for I made the original comment. I'm sorry for that. Had I realized he was within earshot, I would not have said it. Nonetheless, I would thank you to lock him up. I have no wish to be the next with a ball in my chest."

With some difficulty, Rob maintained his grip on his temper. "I think it highly unlikely that Prince Vijaya is the culprit."

"Oh, come now. Just because he is your friend—"

"He is, but that is not my reason for doubting your assumption." Rob held the older man's gaze with his. "I have known him for many years, and I do not believe that Vijaya would seek to avenge an insult in secret or with a pistol. A firearm would not be…personal enough. He would have used a blade."

Rob experienced an unkind glow of satisfaction when Lord Alton blanched. "If that is supposed to comfort me, Duncan, you are fair and far off. I have no more wish to have a blade in me than I do a ball."

"I do not think you are in any danger from Vijaya, Alton, but I assure you that we will leave no one out of consideration."

Lord Rosley cleared his throat. "Indeed not. Will you kindly tell us everything you can remember about the incident? I believe you were among the first to arrive on the scene."

Lord Alton's recollections revealed nothing that Rob had not seen for himself. The man refused to list any of the people whom he remembered being present. "This is foolishness, Rosley. Who else but the Indian would have had reason to do it?"

Rob stood, signaling that the interview was ended. "When we know that, my lord, we will likely know who did do it."

And he firmly showed the diplomat to the door.

Late in the afternoon Rob sought Iantha in her sitting room. "I've talked to everyone who was near the scene of the shooting, but I haven't learned a damn thing of use. No one remembers exactly who was seen in the corridor outside the door before I opened it." He commenced to pace back and forth in front of the sofa on which Iantha sat. "Alton is convinced that Vijaya killed Carrock because of the insult on Christmas Eve, and he fears for his own life. I suspect he has influenced Lord and Lady Kilbride also to believe that Vijaya murdered their son. They indicated as much when I visited them. Several others mentioned it, too."

"How are the Carrocks? Mama and I intended to go to them, but we were told they did not want visitors."

"They are taking it better than I expected, but grieving, of course. I'm sure Cosby must have been a trial to so quiet a couple, but he was still their son."

Iantha nodded. "I can't believe Vijaya can be guilty of so foul a deed. He is so placid and kind."

"Nay, it is not his way at all. I am afraid that Carrock was, in fact, involved in the attack on you, and that someone silenced him when you recognized his laugh. Several people have hinted at it. Sam, Sebergham and Mr. Farlam, among others, have worked that out. So we have two prevalent opinions. There may be others. Wycomb was the last to see him alive, but he was in the corridor outside the locked door, so it cannot have been he.''

Rob ceased his pacing and sat beside Iantha. He reached for her hand, but sensing her tension, quickly released it. ''Iantha, I don't want to frighten you, but I am seriously concerned for you. Your father and I discussed it this afternoon. He and I both believe that I can protect you more successfully here than he can at Hill House. I would like for us to be married as soon as I can obtain a special license.'' He smiled. ''This is, after all, a fortress.''

''And we are trapped in it with a rapist and murderer.'' Ignoring his proposal, Iantha shivered, as if cold. Rob sighed inwardly. Well, let that be for the moment. Obviously, she was going to require some persuasion.

''It seems so. But do not be afraid, Iantha. I will take every precaution to ensure your safety until the roads clear. It will be tomorrow or the next day before carriages can leave. When that happens, I expect a precipitate departure from most of the guests, including the killer.''

''And he will get away again.''

Rob's heart twisted at the bleakness in her face. ''That is certainly a possibility. We have at most two days to unravel the puzzle, and I do not see how, without new information, we can do that.'' He brushed a fallen lock of hair away from her forehead. ''But at least he will be gone from here, and you will be safe.''

''I will never be safe again.'' Iantha's voice sounded choked.

''Unhappily, that may be true. Not until we find the killer or others who still might wish to silence you. But we need time to do that.'' In spite of her rigidity Rob lifted her fingers to his lips. ''So please say that you will marry me immediately. Nothing need change between us. We will continue to feel our way along until you are completely comfortable.''

"But then you will be irrevocably committed. What if we never succeed in—''

Rob placed a finger against her lips.

"I have never considered that a possibility.''

A very tense two days ensued. Rob went through the motions of playing host to a group of very frightened people—people who locked their bedchamber doors at night and refused to open them to anyone. People who, even with the presence of patrols in the corridors, could not ignore the fact that someone among them had murdered a fellow guest.

Rob certainly could not.

He found himself eyeing everyone with whom he had conversation. He and Sam played cards with the men, their ears open for further information, but the gentlemen, while continuing to make serious inroads on Rob's supply of liquor, no longer showed the noisy good spirits of the Christmas celebration. Nor did they reveal anything to the purpose. They still argued politics, gossiped about the royal house and their absent neighbors and eyed the respectable young ladies, who were the only unmarried females in the party, with disappointment.

Clearly bored, Horace Raunds struck up a desultory flirtation with Meg Farlam—much to the visible annoyance of Thomas—and Stephen Wycomb made an abortive attempt on Lady Kendal's virtue. Lord Sebergham drank steadily, but without noticeable effect, and Lord Kendal prowled through the house like a wolf in the sheepfold.

A knot of older gentlemen that formed around Lord

Alton and Mr. Welwyn grumbled about Vijaya's presence in the house, much to the—*in*visible, he hoped—annoyance of Rob. The subject of their suspicions stayed in his own quarters. Sam did his jovial best to help keep everyone cheered up, but no one could forget the stiffening corpse lying in an unheated chamber above stairs. Everyone prayed for warm, sunny weather.

Especially Rob.

Iantha avoided the ladies' entertainments arranged by Lady Dalston. She kept to her sitting room, visiting only with her mother. But even with mama she could not relax. She simply could not make polite conversation right now. Dinner last night had been a nightmare, with every guest gazing suspiciously at every other, and with Iantha feeling that every one of them eyed her threateningly. She lived with held breath and slept with either Burnside or Feller or Rob himself guarding her door. It seemed that Rob did not even completely trust the newer members of the staff. A cold lump formed in Iantha's stomach.

That staff would be with them after the guests had gone.

She tried to work on her writing project, but found herself starting at every sound. Why had God let this happen to her? Iantha always tried to be good—to be loving and kind to everyone. Was it that God valued women as so many men did—in other words, not at all? Had He really made men to be the masters of women, to use them as they saw fit?

How could He!

Iantha flushed at this blasphemous thought. She was angry with God. Reason as well as piety reminded her that humans of all sorts suffered injuries and disasters—men and women, noblemen and yeomen. Surely God did not send those calamities deliberately. Surely they were only the result of the natural order of the world. She was being unjust to God.

She had to smile at that. It was hardly her place to judge God. Rather the reverse. She could only hope that He would treat her lapse of respect kindly. But she could no longer pray for Him to protect her from further harm.

She was no longer sure that He could.

By the end of the second day sleep had become impossible. Iantha almost shrieked at the light tap on her sitting room door. The hour was late, the fire had burned low and the candles guttered in their sockets. Who…?

"Iantha?" Rob's voice, of course, his usual booming accents reduced to what he no doubt considered a whisper.

She gathered up her shawl, opened the door a crack and peeked out. Yes, it was his lordship. Iantha opened the door.

Rob came in and walked straight to the fire, which he built back to flames before sprawling on the sofa with a sigh. "What a day!" As she came to sit beside him, he took both her slender hands in his big ones. "And you are, as usual, half-frozen."

Automatically, Iantha started to retrieve her hands, but once more decided that the warmth of his felt very welcome, even though she had to lean against his shoulder to maintain the contact. "Have you been having a bad time? I confess that I have completely given in to cowardice and have kept to my room all day. I even had dinner here."

"I know. I'm sorry you have been alone, but I had just as soon you stay in a secure place." She shivered, and he touched her cheek. "You are going to catch your death one day.'' He moved one hand and placed his arm around her shoulders.

''When I am working I just don't feel the cold until I stop.'' Iantha gave in to the comfort of the heat coming off his big body and rested her head on his shoulder.

''Have you been very lonely?''

''No, I am accustomed to being alone. I rather like it, but today… Today I was so afraid. I…''

''I'm sorry I could not come sooner. I need to keep my eye on things. Somebody in this house pulled that trigger, and I want to know who. And I certainly don't want him to have another opportunity.''

''You have too many guests. You can't watch them all at once.''

''True, but Sam is helping me, and in fact, everyone in the place is watching everyone else. I doubt our killer will have much chance to repeat his crime, in any case.'' Rob brushed a wayward lock of silver hair away from her face, looking solemnly into her eyes. ''I wish I could stay with you all night and keep you safe. Being married will give me that opportunity, but it would cause too much talk to do it now. I don't want any more gossip about you.''

''A bit more will hardly matter.'' The warmth of the fire and of Rob's body seeped into Iantha, and she could feel the tension sliding out of her. She relaxed against his shoulder and returned his gaze. Suddenly she became aware of how handsome he was, in spite of tired circles under his eyes and the slight roughness of a day-old beard. Something stirred deep inside her, and her lips opened on a little breath. He hesitated a moment, then slowly lowered his face to hers. She had ample time to draw back.

But she didn't.

The warmth of the room and the warmth of his mouth fanned the heat inside her. Iantha slipped one arm around his neck, and he pulled her across his lap and held her tighter. She heard the depth of his breathing increase, echoed by her own. After several heartbeats Rob lifted his head and gazed into her eyes again, a question in his own.

And she didn't know the answer.

She buried her face in his cravat, and he laid his cheek against her hair.

Several moments later, he set her upright and stood. "You need to go to bed. Don't be afraid. Someone will be outside your door all night."

And while she was still searching for the answer, he went out the door and closed it softly behind him.

A thrill of panic traveled up Iantha's back as Molly brushed her hair. Tomorrow she would wed Lord Duncan. After the roads had cleared and the grateful company had departed, it had taken only a week for the special license to arrive from London. She had not even had the opportunity to go home. Papa and Rob feared that she might be vulnerable in the carriage. God knew that she did not want that!

If only she could be as confident of success in this venture as Rob seemed to be! True, the more she was near him, the more comfortable she became with that nearness. At times she had even begun to feel protected by having his arms around her. But always afterward she felt the need to withdraw, to put him at a distance. And she knew the courteous and affectionate touches he bestowed on her were only faint shadows of the intimacy he desired.

The very thought shook her to the core, turning her

hands clammy and making her breath short. Even the warm sensations his presence sometimes created in her body were a threat. They made her want more of him. More that she might not be able to stand.

A loud sniff drew her attention away from these disturbing thoughts. She turned around to discover large tears running down her maid's face. "Why, Molly, whatever is the matter?"

Molly sniffed again. "It ain't nothing, Miss Iantha."

"Obviously, it is *something*. Why are you crying?"

A small sob joined the sniffle. "It…it's just that you and me will be staying here at the castle instead of Hill House."

"And you are homesick?"

Molly nodded and a louder sob emerged. "And Daniel will go back with Lord Rosley. His old mother lives near Hill House, and he has to look after her."

Now a torrent of sobs tumbled forth, and Iantha began to appreciate the problem. "I see. You and he are keeping company?"

"Yes, ma'am." The maid nodded, then hastily added, "But not when we've work to do."

A small smile curved Iantha's lips. "No. Of course not." She envied Molly. To be frankly and happily in love, without fear of her beloved… "Has Daniel spoken to you about…about the future?"

"Oh, yes, ma'am. He wants us to marry, but he needs to save his wages first." With a wail she added, "It will be so long!"

*How cruel life is,* Iantha thought. She stood on the brink of a marriage she both desired and feared, and that marriage was separating Molly from her lover. Daniel was a steady young man. Her maid could do worse. "Don't cry, Molly. I will miss you, but I can employ another maid. Let me speak to my father. I'm sure he will make arrangements for you and Daniel if you will help me until I can hire someone.''

''Oh, Miss Iantha. I will be almost as sad to leave you as to leave Daniel.'' Molly sniffed and hunted for her handkerchief.

''Thank you, Molly. But Daniel is your future, I think. You must go back to Hill House.''

''I'll never forget you, Miss Iantha.''

''Nor I you, Molly.''

For perhaps the thousand-and-first time, Rob asked his reflection in the mirror if he were, in fact, doing the right thing. As ever, his reflection was not a great deal of help. Was it sheer arrogance on his part that led him to believe that he could find the key to unlock the prison in which Iantha confined her feelings? Was he letting his desires cloud his judgment, or succumbing to the temptation to play the hero?

As Rob strove to subdue his thick brown hair, his reflection remained stubbornly silent.

Once more, unbidden, an image of Shakti's warm body formed in his mind. Perhaps he should not wed another as long as he still thought of her with desire. Although in truth, she had never engaged his mind as his present bride did. Shakti had been always welcoming, always pleasant, always attentive, but she had possessed no inclination to intellectual matters at all, preferring to while away the day in lazy pursuits or playing with Laki.

Which had seemed enough at the time.

He had not realized how important a companion who shared his interests might be until his present lady had spent two days under his roof.

Still, without her physical response to him, he felt empty.

Rob sighed. Be the answer to those questions as they may, he had promised to protect this lady. And he had also promised to marry her. It went without saying that he would do both.

The vicar awaited him downstairs.

Rob left the mirror and shrugged into the dark coat that Burnside held. Another glance into the glass assured him that his snowy cravat remained crisp and that his dark waistcoat and knee britches displayed no spots or undue wrinkles. Satisfied, he turned to Burnside. ''Well, what do you think?''

His henchman surveyed him with his head to one side. ''You'll do.''

''Do I look like a bridegroom?''

''As far as I know, me lord. I never was one.''

Rob laughed. ''Did you ever want to be?''

Burnside, his own hair rigorously slicked down, thought for a moment. ''Maybe once or twice. But I come to my senses.''

Rob burst into laughter, and Burnside opened the door and followed him down the stairs.

The wedding guests had already gathered in the drawing room. There were not many—Lord and Lady Rosley, Iantha's younger brothers and sister, Vijaya, the Farlams and Sam Broughton's wife, Amelia. Burnside, Feller, Mrs. Lamonby and Gailsgill, the butler, would also stand in the drawing room. The rest of the staff were welcome if they could find a space.

Rob found the vicar, tall and balding, and Sam, who was to stand with him, by the fireplace. He joined them while Lady Rosley fussed with Valeria's ribbons. Iantha had chosen the girl to be her bridesmaid, and Valeria was quivering with excitement. The musicians from the Christmas party had been retained for the wedding, and they now struck up a march. Iantha, on her father's arm, appeared in the far doorway.

And seeing her, suddenly Rob knew, without a doubt, why he was doing this.

He wanted her.

All of her.

# Chapter Nine

Iantha clutched her father's arm and trembled. The moment was upon her. She had lost the opportunity to cry off. Her bridegroom and the vicar waited, and she approached them with what dignity she could muster.

She had flatly refused to wear white. In spite of her mother's many arguments, she chose instead a heavy silk in a lavender shade that reflected her eyes. The fabric of the bodice crossed her breasts at a stylish, if modest, level, and the skirt draped gracefully from the high waistline. She relented enough to allow Mama to pin a white lace veil over her upswept hair. It fell behind her to the small train of the gown.

She did want to look her best for her wedding—whether or not she wanted the wedding, something she had been unable to decide. But Iantha did not want his lordship to feel that he was getting a bargain any more doubtful than it already was. At least she would not shame him with her appearance.

Cautiously she raised her gaze to his and, seeing his expression, quickly lowered it. Even with her lack of experience of the opposite sex, Iantha had no difficulty interpreting *that* look. In spite of her recent argument with God, she sent up a prayer that she would not fail this man—this man who had both the courage and the kindness to take her as she was.

The music stopped, and she lifted her gaze once more. Valeria stood beside her, all but bouncing in her excitement. Over her head Iantha saw her mother with a rather damp smile on her beautiful face. The vicar, whom she had known since she was a child, gave her a warm smile of encouragement. She dared another glance at Rob.

He winked at her.

A giggle almost escaped Iantha. She pressed her lips together and strove for appropriate decorum. Heavens, she was verging on strong hysterics, terrified one moment and giggling the next! Drawing in a long breath, she grasped at her control. In a moment her mind quieted enough to hear the vicar beginning the service.

The clerk's familiar deep voice boomed into the silence. "Who gives this woman in marriage?"

Her father's voice, also familiar, and very dear, replied, "I, her father, do."

And then he placed her hand in Rob's.

Iantha's heart almost stopped, and she fought the impulse to pull away. After this she would be his. It would be her duty to... But the vicar was continuing. In a few moments she would be asked to make a vow she could not take back.

How would she answer?

And then Rob was speaking *his* vows, looking deeply and steadily into her eyes, and suddenly Iantha knew that she would rather die than disappoint him.

When her turn came, her reply was firm and clear.

"I do."

\* \* \*

Inevitably, the wedding guests and Iantha's family took their leave. Evening fell, and she found herself seated before a cheerful fire in her new sitting room. She found it very comfortable and attractive, a bit larger than the dowager's, which she had been using. The furnishings that she had especially liked from the old one had been moved into it, and Iantha loved the view. Carved from the corner where the master's and mistress's bedchambers adjoined, the room had windows on two sides, revealing mountains as far as the eye could see. It had only one drawback.

The door leading to his lordship's bedchamber.

Iantha tried to tell herself that she would feel safer knowing that Rob lay on the other side of that door, near at hand. But safe from what? Which danger was the greatest—those vague figures that possibly threatened her life, or the strong, muscular figure who slept next door and evoked such conflicting feelings in her?

Tonight, her wedding night, Iantha had no doubt about that!

Rob would make no demands on her. She knew that. But she felt guilty that this good, virile man could not come to his bride joyfully, as a bridegroom would naturally wish to do. She wanted to offer him what he had a right to expect.

And she couldn't do it.

A tear leaked quietly onto her cheek. Iantha quickly dashed it away and groped for control. She could not let her feelings overcome her. Resolutely, she pushed them into the back of her mind.

And, oh God, he walked through the door.

Iantha smiled with what determination she could muster. ''Good evening, my lord.'' She resisted the urge to pull her white brocade robe closer together at the neck. It already buttoned to her chin. But it was a *night* robe. A garment for the bedchamber. For the marriage chamber. Dear heaven! She felt so *vulnerable*.

His lordship returned her smile and went to stand with his back to the fire, his hands in the pockets of his dressing gown. "At least having you in this parlor, I can prevent your freezing to death."

She tried to laugh. The sound that emerged seemed strangled. Rob crossed to the sofa and stood beside her, gazing down into her face. "You look terrified."

"I...I'm sorry, my lord. I know you won't..." Iantha flushed and looked at her hands.

Rob went to the decanter and poured two glasses of brandy. Sitting beside her, he handed her one. "No. I won't." He leaned back and sipped his liquor. "So relax and have a little brandy."

"I have never drunk brandy before." Iantha studied the dark liquid. "It is so strong, and I find I need to be careful even with wine...."

"Why?" He looked at her with narrowed eyes. "What happens when you drink wine?"

"I...well, it is rather like what happened after the snowball fight."

"You want to weep?"

"Yes. That, and I feel...other things...." She looked up from her glass at him. "I have thoughts that frighten me."

"Thoughts of harming yourself?" His brows drew together.

She glanced down again, biting her lip. After several heartbeats she brought her gaze back to his. "No. Not myself."

"Ah!" His frown cleared. "Of hurting someone else then?"

Iantha nodded. "But that is foolishness, of course. Those I wish to injure are not even known to me."

"Not by name." He took a sip. "But known by their actions."

"Yes, of course. But then…" A wave of unnamed distress flowed through her, and she closed her eyes.

Rob looked at her steadily. "Then what?"

"I begin to think of other people—people I do know, and I have such thoughts…." She couldn't go on. It was too horrible to think about, much less say. "I become a monster."

"No, Iantha, that is no monstrous inclination." He set his glass on the table and took her hand. "Your anger, denied its logical prey, simply spreads to others. Listen to me, Iantha. When my family died, when I lost my beautiful, innocent little girl, I felt all the things you describe. At first I wept. When I could weep no more, I brooded. I drank myself into a stupor every night so as not to feel the pain. When I realized that I could no longer allow myself that luxury, at last I began to rage."

He leaned away from her then, against the arm of the sofa, his eyes focused on something far away. "But at whom could I rage? Against the fever? God? What good would that do? So instead I instigated quarrels so that I might shout at someone. I went to the docks and into low places and started fights so that I might hurt someone. I rode through the jungle and killed every animal that crossed my path."

Iantha shook her head in wonder. "I cannot imagine you thus."

He turned his gaze back to her. "I know. It is hard for me to recognize myself in that time. Yet thus I was. And eventually I returned to myself. There is a natural rhythm to grief, Iantha, one that you have given yourself no opportunity to pursue.'' He indicated the glass in her hand. ''So enjoy your brandy, and we will weather together whatever happens next.''

Iantha, watching him over the rim of the glass, sipped the liquor cautiously, choking a little at the fire in her throat. Rob turned to stare into the flames, taking a swallow of his own drink from time to time. She relaxed against the back of the seat and tried another taste. This time it went down more easily.

When Rob had finished his glassful, he brought the decanter and refilled not only his own, but Iantha's portion. Now as he sat, he turned so that he could watch her. Slowly the level of liquid in her glass dropped to the bottom. At some point, which Iantha never quite remembered, the tears she had so ruthlessly subdued earlier bubbled to the surface and trailed down her cheeks. She tried in vain to again cap them off, but they would not stop, and she felt too weak too struggle.

Rob set his glass aside. ''Why are you crying?''

''I am *not* crying.'' Iantha sniffed and searched for her handkerchief.

He smiled at this gross departure from the truth. ''Of course not. What are you thinking then?''

''That…that…'' Another loud sniff. ''I just wish that I could do what we should be doing right now. That you could do what bridegrooms do on their wedding night. You said it is life's greatest adventure, and I will never be able to…'' The rest trailed off into a wail.

Her bridegroom gathered her into his arms and pulled her across his lap, holding her against his chest. ''Yes, we will, my beautiful bride. We will conquer that adventure in due time.''

Sobs choked her now, but she managed to blurt out, "I'm so sorry."

He drew her closer and began to rock her gently. "I am sorry, too. Sorry that you must endure this pain. But it will pass if you let it, Iantha. I know that. Let it go, and one day we will explore heights you never imagined."

His words did not make much sense, but Iantha nodded anyway, clutching the collar of his dressing gown and muffling her sobs in the fabric. She thought they would never stop, but of course, eventually they did. She lay exhausted against his chest, half sleeping, until at length the fire died.

At last Rob lifted her in his arms and carried her into her own chamber and set her on the bed. "Can you get out of your wrapper by yourself?"

She nodded.

"Then I will say good night." He kissed her on the forehead and went through the door that led directly to his own bedchamber.

Iantha sat staring at the closed door until the chill began to make itself felt. Then she fumbled out of the robe and slipped under the covers, pulling them tightly under her chin. She lay there, feeling strangely separated from her body and thinking about the man she had just married.

And she didn't feel afraid.

It was not exactly the experience he would have chosen for his wedding night, but nonetheless, Rob felt exhilarated. He had held her longer this time than ever before. And she had wept, really wept, possibly for the first time since she had been attacked. He viewed that as progress. Like the first crack in the ice after a storm, it was a small thing. But as the sun continued to shine, that crack would grow larger and larger until the whole frozen lump disintegrated and tumbled down the hill.

His elation diminished a bit when Iantha appeared at the breakfast table, again withdrawn and with downcast eyes. Damn! He was still taking a step forward and a step back, like a dance. But sooner or later the steps of the dance must break out into a new, more energetic pattern.

Rob rose and drew back a chair for her. She thanked him without looking at him. Hmm. Not a good sign. Well, he was not going to sidle around the problem this time. He filled a plate from the buffet and brought it to her, gazing directly at her. "What troubles you, Iantha?"

She put her fingertips over her lips, shook her head and winced. "I—I have the headache."

"No wonder in that." Rob suppressed a grin. "You drank more spirits than you have had before. It takes some getting accustomed to. The headache will pass after you eat." She nodded, but kept her eyes downcast and pushed her eggs around with her fork. "But that isn't the only thing troubling you, is it?"

Iantha sighed. "No, my lord. It isn't. I…I owe you an apology."

Rob raised his eyebrows. "Oh? For what?"

"For the scene to which I subjected you. I completely lost control of my emotions. I will do better in the future." She took a deep breath and lifted a forkful of eggs to her mouth. "In the future I will watch what I drink more carefully."

He suppressed an oath. Had he made his confession for nothing? Well, perhaps the significance of it would come to her with time. In the meanwhile…

He placed his hand on her chin and turned her face toward him until he had captured her gaze.

"Iantha, why do you think I gave you the brandy?"

* * *

The tang of fresh air and the broad expanse of the sky were wonderful after so many days mewed up in the castle. While Iantha was still trying to puzzle out the meaning of his lordship's remark about the brandy, he had abruptly changed the subject by suggesting a ride.

"I'm sure you need to get out as badly as I do. You cannot stand being inside all the time, and neither can I. I think it will be safe enough. We will not be trapped, blind and deaf, in a carriage, and there is little cover in this area for an ambush. And of course, Feller and I will carry arms. Perhaps Vijaya will also accompany us."

Iantha had much rather have gone alone. She missed her solitary rambles with no one but Toby for company, but while the little horse had mended from his injuries, her gig remained a wreck. She suspected it would stay that way for some time to come. And, of course, with a killer in evidence who might want her life, she could not justify going about with no protection.

It took her but moments to dash upstairs and change to the midnight-blue velvet riding dress that had been a wedding present from Mama. At last Iantha had an opportunity to wear it. It would add a striking contrast to the dainty dapple-gray mare that had been her father's gift.

Just as she dismissed her new maid, Rob had appeared in their connecting doorway. He nodded approvingly. "That color is lovely with your hair."

He circled her, examining her from all angles. Then suddenly, before she had any idea what he was about, he clasped her waist with one arm and with his free hand pulled her skirts to her knees. "Ah!"

The pistol strapped to the top of her boot shone dully. Iantha flushed.

Rob laughed.

"As I thought. My pistol-pointing lady still goes about armed." Dropping the velvet fabric, he released her. "Don't look so guilty. I am happy to know you are able to protect yourself, even though I see it as my responsibility. Would you like also to carry one of my pistols on your saddle, as I do? Horse pistols are heavy, but mine carry two shots."

Iantha had not even paused for consideration. "Thank you, my lord. I would like that very much."

So now here were the four of them—looking exceedingly warlike for a ride in the fells—trotting along a crest with air and sky all around them. She began to long for her paints. Everywhere she looked, snowmelt waterfalls raced down the hills into the shallow valley. She turned to Rob. "Do you think we might come out again tomorrow? I would love to paint the cataracts."

"I don't see why not." He turned to her, his smile revealing his strong white teeth. She had never before noticed at what a jaunty angle he wore his soft, wide-brimmed hat. It made his steady person look…well, dashing. But he was continuing. "You seem to like waterfalls."

"Oh yes, I do. They move me in some way that I cannot quite describe. I love to paint them."

"Ah, then you will have a treat when spring comes. There is a cascade behind the Eyrie that emanates from a cave. It is a hard climb down, and worse up, but I think a daring lady might accomplish it." He gave her a roguish smile. "And there is a pool deep enough to swim."

"Swim?" Iantha frowned. "Oh, dear. I don't know how, but the waterfall sounds beyond anything."

"It is quite breathtaking, but I will teach you to swim.

Perhaps by then…'' Casting a cautious glance at their companions, he let the sentence trail off.

Iantha was about to ask him for the rest of it when she saw a mounted figure on the road at the bottom of the hill. She pointed with her riding crop. "Who is that?"

Rob squinted. "Looks like Sebergham. Come, we will ride down and meet him." As Iantha hesitated, he added, "Come now. I doubt he is bent on mischief, and in any event, the odds are four against one."

They let their horses pick their way down the muddy slope while Lord Sebergham drew rein at the bottom, waiting for them. He tipped his tall-crowned hat as Iantha rode up. "Good day, Lady Duncan." He bowed toward Rob. "Servant, my lord."

Rob reached out for a handshake. "Sebergham. What brings you out today?"

"The need for a little air. Snowy weather becomes very confining after a while." His cold blue gaze rested on each of them for a moment, without conferring any friendliness at all. Sebergham continued, "I hope you have had no more alarming occurrences?"

"I am happy to say we have not." Rob shifted in his saddle to glance at Iantha. "And your own life has been uneventful?"

Sebergham's mouth quirked up at the corners, but still conveyed no warmth. "Quite tediously so, but thus it is in the country. I find boredom quite difficult to tolerate. Perhaps I will call on you in the near future, if that is agreeable to you?"

"Of course, we should be happy to see you." It seemed to Iantha that Rob's voice did not sound exactly *happy* at the prospect.

Lord Sebergham tipped his hat again. "Well, I'll be on my way. Your servant, my lady. Duncan."

They watched him turn his horse and ride off the way he had come. Iantha shivered. "What a strange man!"

"A bit, aye." Rob watched his neighbor disappear into the distance.

"Wary." Feller spoke for the first time since the meeting.

"Like a tiger in the forest." Vijaya's bright eyes followed the rider. "Ready to pounce."

Rob nodded. "He lived a long time in environs much less civilized than England. It makes one wary."

Startled, Iantha thought she saw a certain wariness in Lord Duncan's eyes. It did not seem to fit his open character. But then, he had lived a long time himself in uncivilized places.

A new notion about her new husband.

No doubt one of many to come.


His new wife had allowed him to lift her down from her horse without pulling away. Perhaps she had gotten over her embarrassment at her tears. The ride had been a good idea. Active pursuits brought her out of her self-imposed emotional confinement.

As they came into the entry hall, Vijaya hurried to the stairs. "Forgive me, but I am not bred to these frigid climes. I must seek a fire."

Rob chuckled and turned to a pile of mail on the table. Someone had gone down to the village and brought the post. Sorting through the letters, he came across one addressed to Iantha. He was on the point of handing it to her when he saw another, written in the same awkward hand, bearing his name.

He drew the letter back from her outstretched hand. "Just a moment."

He unfolded his sheet and scanned the brief message.

Duncan—
You have chosen to marry a slut, so may you have
whatever joy sluts bring to a husband. But if she
speaks one word against us, you will not have that
dubious joy very long. When she does that, she will
die, and you along with her.

With an oath, Rob crumpled the letter in his fist. He
held the still-folded note out to Iantha, but did not allow
her to take it from his hand. "Have you seen this handwriting before?"

She blanched, but answered steadily. "I think so. It is
another of them, isn't it?"

Rob ripped the note open and glanced at it. "Aye."
He made no move to give it to her. "But it was not
written by the same person as the one that was slipped
under your door Christmas."

She shook her head. "No, I think not, but I have seen
both styles before. This one looks as if the writer deliberately disguised his writing."

Rob scrutinized her face. She looked perfectly composed. He himself shook with fury. "How can you be so
calm?" His voice emerged in a shout. She winced, and
he quickly moderated his tone. "I'm sorry. I did not
mean to shout at you. But aren't you angry?"

Her hands were shaking, but she shrugged. "There is
no profit in being angry."

"But you should be. You should be furious."

She turned to look into the distance. "I prefer not to
be."

"No wonder you find your anger directed at innocent
parties. Send it against those who deserve it." He shook
the crumpled paper in his hand. "Send it against these
bastards."

She turned her still face back to him, and her answer left him with nothing to say.

"How?"

How indeed. Rob had never been so frustrated in his life. His hands itched to close around the throat of the man who had written that letter, but that fellow remained safely anonymous. Rob longed to shake Iantha until he broke her icy calm, but he had never raised his hand against a woman, and he did not intend to start with his wife—his small, fragile, frozen wife. Shouting at her had been bad enough.

So, not knowing what to do, he sat with her in their parlor after dinner and resorted to small talk. "Is your new maid satisfactory?"

Tonight Iantha had consented to drink a little sherry, firmly refusing even the suggestion of brandy. She took a minuscule sip. "Oh, yes. Camille is French, you know, and very skilled. She came here as a chambermaid, but Gailsgill suggested her for me because she had previous experience as a lady's maid." Iantha smiled. "I feel very stylish with a French maid. She has such a lovely accent."

"I'm glad you are pleased with her." He cast about for something else to say. Drat! He did not want to make idle conversation. He wanted to hold Iantha again. Still staring at the fire, Rob reached out and closed his fingers around the slender hand that rested on the sofa beside him. She stiffened for a heartbeat, then with an audible breath, relaxed. Rob took another sip of his brandy.

She opened her mouth as if to speak. And then closed it again, as if she knew no more than he what to say. Rob set his glass on the end table and turned to her. "Will you sit a little nearer to me?"

"I…" She considered for a moment. "Yes. I will."

She slid over until their shoulders were touching. "Rob, I…I want you to know that I *do* appreciate your anger on my behalf. I would express my own if I dared, but I honestly don't know how, and I am afraid of what I might do."

Rob could say very little in rebuttal. He knew all too well how the anger of grief could turn to violence. He put his arm around her shoulders and pulled her closer. "Perhaps together we will find the key. May I hold you as I did last night?"

A long pause followed. Finally she nodded. "I think that would be pleasant."

Rob wanted to leap into the air and shout for joy. Instead, he turned her in his arms so that she lay across his lap again, her head on his shoulder. Commanding his body to remain quiet, he sat with the scent of her hair in his nostrils and the softness of her breasts against his chest.

Pleasant. Aye, it was that.

And he wanted so much more.

So much.

*He drew on the cigar and let the soothing smoke flow out of his nostrils and into his blood. Carefully pouring the water through the sugar into the clear green liquid, he watched it turn milky before taking a swallow.*

*They should have the threatening letters by now. In truth, at this time he was only toying with them. He would kill them both someday when he found a likely opportunity. She had recognized Carrock's laugh. She might remember something incriminating about himself. And Lord Duncan was just such a man as might interfere with his plans if he let him remain alive. In the meantime, he would keep her too afraid to think—to remember.*

*But before he killed this fine lady, he would bring her to a proper sense of her worthlessness—she who held her defiled self apart from lesser mortals. From lesser men than her own top-lofty class. Well, she would find that his sword fit her sheath just as well as her lordly husband's.*

*And she would find it a sharp sword.*

# Chapter Ten

"Sam and Amelia are here. Thursby just came up to tell me." Three days after the receipt of the hateful letters, Rob strolled into Iantha's bedchamber to find her at her desk apparently lost in whatever she was writing. Her graceful back was carefully erect.

"Oh!" She jumped at the sound of his voice and spun around. Her hand swept across the desk, and papers went flying in all directions. "Oh. You startled me."

"Forgive me." Rob knelt and began to pick up the scattered sheets.

Iantha quickly took them out of his hands. "Never mind. I'll get them."

"I think that is all of them. No, here are two more." Rob scrunched down and groped under the desk.

"Really, my lord. There is no need for you…"

Rob got to his feet and glanced down at the papers, puzzled. "'Dear Lady Wisdom'?" He turned one over. "This is addressed to *La Belle Assemblée*. Did you receive it by mistake?"

Before he could lay the sheets on the desk, his polite new wife snatched them out of his hand. "This is my personal correspondence, my lord!"

"Hmm." Rob regarded her thoughtfully for a moment. She looked seriously distressed. What did that imply? He had no idea, but if she were that upset, he had best find out. He strove for a light note. "It seems my bride is conducting a secret correspondence. Should I become alarmed?"

The expressions flitting across her face almost made him laugh, but he had enough experience with matrimony to know that laughing would rapidly put him in a position into which no wise husband would corner himself. He suppressed a smile and contented himself with raising his eyebrows questioningly.

She flushed very prettily and looked quite as guilty as any wife ever looked. "My lord, you know... I mean, I would never... I mean, you realize..."

In spite of himself, Rob let the smile escape. "As you say—you are the last person of whom I would suspect a clandestine relationship. So what is the source of these blushes?"

Iantha looked down at her hands. "I had rather not say, my lord."

"Now I *am* beginning to worry." Rob sobered. "Surely a woman's magazine such as *La Belle Assemblée* has nothing to do with the other correspondence you have kept hidden?"

"Oh, no, my lord! It has nothing to do with that."

"Then I would appreciate very much your telling me what this is all about."

His wife let out a long sigh. "Very well. I do not want you to be concerned."

Iantha studied her hands.

Rob waited.

"I...I have an...an association with *La Belle Assem-*

*blée.''* Had she been confessing to a flagrant affair, she could not have looked more conscience-stricken.

Puzzled, Rob frowned. "I don't understand. What sort of association? Why are you so secretive about it?''

"Well… Most people—most men, at least—think women's magazines are very silly. And in some ways they are—all about clothes and pretension. But some of the articles are very helpful. *La Belle Assemblée* encourages their readers to write to them for advice.''

The light broke in Rob's mind. In spite of himself a laugh broke through his guard. "And you are Lady Wisdom?''

Iantha bristled and turned back to her desk. "I knew you would laugh.''

Rob hastened to make amends. He had well and truly made a mull of that! "I'm sorry, Iantha. I am not laughing at *you.* I—I believe that I am simply relieved.'' He placed his hands on her shoulders and turned her to face him, looking as earnest as he knew how. "Truly, I do not think you, of all people, silly. You are serious to a fault.''

Rob gazed into her face. Hmm. He did not seem to be making much progress in reinstating himself in her good graces. Maybe that last was not the thing to say, either. "Come now, Iantha. I didn't mean…''

The color in her face now was not due to embarrassment. She stood and began to pace. "That is always the way with men. They continually think women too silly or too serious or lacking in wit or having too much of it. They take nothing we do seriously. Women cannot handle oils. Watercolors are too missish. Poems too sentimental. Novels too florid.''

She took a deep breath and clamped her mouth shut, crossing her arms across her breasts. Well, Rob had wanted her to get angry. But not at him. He decided on diplomacy. "I can see why that is frustrating to you. But I assure you, I do not feel that way about women and their achievements. I would like to read something you have written—perhaps the answer to that letter on your desk—if you would allow me?"

"You would laugh."

"Is the letter humorous?"

"Definitely not."

"Then I shall not laugh." Rob waited for her permission to pick up the letter. For a moment he thought it would not be forthcoming.

Finally she nodded. "Here is the original question. And this is my answer."

Hoping against hope that there was nothing in the letter that would make him smile, Rob perused the two documents. The writer had asked what she should do when her husband stayed away from home until late in the night. She feared that he had a mistress, especially since her own latest pregnancy. Signed with tears—"B.T."

The cad! Rob turned to Iantha's answer.

Dear B.T.—

I am sure it is very difficult for you to accept your husband's resorting to another. But men are not creatures such as we. They do not exert control over their needs and desires as we must do. They appear to require variety. Nonetheless, you have no recourse but to control your tears and your anger. They will gain you nothing but further anguish.

With my best wishes for your happiness, I am,
Lady Wisdom

For an eye blink Rob wrestled with his own annoyance. So she thought that men did not practice control over their desire? What the devil did she think he had been doing ever since he had known her?

Or rather, *not* known her.

He took a calming breath and handed the letter back to Iantha. She regarded him with a question in her eyes. But he had a few questions of his own. "Is it always thus? Men may do as they wish, and women must contain their emotions? Is that always your advice?"

"Nearly always. Most of my corespondents are angry with their husbands, but it will not help them to show that. And men hate tears."

And where did she get this comprehensive information about men? No wonder she had apologized for crying. Had she paid no attention to anything he had said or done?

Or not done?

Irritation prickled him again. "So you always advise self-control."

"I have always found it to be the most comfortable policy."

"I see." Comfortable, no doubt, if very limiting. But they did not have time to deal with that at the present. "I have no objection to your pursuing this relationship with *La Belle Assemblée* if you enjoy it. But now we need to go down to Sam and Amelia."

She nodded, and Rob opened the door for her. At least he had learned something. It appeared easy for women to direct anger toward their husbands. And anger tended to spread. And today they were both a bit indignant.

Perhaps he could use that.


Sam Broughton rose and extended a hand as Rob and Iantha came into the small parlor.

"How are you, Sam?" Rob shook the proffered hand,

then leaned down to place a cousinly kiss on Amelia's cheek. "You are looking well. Is Sam treating you as he should, or should I thrash him for you?"

"You wouldn't dare." Sam grinned and turned to Iantha, taking the hand she held out and jerking his head toward Rob. "He thinks himself formidable."

Iantha thought Rob rather formidable herself. And one would think the tall, lanky Sam at a serious disadvantage against Rob's breadth and muscle. The cousins hardly looked as though they were kin—Sam with straight, reddish-blond hair and Rob with brown curls.

Rob laughed and punched his cousin playfully on the arm. "I'd dare if you were mistreating the fair Amelia."

Amelia shook her head, black curls bobbing, and smiled at Iantha. "Pay no attention to these two. They are always harassing one another."

"Have to." Sam lowered himself back to his chair as Iantha chose the sofa near the tea table. "It is the only way I can compete with my lord Duncan."

Iantha wondered if she detected a hint of envy in the voice of Rob's agent. Rob did, indeed, seem to have all the advantage—not only size and strength, but a title and wealth as well. Sam must content himself with being his employee.

Rob laughed aloud. "You gave a good enough account of yourself when we were lads. Always scrapping about something."

The conversation paused briefly while Gailsgill brought in the tea tray and set it beside Iantha. When she had poured and distributed the tea, Sam turned to Rob. "Have you made any progress on discovering who killed young Carrock?"

"Not one iota." Rob shook his head and set his teacup

on a small table. "As you know, all the possible parties departed in great haste as soon as the roads cleared. Nothing has happened since to cast any light on the subject."

"I saw Lord Alton recently when I went to London to talk with Welwyn about that shipping venture we are interested in. He is still sure that Prince Vijaya is the guilty party."

Rob scowled. "He is letting his prejudices influence his judgment. The devil's in it, though, that no one remembers when Vijaya appeared in the crowd outside the door."

"I can't think it of him, although I don't know him as well as you do." Sam sipped his tea.

"Well, they do say that still waters run deep." Amelia blotted her lips daintily.

"Not that deep." Rob's brow furrowed again.

Iantha felt tongue-tied. She disliked the imputation that Vijaya was the murderer, but had no wish to bring up the alternate theory that Cosby had been silenced by someone involved in the assault on her. She caught a speculative glance directed at her from Sam. Did he know something of use that he was not willing to say to Rob in her presence?

She swallowed the last of her tea and turned to Amelia. "We are changing the furnishings in my bedchamber. Will you come up and give me your opinion on the drapes?"

"Of course! I would love to see it. I have never been in that room."

"Nor have I, nor the master's, either." Sam set his cup aside. "Although we roamed everywhere else, my uncle never admitted the rabble into his sanctum."

"Especially not two rowdy boys." Rob stood as the ladies withdrew. When they could be heard climbing the stairs, he turned back to his cousin. "Come into the library. I have some tolerable sherry there."

"That sounds a welcome relief from tea." Sam followed Rob down the hall to his favorite haunt. "How are you and your lady faring? Does marriage suit you?"

Rob poured two glasses of the wine and settled behind his desk, propping his feet on it and leaning back in his chair. "Marriage has always suited me. I have missed the companionship."

Sam took the chair by the fire. "I wish I might have known your first wife." He sighed. "But I have always been stuck here in England."

"That has its good aspects." Rob drank a bit of the sherry. "You know a great deal more about how things stand here now than I do. Did you learn anything else of interest in London?"

"Only that there is friction between Welwyn and Wycomb. I'm not sure the source of it, but it was pretty obvious in my meeting with them."

"Hmm. I guess that is not surprising. They are of two different generations—and from the argument here Christmas Eve, I'd say they don't agree on politics."

"No, they don't." Sam stretched his long legs out to the fire. "And sometimes I can see Wycomb's point of view. Bonaparte's strengths show our monarch's weakness, to the advantage of the French."

"What do you think? Will we go to war with him?"

"Oh, certainly. He is preparing for that even as we sit here and drink French wine." Sam emptied his glass, and Rob stretched across the desk to refill it. "But about the subject you asked me to explore... I can find no hint of who Iantha's attackers might have been, except that Carrock ran with some rather wild companions. It is quite possible that they entertained themselves with rape."

"But which of them was here—at my invitation? That's the bastard I want my hands on now." Rob's fist closed convulsively around the wineglass, and he made himself set it carefully on the desk. "You know that they still send her filthy letters?"

"You told me."

"Well, now I have also received a threat, and the same person sent one to her. Thank heaven I was able to intercept hers." He pounded his fist on the desk. "God, I wish I knew who the bloody scoundrel is."

"If you knew that, you would know the rest."

"Yes. And it is only a matter of time until I do know." He looked his cousin in the face. "I promise you that, Sam."

Dinner had been a quiet affair. Rob still felt the pricks of vexation brought on by Iantha's bias toward men and the injustice to himself that he perceived, and she apparently felt no more amiable. He spent some time studying with Vijaya afterward, still grumbling to himself. But grumbling would get him nowhere. Time to have a frank discussion with his lady.

As he opened the door of his bedchamber to divest himself of coat and cravat, he started at the sight of Camille, Iantha's new maid, turning down his bed.

Rob frowned. "What are you doing here?"

The maid curtsied, eyes demurely downcast. "Lady Duncan told me I might retire. I thought I would prepare your bed before I go."

The glance she now cast at Rob ranked a long distance from *demure*. He narrowed his own eyes as he watched her finish her task. What was this about? Tending to his bed certainly constituted no part of her duties—nor did being in his bedchamber for any other reason. The answer he expected was not long in coming.

Her task finished, she walked toward the door, pausing close beside him. "Will there be anything else, milord?"

The languid gaze she now bestowed on him, her chin lifted, her eyes sleepy, explained the whole matter. No doubt she knew that he and Iantha had yet to share a bed. Little baggage!

Her scent wafted up to him, and Rob's body stirred. It had been a very long time since… He drew in a long breath. With her neatly coiled black hair and light olive skin, she reminded him for a moment of Shakti. But he had never seen that calculating look in his first wife's gentle eyes.

And he had no intention of tupping his wife's maid.

Even if his present wife thought men required variety.

"No, I thank you." He made his voice cold.

Camille hesitated but a moment before curtsying again and slipping out the door.

Rob feared he had not seen the last of her.

He was still pondering the question of what to do about the encounter when he strolled into the sitting room he shared with Iantha. He found her on the sofa before the fireplace, reading. He poured himself a glass of brandy and went to stand by the fire.

Iantha set her magazine aside and favored him with a cool look. A bit too cool. Rob bristled. Why was he putting out so much effort to be understanding of her, when she apparently had no understanding of him at all? Nor appeared to want any. And what was he getting in return for his effort? Very little.

Unless he counted the offer from her maid.

Which he had nobly refused.

Rob did not like the way he felt. He wanted the air

cleared. But where to start? Her expression gave him not the least notion. Oh, the devil with it!

He took a fortifying sip of his drink. "Iantha, we had little time this afternoon to discuss your approach to being Lady Wisdom."

She cocked her head to one side. "True. Did you have a comment?"

The icicles in her tone warned Rob that any comment he might have had best be complementary. He was not, however, in a mood to be obliging. "Not exactly. I was wondering why you have the opinion of men that you do."

Her delicate brow wrinkled. "I am not quite sure to what you refer."

"In the first place, where did you get the idea that all men are alike? That all of us hate tears? Or that we exercise no control over our desires or our temper? Or that women must simply tolerate our 'need for variety'?" He sounded angrier than he had intended.

"One hears things, my lord. Even I."

"But what things? From whom?"

"My lord, I have a father and three brothers. I can assure you that they all abhor tears. And Mama always says, when Papa is in a temper, that we must avoid him and be careful what we say. She will not allow us to annoy him."

Rob grinned. "And I can assure you that your papa knows exactly when your mother is not pleased, and makes every effort to ameliorate the situation. Nor does he seek variety."

Iantha had to think about that. "That may be true."

"Of course it's true." Rob grimaced. "There is not a man alive who wants to live with his wife's displeasure."

"If you saw and read what I do, my lord, you would

not be so sure. This very magazine has an article advising women not to seem too intelligent. Men don't care for intelligent women, it seems. I have heard that all my life.'' She shook the pages in her hand, thinking of the many unhappy letters she had read. "And the questions I receive... This writer's husband forbids her to visit her family. That one reports that her spouse strikes her if she speaks at all sharply to him. Another one—''

"But those women write because there *is* a problem. They don't represent...'' He took a breath and smoothed out his frown. "I *enjoy* your intelligence! It is one of the things... Iantha, look at *me*. Not them—me! Have I failed to control my desires? Have I fled from your tears? No!''

He began to pace. "I have urged you in vain to express your anger. You refuse to do it. Now you tell me that *men* will not tolerate it in women.''

Oh, dear. Now *he* sounded angry. Iantha hastened to make amends. "I...I'm sorry, my lord. I did not mean to imply...''

"It isn't just your anger, Iantha. It is all your feelings. You rarely let yourself laugh. You apologize for weeping. You don't even know when you are getting cold. How do you expect ever to...''

"I don't expect it, my lord.'' Iantha felt the flood of indignation rise in her chest. "I told you how it was with me, but you were so sure...''

"You have to try. You will not even make the attempt to feel anything, but rather you make every attempt to restrain—''

"You are unjust, Lord Duncan! I have tried. I have kissed you. I have...'' The anger grew stronger. She must flee, or else she might... "If you will excuse me...'' She rose and made for the door.

He beat her to it and barred her way. "No. We will finish this discussion."

She stopped a foot away from him. "I cannot, my lord. Please get out of my way."

He crossed his arms and held his ground, his mouth a grim line. Before she could stop herself, Iantha's hands came up, and she gave him a hard push.

He didn't budge.

She began to feel panicky. "Please, my lord. Look what I have done! I do not wish to resort to violence. I must leave before…"

"Before what? What will happen if you don't leave?" He watched her implacably.

"I…I don't know."

"I do. You will act and speak in anger. Is that so terrible?"

"Yes! Yes, it is!" She wrapped her arms around herself and held on tightly.

His face softened. "Why, Iantha? You haven't the strength to harm me physically. What can happen that is so bad?"

She dropped her arms and looked at him helplessly.

"I will go mad."

## Chapter Eleven

God knew he wanted to deny it, to comfort her, to tell her she would not lose her mind no matter how angry she felt. But he could not do it.

Who was he to say she wouldn't?

When he remembered the days of his own fury, he could not be sure that he had been quite sane. But he had not lost his reason altogether. After a time his rage had abated. He began to see for himself what he was doing. He became able to stop doing it.

But last night all Rob could do was mutter a reassurance and let her pass. This morning he felt disappointed that he had not made better use of the opportunity. Earlier he had planned to make her angry at him. Well, he had accomplished that! His own irritation had fueled hers. But she still had not been able to express it.

He put aside these thoughts when the library door opened and the subject of his reverie came into the room. She looked as subdued as he felt. In her hand she carried two letters.

"I found these in the post." She laid them on the desk.

"I did not open mine. I think they are…more of the same."

Rob opened the note addressed to him, then crumpled it in his fist. "Aye. That is what they are." He started for the fire, and then thought better of it. He examined the writing carefully. "But this seems to be yet another writer. How many of the bastards—" He broke off as he realized how difficult the question might be for her. "I'm sorry. I…"

Iantha shook her head. "It's all right. But I don't know the answer. They all wore identical masks, so I don't know if any of them…"

Rob crumpled the paper again, shaking it in his fist. "They should be hung, and if I could but identify them, I'd *see* them hung if I had to do it myself. Is there anything at all you remember about them?"

"I try very hard not to remember." She stared at her clenched fists.

Feeling like the greatest brute in nature, Rob persisted. "I can only imagine how harrowing this is for you, but even the smallest detail might help identify them. Were they all young?"

"Again, I can't be sure." She gazed into the fire thoughtfully. Rob didn't rush her. Finally she said, "It is very hard for me to think about it. But I do believe most of them were probably young. They all seemed…very…" Her chin quivered, and she set her jaw. "Very strong."

Could she stand another question? He must know everything in order to stop this horror. Perhaps one more. "What about their clothes, their horses?"

Iantha shrugged, withdrew into herself. "I don't know. They weren't ruffians." She whirled toward him. "Please, Rob, I can't…"

Rob walked around the desk and put his hand on her shoulder. "I'm sorry. I know it is painful for you."

"Yes." She looked down at her tightly clasped hands. "When I let myself remember, it all comes back and…and I become very agitated." She dropped her face into her hands. "I don't know what I might do."

"Look at me, Iantha." Rob gently moved her hands and lifted her chin. "I cannot tell you that you will not go mad from fear and anger. All I can say is that I did not. And I don't think I would ever have recovered from my grief and bitterness without acting on that anger." He smiled. "And I think it likely that I did a great deal more damage than you possibly could."

"I don't know about that. Sometimes I believe that I would be capable of anything. I don't want to hurt you…or anyone…."

He brushed his lips across her forehead.

"I think that highly unlikely."

He would be careful not to let her.


Iantha burst from sleep with a scream in her throat. She clapped her hands over her mouth and refused to allow it birth. When she was sure it would not emerge, she sat up and covered her face with her hands. This was the third night in a row that the events of that terrible night had come back to haunt her dreams—the cold, the masks, the pain. She could no longer shut them out. In hearing that hated laugh, in knowing that some of them had been in the house with her, in answering Rob's questions about her attackers, she had been forced to remember. It had opened Pandora's box.

And now she could not close it.

For three days, whenever she had shut her eyes, images

of grotesque, bloodred masks leapt up behind her eyelids. Animal sounds assaulted her ears. The smell of spirits sent a lash of panic through her. But she could not tell Rob that.

She could not tell him anything.

He had shattered her control. He made her laugh. He made her weep. She had danced with him, kissed him. His vigor, his manliness assailed her senses and started feelings in her body that she feared to allow expression.

She stayed in her bedchamber during the days, but her brain refused to consider answers to the letters she received from *La Belle Assemblée*. The endeavor to put her confusion into poetry died aborning. The painting she had attempted devolved into a dark, swirling mass. Iantha had cast it into the fire.

She got up and walked to the window. A hard wind was blowing, but no snow fell. Just like that other night.

And now she again felt the cold.

Iantha climbed back into bed and pulled the down-filled quilts up under her chin.

And lay there, awake and shivering, until dawn.

Just like that other night.

He did not know what to do for her. Rob had watched her tired face and trembling hands all through dinner. She hardly ate at all. Clearly, her fear had gotten worse. When asked how she was, she simply said that she had not slept well. When he put an arm around her shoulders, she froze so completely that now he was afraid to touch her.

When Rob came into the sitting room that night, he found a shivering Iantha huddled on the sofa, wrapped in several shawls, her arms hugging her body.

"Are you that cold, Iantha?" Rob crossed to her and placed a hand on her forehead, expecting to find her feverish. Instead her forehead felt chilled and clammy. "Do you feel ill?"

She shook her head. "No, just cold. I haven't been able to get warm for several days."

Rob studied the dark hollows under her eyes. "You're sure?"

She nodded, but did not speak.

Kneeling by the fireplace, he set another log on the blaze and reached for a second. The one he picked up had the remnants of a small branch sticking out at an awkward angle. It might keep the log from lying securely on the pile. Rob laid it on the hearth, pulled his knife from his boot top and attacked the projection.

Suddenly, from behind him he heard a strangled, "No!"

He turned to find his wife standing by the sofa, the shawls in a pile around her feet. "What is it, Iantha?"

"No, no, no." He took a step toward her, only to have her back away, the scarves tangling with her feet.

"Be careful! You will fall." He reached for her, and she uttered a muffled scream. What? And then he remembered. The knife. The first time he had met her.

He tossed the blade aside, but she continued to stumble back, kicking at the shawls and trying to turn, all the while muttering, "No, no."

Her eyes were wide and wild, and he thought she did not really see him. He reached for her again, but as his hand closed on her arm, she tried to jerk away and fell. His own feet now in the scarves, he lost his balance and followed her down to the floor, one arm across her body.

She pushed at him frantically. "No! Get away!"

As she fought to escape his arm, Rob became frightened himself. Had she, indeed, lost her mind? She obviously did not know who he was. "Iantha, it is I—Rob! Look at me."

Instead she turned her face away and attempted to roll out of his reach. "Leave me alone! Leave me alone!"

But he could not leave her alone. She might hurt herself. She clearly did not know where she was or what she was doing. He tightened his grip on her, and she flung her free hand out, groping for the knife. He could not let her have *that!*

Rob rolled his weight onto her, immobilizing her. She screamed again and began to beat on his face and chest, crying, "Let me go! Let me go!"

He began to understand. Somehow her mind had returned to the night she had been raped. What should he do? He couldn't release her, and if he continued to restrain her... When she clawed at his eyes, Rob clasped his arms around hers, pinning them to her sides. She continued to fight him, kicking and twisting, crying out and then struggling in grim silence.

He had no idea how much time passed. Then, suddenly, her voice changed.

In a completely different tone she said, "Please stop," and began to cry.

Rob rolled off of her, but he could not bring himself to take his arms from around her. Instead he pulled her to his chest and stroked her hair.

Through a muffled sob, he heard, "Rob?"

"Aye. It is I. I have you."

"Thank God." She wept quietly now. He held her as

gently as he could. At last she asked, "I was beside my-self, wasn't I?"

"Yes. I think that would describe what happened."

"I *have* gone mad!" A sob threatened to choke off her voice.

Rob thought for a moment. "Nay, I think not. Strong emotion often takes us outside ourselves."

"Did that happen to you?"

"Not quite the same way, but there are times I can't remember. Do you recall what just happened?"

A long silence ensued. At last she shuddered. "Yes. I don't want to...but I do. I was there again...with—with *them*. He had the knife.... It still had Nurse's blood on it." Another paroxysm of sobs shook her. "He cut her throat, and then he held the knife against my neck and would not let me move or cry out...not even when he... When I screamed at the pain, he cut me."

Behind her back, Rob's fists clenched, but he kept his voice quiet. "It is all right now. You are safe here with me."

"He...he hissed at me." Her voice, between sobs, sounded weak.

"Hissed?" Rob drew back far enough to give her a puzzled look.

"Through his teeth." She sobbed again. "I can't remember his voice because he hissed everything—'Don't move,' 'Silence!' Only a few commands. He was the first." She grasped Rob's shirt and hid her face in it, weeping again.

She was shivering in his arms now. Rob fumbled with his feet and finally raked one of the shawls within reach of his hand. He spread it over both of them.

Again she choked back her sobs long enough to say, "And then another one came and another one and...I don't know.... They cut my clothes and hit me...and one of them bit me." Her voice broke and silent sobs racked her slight form.

"Bloody hell!" Rob could not hold back the oath. "Killing is too easy for them."

He got to one knee and gathered her into his arms. After he had laid her on her bed, he wrestled off his boots and lay beside her, pulling the covers over both of them.

Iantha drew in a long shuddering breath and looked up into his face. "Please don't leave me."

Rob gazed into her tearstained face. "At this moment, not all the forces of hell could take me away from you."

The cold bit at her again. Iantha woke to a frosty dawn and the realization that her husband was in her bed. Oh, dear heaven! Pulling the covers tightly around her neck, she lay on her back, shivering. A few tense moments later she felt movement and heard a rustle from the other side of the bed. Without turning her head, she slid her gaze in that direction.

Rob's face, propped on one hand, smiled down at her.

Iantha quickly looked back at the ceiling and clutched the quilt tighter.

Her husband chuckled. "Don't you find the bedding a bit redundant? You still have on your robe, and I am wearing both shirt and britches."

She dared another glance out of the corner of her eye. "But we are in bed."

"Not an unusual circumstance for a man and his wife."

Iantha clutched the quilt tighter. "But we—we don't…"

Rob's grin disappeared. "I know. We don't. But if you will allow me to hold you, I will warm you."

Did she dare? Last night had been so intense. So frightening. But having Rob hold her later had been…very comforting. Her teeth began to chatter, and she nodded. "Th-thank y-you."

She rolled toward him, and he took her in his arms. "How are you this morning?"

"I am not sure, but I must know…" Iantha pulled back and gazed into his face. "Seeing what you saw last night, hearing what I told you… Have—have you taken me in disgust?"

*"No."* His voice firm, he did not hesitate for a second. "How could I? You are no less beautiful or interesting than you were yesterday. No less intelligent. No less fascinating. What they did has no bearing on that. I only regret that I was not there to defend you."

"Thank you." He sounded as though he meant every word.

The heat of his body enveloped her, and his big hand stroked her back. They lay quietly for a few heartbeats, then Rob asked, "But how do *you* feel?"

"Other than being cold—" her throat closed, and Iantha choked on the words "—I don't *feel* insane." She hid her face against his chest.

"I do not believe that you are mad—although an experience such as you had is enough to challenge anyone's reason." He moved back slightly to look into her face. "You are a very strong woman, Iantha. You do not give yourself enough credit for that. You *will* heal if you determine to do so. Do you realize that you told me about the attack last night? I have never heard you do that before.''

"No. I never have—not even just after it happened. I...I couldn't. But no one asked me, except about their clothing and appearance. They just put me to bed and tended my wounds and tiptoed and whispered around me. And *no* one mentioned the incident in my presence, even after I grew better. I did my best to shut it all away.''

Leaning back again, Rob traced the faint, white scar on her neck with one finger. She felt a rumble in his chest, like a growl, but he said nothing. He just pulled her close once again and wrapped his arms tighter around her. Slowly Iantha began to thaw. She relaxed against him, absorbing his warmth. The terror of the night before grew dimmer. A sense of peace crept over her.

How long had it been since she had felt peaceful? The past six years had been one long, grueling battle to wall off the horror that had erupted from her mind last night. To crush all the distressing emotions. Now that she had lost the fight, the memory seemed to have lost its power over her. Sheltered in Rob's arms, she could think about it without fear.

Rob's arms. Her husband's arms.

She had not thought it possible.

Other than being very tired, Iantha was amazed at how well she felt that day. Her writing went smoothly. Her thoughts flowed more freely. She enjoyed a walk with Rob. She even enjoyed having his arm around her to help her back up the steep road.

Supper tasted wonderful. Iantha had not realized how much her appetite had diminished in recent days. Burnside had overseen the preparation of a curry he was teaching the new chef to prepare, and she wolfed it down as though she were starving. She drank a whole glass of wine, and later as they relaxed before the fire in their private parlor, she accepted the glass of sherry that Rob poured for her.

They sat in companionable silence and watched the fire. Iantha realized that she no longer felt the need to sit as far away from him as possible. She turned to study his profile. In his rugged way, he really was a very handsome man. The recognition stirred something deep inside her, but she didn't look away.

As though he felt her gaze on him, he suddenly looked at her and held out an inviting arm. She slid across the sofa, and he laid the arm around her shoulders. After an awkward moment or two, Iantha snuggled a bit closer and let her head rest against him. Briefly she felt the soft warmth of his lips on her forehead. Sighing, she smiled up at him.

He set his glass aside and shifted so that he could look into her face. A strong hand came up and gently brushed the hair back from her cheek. "How could you think anything about you could ever disgust me? You are so…so innocent. And so lovely."

He leaned closer, and Iantha now felt his lips against hers. Only a fleeting touch. And then he was gazing into her eyes. "Your eyes are like the mountain sky in summer. I want to fall into them and fly away with you."

Love words. She had never before heard them.

His mouth came down on hers again, this time more strongly. She lifted her arm and tentatively touched his face, exploring the slight roughness of his carefully shaved cheeks. His arm tightened around her shoulders, and the pressure of the kiss increased. After several breaths he leaned back and looked questioningly at her.

She smiled. "I found that rather pleasant, my lord."

"Rather pleasant?" Rob grinned. "Surely I can do better than that."

Before she realized what he was doing, he leaned back and pulled her across his lap, cradling her head against his arm. He kissed her again, harder. Iantha reached up and rested her hand on the back of his neck, cautiously weaving her fingers through his thick hair. His faint, smoky scent rose to her nostrils. She took a deep breath to savor it, and her mouth opened slightly. His tongue slid along her lower lip.

Iantha didn't know what to do. But apparently she was not required to do anything. Which was a fortunate circumstance, as the sensation of his tongue on her mouth seemed to take all her attention. For several minutes he tasted her lips, nibbled at them gently, kissed her eyelids and returned to her lips.

Then, through her robe, she noticed the warmth of his hand against her hip. The hand slipped upward to her waist, competing for attention with what his mouth was doing. Iantha seemed to be floating on a vast, balmy zephyr. Her breath came in little sighs, and she could hear Rob's coming faster. His hand moved to the side of her breast.

A tension developed between her legs, only to increase when he brushed his thumb across her nipple. She gasped and ducked her head against his chest. And now she noticed that under her in his lap was a growing bulge. For a moment she wanted to move away, but as he continued to tease the nipple, the impulse died, and she relaxed against him again. Iantha heard herself moan. At the sound, Rob pulled her tighter against him, again finding her mouth with his.

And suddenly his hand was gone from her breast, and he was clutching her to him, breathing as though he had been running. She looked up into his face. He smiled down at her. "I think…" He drew a long breath. "I think we had better stop this. If we don't, I am afraid I will push you too far too soon."

Iantha rested her head against his chest and sighed, half disappointed, half relieved. The sensations had been so…so *compelling*. She had not felt in control of her body; rather, *he* had seemed to control it. The thought frightened her. Could she tolerate that?

Did she trust him that much?

Now *that* was progress. She had actually responded to his lovemaking. Rob took heart. If he could but control his own urgency for a while longer, surely she would learn to enjoy him as he enjoyed her. Last night his blood had heated to the point that he'd doubted his own restraint. The sensation of Iantha's delicate body in his arms had inflamed him until… He must be careful of demanding too much from her. He feared another frightening experience would freeze her forever.

Rob looked forward to his next opportunity to woo her. Unfortunately, there would be none that day. They were on their way to visit Iantha's family and would spend the night.

He had debated the safety of traveling in the coach, but decided that, with both Burnside and Feller as scouts, an ambush was unlikely. Both he and his henchmen were seasoned by travel in hazardous places. They would not be caught unprepared like the inexperienced English country lads who had accompanied Iantha on her ill-fated journey.

To Rob's surprise, when they drew up in the drive at Hill House, another carriage was being led away toward the stables. Now who could that be? The question was answered as soon as they were escorted into the drawing room. Across the flurry of greetings that followed their entrance, Rob saw the rotund figure of his banker and the hawklike visage of his young protégé.

"Welwyn!" Rob hastened to shake hands with both of them. "Wycomb. What brings you here?"

The banker bowed. "Looking into some investments. Lord Rosley has very kindly agreed to discuss his gunpowder mill with us."

"In that case…" Lady Rosley smiled graciously at the company "…Iantha and I will leave you gentlemen to your business." The men all stood until both ladies had cleared the door.

"Sit down, sit down." Lord Rosley motioned them to comfortable chairs. "Madeira, gentlemen? Or would you prefer tea?"

All of them quickly indicated a preference for the wine, and Lord Rosley passed it to them. Seating himself, he carefully lifted one leg onto a footstool. His gout must be bothering him again. "What may I tell you about the mill? Have you a party interested in investing in gunpowder?"

"We have several." Welwyn sipped his wine.

"Everyone is interested in gunpowder. It is only a matter of time until we find ourselves at war with Bonaparte, and then…" Wycomb took a deep swallow.

"We are researching several possible mills in this area." The older banker set his glass aside and rested his hands on his ample belly. "If you would consider taking in additional investors, we may be able to send them to you."

Wycomb tipped his glass up and drained it. "We will need to know a bit more about the operation, of course."

Rob listened with interest. If his father-in-law needed additional capital, he might consider investing himself. It sounded like a good investment. He would speak with him about it later. If England went to war, a need for the production of more gunpowder would certainly be the result.

At length Lord Rosley agreed to have his agent forward the information that the bankers needed on the profits and output of the mill, and the conversation turned to more general topics—the European situation, their king's increasing madness and several salacious tidbits of gossip from town. An enlightening afternoon.

But Rob would rather have spent it with his wife.

# Chapter Twelve

Iantha and her mother repaired to Lady Rosley's cozy sitting room. "Oh, Iantha!" The older woman gave her a quick hug and a peck on the cheek. "I have missed you so. Are you well? Are you happy? Is Lord Duncan…?"

"I am fine, Mama." Iantha returned the kiss and settled into her favorite sofa. "I assure you, Lord Duncan is the kindest of husbands." She gathered her skirt in so that her mother could sit beside her.

"He—he is…considerate of…?" A red stain climbed Lady Rosley's throat.

Iantha smiled to herself. She understood well what her mother wished to know. But how to convey that information delicately? "I could not ask for more consideration. He is in no way demanding."

"Oh. Well, I am very glad to know that." In fact, her mama, a confirmed romantic, looked a bit disappointed.

"I'm sure we will grow closer with time."

"Of course." Lady Rosley brightened. "It takes months to become comfortable with one another."

"I am feeling quite comfortable with him, Mama. You have no need to worry about me at all."

"I *do* worry. I am very sorry, but I can't help it. Someone actually committed murder in your home, and those horrible letters... You don't still receive them, do you?"

For a moment Iantha contemplated telling her parent a lie.

But that was not her way.

Besides, Mama would know.

She took a sustaining breath. "Yes, Mama, I have received three more. But you must not be concerned. The writers have never acted on their threats. And Lord Duncan becomes extremely fierce when he thinks of what happened. I have no doubt that he will keep me safe. He is also making a renewed effort to find them and bring them to justice."

Lady Rosley sighed. "Your papa tried. He left no stone unturned. We hired Bow Street to investigate, but they never discovered anything of use."

"I know, Mama. But I...I have begun to recall more about that night."

"Oh, Iantha! No!" Her mother leaned forward and clasped her daughter's hand. "I do not want you to think about it."

Iantha grimaced. "I have no choice, it seems. Recently... Recently..." How could she explain it? "The other evening, the events of that time... They just suddenly burst upon me. I felt that I was there again—although I knew that, in truth, I was not." She twisted her handkerchief in her lap. "I...I thought I had gone mad."

"Oh, my darling!" Lady Rosley flung her arms around her. "You cannot be mad. You of all people. You are too restrained, too intelligent."

A tiny smile curved Iantha's lips. "Thank you, Mama, but I do not believe that madness and intelligence exclude one another."

"Well, no, they don't. I have heard of some very brilliant individuals who... But..." She stopped for a moment and stared out the window, before turning back to Iantha. "Terrible experiences do sometimes return to us. When your baby brother died—you were only two, so you may not remember—I kept waking to the belief that he was still with me. I could not be sure until I went to the nursery and looked in the cradle. And then, seeing it empty..." She paused to wipe away tears. "Then it would all come back to me. I would understand that he was dead, just as I had when he died." A sob escaped her. "I lost him again, time after time."

"Ah, Mama."

For the first time in six years Iantha returned her mother's embrace, their tears mingling.

Between Lord Rosley's dry wit and Mr. Welwyn's hearty laugh, dinner had been a convivial occasion. Rob had a visit earlier with the younger Kethleys. As much as he enjoyed the children, he could not gaze at Valeria without picturing Laki and wondering how she might have looked at that later age. Not blond, as Iantha's little sister was, but he thought she would have the same quiet charm. In spite of himself sadness overtook him, and he appreciated the company over dinner.

But what he really wanted was some time alone with Iantha. His gaze persisted in wandering to her, even when he pretended to be listening to the conversation. As usual, she ate quietly, keeping her reserve, but Rob noticed that she laughed more than she once had at her father's sallies.

She did not give much attention to Stephen Wycomb, who sat on her other side. Rob could feel her leaning toward him, ever so slightly pulling away from the young banker. Perhaps she would always be guarded with men she did not know well.

Rob heartily hoped so.

At last they had been able to excuse themselves and retire. Rob thought he saw knowing looks in the eyes of the bankers and speculation in the eyes of her parents. Well, the two of them *were* newlyweds. He just wished that they were hurrying away for the reasons newlyweds ordinarily did. But he sensed progress. Full victory would shortly be within his grasp.

Once in his bedchamber he divested himself of his coat and cravat and let Burnside pull off his boots before dismissing him for the night. Rob didn't bother with a dressing gown. His muscular build usually kept him from being cold indoors.

Lady Rosley had diplomatically assigned Rob and Iantha adjoining bedchambers. Rob smiled as he tapped on the connecting door. He suspected he had a staunch supporter in his new mother-in-law.

Iantha opened the door and peeped through. On seeing him she opened it wide enough for him to enter. Damn. Now she seemed wary of *him* again. Rob sighed. "I just came in to say good night." He could see some of the tension drain out of her, and chanced putting an arm around her. Her body still felt stiff. "Is something amiss?"

She shook her head. "No. I only… I am not comfortable with strangers."

Rob hoped that was the problem, but he doubted it. "Did I frighten you again last night?"

For several heartbeats Iantha looked at her hands. At last she lifted her gaze to his face. "Not frightened, no."

"Then, what?"

"The experience was quite interesting and not unpleasant. I just felt… I don't know… That I was not in control of my person, that you were creating sensations in me that I could not stop.''

"Did you want them to stop?"

A thoughtful pause ensued. Finally she said, "Not at the time.''

A deep chuckle rolled up from Rob's chest. "That, at least, is encouraging.'' He placed both hands on her arms and began stroking them. "The nature of lovemaking, my dear wife, is just that—to be out of control and not want to stop.''

"And you enjoy that?"

"Oh, aye. I think most people do, once they become accustomed to it. Certainly most men like it. And many women, also.''

Iantha considered that, her head a bit to one side. "It seems one must place a great deal of faith in the other person.''

His hands paused for a moment. "Yes, it does, and I think that is harder for women. Men are so much stronger. But it is important for us, too. The very strength of our passions makes us vulnerable—gives women power over us.''

"I find it hard to think of you as vulnerable. You are so wise and steady, and of course physically very large and strong. And you have such an aura of power.''

Rob read a question in her eyes. "But I am still vulnerable to you, just as you are to me. I was very nearly not able to control my own feelings last night. You have a potent effect on me.''

"I do?" Iantha pondered that thought. She had once believed that she would someday have a husband who would love her and desire her. And then it seemed that she never would, that no man would ever want her. But

now she *did* have a husband, and he was saying he desired her. Perhaps he did *not* have all the control over the
situation—over her. She lifted her hands to his shoulders
and turned her face up. "Perhaps I shall get accustomed
to the feeling."

His big palms cupped her face. "I have every intention
of giving you that opportunity."

His mouth came down on hers. Iantha tensed for a
moment. Then she ordered herself to relax, to concentrate
on the feeling of his lips on hers, the warmth of his hands
on her face, the bulge between his legs pressing against
her.

For a heartbeat that sensation threatened to destroy the
others. But why should it? Was it not the evidence of
what he had just told her? Her touch brought about
changes in his body that he could not control, just as his
did to hers. She clasped her arms around his neck and
rocked her hips forward.

With a groan he moved his hands to her bottom and
pressed her against him. Taking a step back, he spread
his legs and leaned against the wall. He lowered his lips
to her throat, holding her body tightly against his erection. The heat of his breath against her skin started a dark,
warm tension growing in Iantha's lower body. It flowed
from her belly down her legs, pooling between them.

Still holding her hips close with one hand, Rob began
unfastening the ties of her wrapper and gown. Brushing
the robe aside, he wrapped that arm around her waist and
pressed his lips against the swell of her breast. The sensations in Iantha increased, and she arched her back, leaning her belly against him and allowing him access to her
breast. Slowly his mouth and tongue made their way
downward, leaving small tingling damp spots in
their wake.

When he lifted her and his lips closed around her nipple, Iantha gasped aloud and clutched his shoulders. His breathing roughened, and his hips pulsed against hers. After several intoxicating seconds, he straightened and turned her so that her back was to the wall.

Kneeling before her, Rob opened her gown and cupped both breasts in his big palms. "God, you are so beautiful." He began to tease her nipples with thumb and finger and looked up into her face. "I will stop if you wish, but…"

Iantha saw the unspoken plea in his eyes. She could only shake her head silently and drop her hands on his shoulders, gripping them hard. He closed his mouth around one nipple, his hand still in place on the other. Iantha heard herself moan, and he pulled her hips close with his free arm. Her legs began to tremble, and when her knees threatened to give way, she slid down the wall.

Rob grasped her waist and eased her to the floor. He stretched them both out side by side on the carpet, then returned his attention to her breasts. Any vestige of control deserted her. Her mind clutched futilely at it for a heartbeat.

And then, very deliberately, Iantha let it go.

She pressed herself upward to his mouth and hand. His free hand rested on her belly. Gradually the warmth of it moved lower, and she felt a tug as he raised the hem of her gown. Before she could react to that, he began to press gently on the focus of her sensation.

Gasping for breath, Iantha lifted her hips against his hand. The pressure increased, slowly circling. The tension became almost unbearable. And then, just as she was about to beg him to stop, it exploded. Every muscle in her body tightened. Feeling rippled outward from her legs, racing all the way to her face and to the tip of her toes. A loud cry sprang from her throat, only to be swallowed by Rob's mouth over hers.

Then, gradually, the feelings disappeared, leaving Iantha limp and gasping.

She sobbed.

And Rob drew her to him, cradling her head in his hand, pressing her close. After a minute her weeping ceased. He eased away and looked down into her face, then dipped his head and kissed her tearstained cheeks. "Why are you weeping?"

Iantha shook her head. "It was just so...so overwhelming. I never felt anything like that."

"It is a unique experience. Were you afraid?"

"I was for a moment," she admitted. "But then...I don't know. I just stopped thinking about it. Did I... Is how I reacted acceptable to you? Am I supposed to do that?"

"Oh, my dear wraith!" She felt the vibration of his chuckle against her breasts. "It was far more than acceptable. Your passion is a precious gift. I am humbly grateful."

"Grateful? Do you mean it?"

"Completely."

"Did you feel it also?"

"Not this time, but one day soon I will. We will feel it together."

Suddenly she became aware of the hardness of his shaft still pressing against her. "Do you want...? I mean, do you need...?" Iantha felt the blood flooding her face. "I believe that men, when they are aroused..."

Her husband laughed aloud. "Not now. This is enough for your first taste of ecstasy."

"But you..." She shifted against his erection.

He groaned and moved back a little. "Enough. Not

now. Unfortunately, men become aroused much more frequently than they are able to do anything about it." He grimaced. "We are used to that. I will be all right. I enjoyed every second of having you in my arms. When you become a bit more comfortable with your own feelings, we will deal with mine. I don't want to repeat anything that happened to you before just yet."

Iantha looked at him in amazement.

"I assure you, my lord, *nothing* that you did this evening happened that night."

Rob felt like a traitor. He had been dreaming of Shakti. Throwing the covers off, he sat on the side of the bed and let the cold air wash over him. Considering his earlier unfinished encounter with Iantha, it was no surprise that he had dreamed erotically.

But why Shakti?

He still felt her supple golden body against him. Felt her desire answering his. Heard her ecstatic cries. But Iantha had also given him her passion this evening. And she had offered him completion. It had been his choice to leave her after tucking her into bed.

The image of the waterfall she had painted for him swam into his consciousness. And her words—*Or will I crumble, shattered by thy power?* God forbid he bring that about. He must wait until he could be sure she was ready.

But, ah, he missed the free give and take of lovemaking.

He missed his family—dancing little Laki, golden Shakti. The empty loneliness welled up inside him. Rob walked to the window and stood looking out, tears trickling down his face. The fells lay bare and cold in the moonlight. No comfort there. He longed to walk into the next room, to lie down beside Iantha and hold her close.

But he did not dare.

He would never be able to contain his need for her.

At least he had some companionship with Iantha. Her bright mind ranged with his over innumerable subjects. He had begun to teach her to read some of his old manuscripts, and she talked with him about her poetry. He had never had that with Shakti.

But Iantha always seemed to be on the other side of some intangible, indefinable wall.

Out of reach.

Rob sighed and went back to bed.


The wall stood firmly in place this afternoon. Rob glanced at Iantha, who was staring out the window on her side of the coach. Last night's experiment had gone well enough, but now they were back to the dance—one step forward, one step back. He had known from the start that he would need patience, but he hadn't realized how hard it would be, being near her, wanting her, to maintain that patience.

In fact, he was very nearly out of it.

Rob leaned back in his corner of the seat and studied his elusive wife. She continued to gaze at the scenery.

Enough of this!

"Iantha, what are you thinking about so deeply?"

She started guiltily and threw him a hasty look over her shoulder. "Why...nothing important."

"If you are thinking about last night, I consider it very important." He kept his tone gentle.

Slowly Iantha faced him, a blush rising to her cheeks. "I... Yes, it is important." She glanced out the window for a moment, then returned her gaze to him. "I feel embarrassed with you. I was so…so *wanton*."

Rob chuckled and reached for her hand, closing his own around it. "Dear wraith, by definition a lady cannot be *wanton* with her own husband."

"Well, no, I suppose not. Perhaps *abandoned* is the word." She scrutinized their clasped hands as though they were some interesting phenomenon which she had never before seen.

But she did not pull her hand away. Encouraged, Rob drew her toward him and brushed a light kiss across her lips. "It is only when both parties give in to abandon that we are able to fully realize the pleasure of making love."

"Yet *you* did not do that last night." She raised questioning eyes to his.

"No. I am afraid I would frighten you if I did."

Iantha considered for a heartbeat. "Then as long as you are afraid of frightening me, you will not fully enjoy the experience."

Rob shook his head. "No, but it is always wise to temper the wind to the shorn lamb. I am willing to wait, as long as we are coming closer. But every time we do, you back away again."

"I'm sorry!" Dismay filled Iantha's face. "I haven't meant to do so. It is all so new…and I am not accustomed…" She sighed. "It has been a long time since I have been able to show affection to anyone, and lovemaking…" A frown puckered her brow. "It is so *revealing*."

Rob took her other hand into his and held them both. "That is true. It reveals our inner selves as well as our bodies."

She nodded. "Yes. That is why it is so hard for me, I think. But I *am* trying."

"I know you are. I shouldn't push you."

"Perhaps I need a little pushing." She smiled shyly.

"In that case…" Rob drew her across the seat and turned her so that she rested in his lap. "Making love in a carriage is no easy task, so we won't attempt that. But you are cold again." He pulled the lap rugs over them, and she snuggled against his shoulder. Rob rested his cheek against her hair.

And some of the loneliness faded away.

It had turned out to be very cold. A leaden sky accompanied them back to the Eyrie, and snow again looked likely. In spite of being in Rob's arms for a large part of the journey, Iantha felt thoroughly chilled by the time they reached home. Even Rob was blowing on his hands to warm them as they came into the entry hall from the old castle. At the sound of their arrival, Gailsgill hurried to meet them.

"Welcome home, my lord…my lady. There is a good fire in the library, if you would like for me to bring tea."

"Oh, thank you, Gailsgill." Iantha let the butler take her wraps. "Tea would be very welcome."

She started toward the library, but stopped to glance back at Rob. He was gathering up a stack of letters from the hall table. "I'm coming. We can look at these in comfort."

Setting the post on the desk, he pulled two chairs close to the fire for them, then scooped the mail into their laps. Iantha found a bundle of letters from *La Belle Assemblée* and one from her older sister. She set these aside to read later, and looked at a small package tied with string.

"Who is that from?" Rob looked up from his own sorting.

Iantha turned the parcel over. "I don't know. I don't recognize the hand."

"Let me." With no further permission Rob took the package from her and tore it open. A slip of paper fell out and floated to the floor.

Iantha leaned over and picked it up, read it and gasped.

The message was written in crude block letters: "SOON."

Dizziness threatened to overwhelm her. She let the paper fall back to the floor and turned to look at the object in Rob's hands. It was a piece of crimson satin fabric. Rob unfolded it, revealing the holes cut for eyes and mouth. "What…?"

But Iantha knew.

Her husband held in his hands one of the masks she had seen in her nightmares for the last six years.

At the look on her face, he swore.

Suddenly the dizziness cleared, and something Iantha could hardly name surged through her. She sprang to her feet and snatched the abomination away from him. Her hands became claws as she dug her fingers into the holes and pulled. The fabric ripped with satisfying ease. Renewing her grip again and again, she rent the satin, her breathing becoming harsh and labored. When nothing but shreds were left of the mask, when she could do no further damage, Iantha turned and hurled the remnants into the fire.

With an outrush of breath she collapsed into the chair.

Her husband was looking at her with astonishment written large on his face. After several stunned moments he knelt and retrieved the note and added it to the blaze. Only then did he speak.

"Well done!"

* * *

Iantha felt strangely... well, strangely eager. And very liberated. In spite of its threat, destroying the mask had somehow banished her fear and allowed other emotions to come forward. How long had it been since she had felt anything but fear?

All of six long years.

Throughout dinner that evening, she had watched the play of her husband's muscles under his clothes, the play of expression over his face. It changed from playful to serious to a warmth that started an answering heat in her. And she was beginning to discover the attractiveness of that heat. Rob's gentle hands and strong body, his tender caresses, were in no wise like the abuse she had experienced from her attackers.

And he was holding back for her sake. Considering all he had offered her in comfort and understanding, a home of her own—in fact, the very opportunity to experience marriage and desire—Iantha felt she owed him a great deal. And all he seemed to want in return was for her to let him teach her to make love.

How could she not?

Tonight as she readied for bed, she had Camille lay out a nightgown that she had never before worn. It had been a wedding gift from her sister Andrea. The pure white silk of the neckline plunged almost to her waist, and the skirt clung in graceful folds to her hips and thighs. The sheer matching robe tied with two dainty bows at the bosom and fell open below the waist. Iantha shivered. She would no doubt be chilled in the ensemble, but wearing it was the least she could do for the man who was willing to give her so much.

Her maid had smiled knowingly when Iantha requested the gown, but as Camille brushed her mistress's hair, Iantha could see a pout reflected in the mirror above the dressing table. Not knowing the young woman very well as yet, Iantha was uncertain whether she should inquire as to its source, or let it go unremarked.

But before she could decide, Camille smiled and tied her hair up with a ribbon. "Now, milady, his lordship will have the pleasure of untying it."

Iantha flushed, not quite knowing how to respond, but smiled back. "Thank you, Camille. That will be all."

The maid curtsied and let herself out of the room.

Iantha stared at the door to the sitting room.

After a few moments she drew a deep breath and marched toward it. When she entered the parlor, Rob was already sitting on the sofa, drinking his evening brandy and studying one of his old manuscripts. Still feeling a bit uncertain, Iantha walked to the fireplace and stood before it, warming herself, instead of sitting beside him.

Rob looked up and suddenly paused with his glass halfway to his lips, an expression of almost comic disbelief on his face. Iantha felt the hot blood flood her face. Very slowly and carefully, without taking his gaze from her, he set his glass on the end table.

After what seemed like a very long time, he grinned.

# Chapter Thirteen

"Good evening, Lady Duncan. You look quite lovely."

Iantha expected him to ask her to come and sit by him, but he did not do that immediately. Instead he gazed at her with an intensity that seemed to burn right through the filmy silk. Then he held out his arms. "You are even more entrancing with the firelight behind you, but I want you nearer." He patted his leg. "Come and sit on my lap, beautiful lady."

She could think of no answer, but still blushing, crossed to the sofa and let him settle her on his lap. She felt incredibly stiff and awkward, yet the warmth of his legs beneath her derriere felt incredibly nice. Iantha tried to smile.

Rob moved the manuscript out of harm's way and set it on the table. Picking up his brandy glass, he offered her a sip. She took a tiny one, then, feeling bolder, accepted a large swallow. The liquor burned a path down her throat, and she coughed.

"Not so fast. We have plenty of time this evening." Rob took a taste, then offered her another, grinning. "Brandy, like other things, is intended to be savored."

Iantha swallowed more cautiously this time. A pleasant sense of relaxation began to spread through her, warming her belly and her legs. Rob reached for the top tie on her robe and tugged gently. The bow came undone, revealing the skin above her breasts. She felt the blood rushing up her neck to her face.

Leaning forward, he placed a light kiss on her throat. "Fascinating. Your blushes go all over you."

Rob held the glass to her lips, and she sipped again. He undid the second tie and brushed the silk away from her breasts. Slowly and carefully he covered one of them with his big palm. Iantha drew in a quick breath as the heat reached her nipple. Giving her one last swallow of the brandy, Rob drained the rest and set the glass aside. Still holding one breast, he kissed the valley between them, then began to kiss his way up to her mouth, leaving hot, moist spots on her skin.

As his lips touched hers, his fingers found the nipple, and Iantha moaned. Under her thighs she could feel his shaft grow hard. She shifted her hips, and suddenly his hand tightened and she heard his quick intake of breath. She shifted again.

"Ah, beautiful wraith, no more of that for now, or our pleasure will come to an untimely end." He set her off his lap onto the sofa and slid to the floor, opening her knees so that he could kneel between them.

Oh, God! She felt so exposed. So vulnerable. Iantha tensed and covered her face with her hands.

Rob reached up and gently moved them aside, gazing solemnly into her eyes. "Shall I move?"

Before she could say, "Yes! Yes, move!" Iantha made herself take a long breath. This was the essence of marriage. She must deal with her fear. She must control… No. Not that. Just… "Just give me a moment."

Nodding, he reached up and pulled the ribbon out of her hair, combing his fingers through it and smoothing the silver curls against her shoulders. Iantha remembered Camille's words. *Now his lordship will have the pleasure of untying it.* She smiled inside at the thought.

Hoping that it *had* given him pleasure, she clasped his hands, holding them against her face. For several heart-beats his thumbs stroked her chin, brushed across her lips. Iantha turned her head and kissed his palms, first one and then the other. She took another deep breath and felt her tension ebb. His hands moved to her shoulders and pushed the robe off her arms, then rested on her thighs. All the while he studied her face.

Iantha managed a smile. "I believe I am all right now."

"You are sure?"

She nodded and felt the warmth shift to her hips. Cupping her bottom, he pulled her closer. Again his mouth found the sensitive skin between her breasts. But now, instead of working upward, the soft kisses moved from side to side, coming closer and closer to her nipples, wetting the fabric of her gown. When at last his lips closed over one of them, Iantha sighed and lowered her hands to his shoulders, pulling him closer.

Immediately she heard his breathing change. And then she could not distinguish it from her own. His fingers moved subtly over her bottom, and his mouth seduced her breasts. Now Iantha heard her own voice, quietly moaning.

Rob grasped her waist and, lowering himself to the floor, pulled her off the sofa on top of him. He lifted her until her breasts were over his mouth, and tugged the gown away. One of his knees came up between her thighs. Iantha felt herself begin to move against his leg.

Was she supposed to do that?

She no longer cared. She could think of nothing but the sensation of his hands and lips on her nipples, the feel of his bulging shaft so near the source of the need between her legs. And then his thumb was pressing against her there and the room began to go dark. She cried out as the world shattered into a million dazzling pieces.

As the glittering shards fell around her and she collapsed on his chest, she became aware of a different pressure between her legs.

He was inside her!

His breeches were open, and he was inside of her.

Panic threatened. Instinctively she tightened, and her body clenched around him. He groaned aloud and began to pulse, faster and faster. Suddenly he gripped her bottom and shouted—a hoarse, rough, triumphant cry. His movements slowed and finally stopped altogether. He clasped her tightly to his chest and held her as their breathing quieted.

It was over. She had made love with her husband.

She had survived.

In fact...

At last Rob let her roll to the carpet beside him, raising himself on one elbow so that he could look into her face. "Are you well? Did I hurt you?"

Iantha shook her head. "No, not at all. I didn't even know exactly when..."

He smiled. "Good. I didn't want you to think about it and be frightened. *Were* you frightened?"

"Only for a moment. I—I was feeling so much when you... I didn't realize it right away. For a moment I felt fearful, but then it was over."

"Hmm. I have been wanting you so long that I seem

to have been a bit precipitous.'' Rob grinned. ''I will have to slow down so that you can also enjoy our being joined, but I think it was best this way for the first time.'' He sobered. ''You *will* come to enjoy our union, Iantha, I promise you. It can be very beautiful.''

''I...I enjoyed most of it this evening, my lord. I experienced a few tense moments, but much of it was very enjoyable—though in some ways disturbingly intense.'' She thought for a few moments. ''I didn't know it could be done as you did tonight. Was I supposed to move like that?''

He dropped a kiss on her forehead. ''You are supposed to move in any way that feels natural to you. That evidence of your passion is a great joy to me. I did it that way because I felt sure that before...''

For the first time, he seemed uncertain. Iantha nodded. ''That I was held down? Yes, I was.''

''I didn't want to do that to you.''

''Thank you, Rob. Thank you so much for understanding.'' Iantha buried her face in his shoulder, and his strong arms closed around her.

Thank God that He had sent her Robert Armstrong as a husband.

She slept in his arms that night. When Valeria was small and had a bad dream, she had sometimes crept into Iantha's room for comfort, and slept with her for the rest of the night. But that had stopped after Iantha was assaulted.

Iantha felt that the situation was reversed. She clung to Rob like a child with a nightmare on a dark night— the nightmare she had shut away with such determination. Now events had demanded that she must think about it. Experience it. Acknowledge it. She sensed that the recognition had been good for her, had freed her to an amazing extent.

Yet it still frightened her.

So she sheltered behind her husband's strength.

But when she woke the next morning, he was gone.

Rob slipped out of his wife's bed as soon as he wakened. After—at long last—enjoying her body completely, he awoke this morning hungry for more. He did not know how Iantha would feel about that in the morning's light, so he took his desire away and let her sleep. He could stand being unfulfilled awhile longer. Now, at least, he had hope. The vision of a loving future opened before him.

Whistling as he shaved, Rob was startled by a tap on the door that opened to Iantha's bedchamber. He turned and called, "Come in."

The door opened a crack and a dainty face peeked through. Rob laid down his razor and wiped the suds from his chin. As he turned, Iantha, white silk billowing behind her, darted across the room and into his arms. He caught her close to his bare chest and laid his cheek against her hair, smiling. "What brings this on, my lady?"

A muffled mumble sounded from the vicinity of his breastbone. The words came out in a rush. "I woke and you were gone and suddenly I felt afraid."

"You are safe. I am here." Rob stroked her soft hair. "Of what were you frightened?"

"I…I am not certain. I am just feeling very vulnerable of late. I have lost my control and every emotion assaults me unaware. I feel like a child in a nightmare." She leaned back and looked into his face.

A wave of guilt flowed through Rob. "I'm afraid I

have done much to bring that horror back to you. I have deliberately undermined your control, because..." He searched his mind and his conscience. "I honestly believed it kept you afraid and unable to enjoy life." What if he had been wrong?

Iantha sighed. "I believe you were correct in that. But this is so...so very *difficult*."

He pulled her head back against his chest. "I'm sorry. All I can say is that I will not desert you."

Rob felt her nod. "I believe that, Rob, and I am very grateful."

Grateful? Was that what he wanted from his wife? Gratitude?

Later that afternoon, Rob knocked on the door of Iantha's bedchamber, and at the sound of a curt, "Yes?" he opened it and stepped in.

And almost stepped back out.

Perhaps he had overdone it. To his dismay he found his formerly over-restrained bride pacing the floor, waving a handful of letters. At the moment she was definitely experiencing all the emotion he could possibly have desired.

He only hoped it was not directed at him.

Rob sauntered into the room as nonchalantly and unthreateningly as he could under the circumstances.

Iantha turned toward him and shook the letters. "Will you look at these!" She thrust the papers in his direction. "Just look!"

He reached for them, but she whirled, charged across the room and flung them onto her desk. "Men!"

Damn. Definitely a hazardous situation here. Rob raised his eyebrows, but forbore to venture a comment.

"They see themselves as masters of the world." Iantha

stamped back across the room and stopped before him, arms crossed over her chest. Rob held his peace. "And women... You would think that God made women just to serve them."

Concluding that biblical quotations were not in order, Rob raised his eyebrows politely.

His irate wife stormed back to her desk and seized a letter. "This lady writes that her husband gambles away their income and then rails at her because she cannot supply the household. And this one..." She threw the first letter on the floor and grabbed another. "This one paws her even in the presence of the servants and demands her compliance at all hours of the day and night—which is no doubt better than this one." She held up a third letter. "This one found the poetry she had been writing and laughed at her and threw it into the fire. Can you imagine? All her innermost fears and desires..."

Suddenly her shoulders lost their militant bearing, and she cast a sheepish look at Rob. "Oh, dear. I am ranting, am I not? Please forgive me."

Seeing the threat momentarily abated, Rob approached her cautiously. He had sufficient experience with members of the opposite sex to know how quickly anger could shift from one man to another.

He did not smile.

"I can understand why they infuriate you. However, I would like to respectfully ask that you recognize that I have done none of those things." In spite of himself the smile emerged.

As he feared, Iantha looked annoyed. "No, my lord. I am aware that you have not. Nor did I direct any complaint against you."

"For which I am humbly grateful." The smile became a grin. "Having observed your displeasure, I would certainly not wish to be the target of it.'' He placed his hands on her arms.

She looked into his face. ''Of course not. I have no reason to be angry with you—and I do not even know these other gentlemen. Yet…'' She sighed. ''It is as I told you this morning—all my emotions are suddenly overwhelming me. I can't keep them back.''

Rob drew her to him. ''You have been denying them so long, it seems understandable for them to bolt once you loosen the reins.''

''I suppose so.'' She pressed her head against his chest. ''But it is very disturbing.''

''I'm sure it is.'' He lifted her chin and gently kissed her lips. His body stirred and, for a moment, he felt inclined to coax her into bed for another lesson in life's greatest adventure. But considering her fury at the husband who demanded compliance *at all hours,* he thought better of it. Best not to test his luck. He stepped back from her. ''Would you like to ride out? Perhaps take your paints? The weather has turned surprisingly warm.''

''I would love to.'' She smiled up at him, and he almost reverted to the coaxing plan. ''Give me a few minutes to change.''

Oh, well. The coaxing could wait until later.

Perhaps he would not have to coax.


Rob lounged against a rock, reading, while Iantha painted the view from the crest of a low, rocky hill. While the air could not quite be described as warm, he did not feel chilly at all. The pale winter sun shone on the knoll they had selected, warming the rocks and making him drowsy. He glanced at his wife from time to time, knowing that her small frame would lose heat much more rapidly than his did, but she did not seem cold yet.

At intervals he rose and scrutinized the surrounding country, alternating with Feller, who meantime had the deceptive appearance of napping in the sun near the horses. Seeing nothing, Rob would turn back to his book.

Just as he was making another survey, a shot sounded from across the narrow valley.

Iantha cried out, and Rob whipped around in time to see her easel go tumbling over the side of the hill. He dived in her direction and, catching her around the waist, pulled her down behind his boulder. He yanked a small pistol from his pocket. Moments later Feller materialized at his side, handing him the larger horse pistol from his saddle. Feller had his own, and Iantha quickly pulled her hidden weapon from under her skirts.

An interval of tense silence ensued.

The trio held their breath. Every muscle in Rob tightened.

When, after several minutes, no further attack manifested, Rob cautiously used his pistol to hold his hat above the rock.

Nothing happened.

He nodded at Feller, and the groom slipped away from the boulder and over the crest to reconnoiter their back. Staying low to the ground, Rob leaned around the stone and studied the opposite hillside. He could discern not the slightest movement among the rocks and small vegetation. Had the rifleman slipped away while they sheltered behind the boulder, or did he still lie concealed, hoping for another opportunity to end a life?

Rob felt Iantha leaning across him, her pistol in her hand, trying to see past him and their barricade. He pulled back, bringing her with him, his voice sharp. "Stay down! Do not let him see you."

Both of them leaned against the stone. She frowned at him. "How can I shoot someone I cannot see?"

"Exactly. If you cannot shoot him, it is likely that he cannot shoot you." He frowned back at her. He was relieved to see that his very determined pistol-pointing lady showed no sign of fear, only a grim resolve. "I don't want him to see you. It was you at whom he fired."

For a moment she looked at Rob stubbornly. "I am sick of being afraid. I want to fight back!" Then she sighed and nodded. "Very well. But I have little doubt that he—whoever he may be—would not cavil at killing you also. Nor Feller." Her voice trembled. "I have brought danger to you both."

Rob cupped her face and ran his thumb across her mouth. "Don't fret, wraith. This is by no means the first time that Feller and I have encountered danger together."

As if he had heard his name, the stocky groom reappeared at their side. "Can't find no one back there. Leastways, no one shot at me. I'd say the bas—uh, pardon, my lady—whoever it be is hid out on the other side of the valley. I never heard but the one shot."

"Nor did I." Rob relaxed somewhat as he thought the matter over. "So very likely, there is only one of them. I wish I could be certain of that."

"If he is still there at all." Iantha craned her neck a little, but kept her head behind their shelter. "Do you think he may have gone?"

"He did not shoot at my hat, but he is probably well acquainted with that old trick." The sun had begun to sink, and Rob was growing aware of the chill in the air. They needed to get home before the cold returned. He turned to his henchman. "What do you say?"

Feller rubbed his chin. "I say I ride out a little way— see what I can scare up."

"No!" Iantha sat up, and Rob pulled her back down. She glared at him. "I will have no one shot in my place. Can we wait until dark?"

Rob shook his head. "It is getting much colder, and it will take us longer in the dark. I say we ride behind the crest as far as we can, then make a run for it."

"Aye, that's no doubt the best." Feller inched back toward the horses and led them a short distance down the far side of the knoll.

Rob signaled Iantha with his pistol, and keeping low, she slid down the hill like a veteran. Aye, she was quite a lady. A glow of pride swelled in Rob. He took the chance of retrieving her paints, before going over the crest of the hill. No sign of further hostilities occurred, so he found the easel and stowed it and the painting in the case.

They walked the horses in the comparative safety of the lee of the hill until the terrain became too broken. Crouching low behind their mounts, they led them over the rise. Rob held Iantha back until he was reasonably confident that no shot would follow.

Once mounted, they threw caution to the freezing wind and galloped for their lives.

They charged into the warm dark of the stable, scattering the startled stable hands. Almost before Iantha realized it, Rob and Feller were off their horses, shouting orders and running to help close the doors. She slid off the sidesaddle, breathing hard.

Rob hurried back to her. "Are you all right?"

"Of course." She nodded. "Just a bit out of breath—probably from the excitement."

"Excitement?" Rob grinned. "I am glad to hear that

you view it in that light.'' He put his arm around her waist and ushered her up the stairs into the old castle.

''Well, I yearned for adventure.'' She smiled up at him, and he suddenly pulled her into his arms and kissed her hard.

After several breathless moments he broke the kiss and gazed down at her. ''This was a great deal more adventure than I had planned for you. I do not want you to be in real danger.''

''Surely there is always an element of peril in any adventure.'' Iantha lifted her face for another kiss, and Rob obliged her.

When they stopped for breath again, he shook his head. ''A little excitement is one thing, being shot at is another.''

''You know…'' She looked thoughtfully into his eyes. ''It is very strange, but rather than being afraid, I found the episode to be oddly exhilarating. Especially the last gallop.''

''Danger does that.'' Her husband searched her face. ''And it also does other things. I think we should go upstairs.''

She agreed and let him guide her through the entryway without even taking time to doff their wraps. An unaccustomed urgency surged through her, and she could feel an answering tension in Rob. He took her directly into her bedchamber.

Iantha did not ask why.

He clasped her to him for a quick kiss and then began to unfasten her coat. Shoving it off her shoulders and onto the floor, he turned her and unbuttoned her dress. When it had joined her coat on the carpet, he pulled her to him, her back against his chest, and covered her breasts with both hands. She leaned against him and sighed.

The cool roughness of his wool coat caressed her back as his warm hands stroked her breasts and stomach. A demanding pressure began to grow in her lower body, and she could feel the bulge swelling between his legs. Rob stopped what he was doing long enough to shed his coat, then sat on the edge of the bed and drew her to him. While his hands stroked her bottom, his mouth closed over a nipple, and Iantha moaned.

"Drat!" He pulled her around onto the bed and tugged at her boots. When they fell to the floor, he sat and wrestled with his own. After several impatient minutes, he at last rolled onto the bed and drew her on top of him. His mouth tasted and teased her nipples. Iantha's head began to swim as her body seemed to float upward on a cloud of sensation.

Suddenly she was pulled back to earth by the pressure between her legs as he slid into her. She tensed, but then he was pulsing gently, his body stroking the center of her desire, his tongue claiming her nipples. The feelings began to escalate once more. Again her mind floated away from her body, aware only of a longing she could not define. Rob began to thrust more strongly, and as the world darkened, Iantha let it go.

When the explosion occurred between her legs, her senses denied everything but the rigidity of her body, the sensations racing from head to feet, and her voice crying out.

Rob's voice in answer.

And then she collapsed onto him. They both lay gasping for breath. Rob rolled her to one side and grinned at her.

"And that, my lady, is the other result of being in danger."

\* \* \*

*A most entertaining afternoon. The fools had thought that he really intended to kill them.*

*And he did.*

*But not yet.*

*No, not yet. He could take no chances, now that the killing might be traced to him, or even bring him under scrutiny. That would render him ineffective in his main goal. But what fun to see them scurrying about, waiting motionless in the cold while he slipped away to a warm house. A low laugh escaped him. How long had they stayed there shivering with fear and the chill?*

*And before he killed her, he would have his pleasure with the high-headed slut. It had been too long since he had stalked a haughty lady and brought her down. Had heard her beg for mercy. Had made her call him "master."*

*Before he killed her.*

## Chapter Fourteen

Having Gailsgill announce the next afternoon that Lord Sebergham awaited her in the drawing room startled Iantha. Their taciturn neighbor had said he might call on them, but she did not expect him to do so. He did not seem the type for polite calls. He must be very bored indeed. Rising to his feet, he bowed as she came through the door.

"Lady Duncan, I hope I find you well." His sharp blue eyes reflected none of the concern he expressed.

Iantha found she could muster no more for him, but smiled anyway, as best she could. "Quite well, I thank you. What brings you out today?"

"Ennui, as always in the winter. And of course, the desire for your agreeable company." Again the ghost of a smile on his lips gave little evidence of the veracity of the comment. Pure gallantry. Before she could respond, Rob entered the room.

"Good afternoon, Sebergham. Gailsgill told me you were here." He crossed to the other man and shook his hand, then turned to Iantha. "Have you rung for tea? Perhaps his lordship would prefer wine?"

Sebergham nodded. "Thank you. I would enjoy some wine."

He smelled to Iantha as though he had already had plenty. No wonder in that. Many gentlemen spent the day as well as the night drinking, although Sebergham did not seem drunk. But she detected something strange in the scent. It was not exactly like wine, but perhaps the smell of tobacco mixed with it changed the odor. An uncomfortable feeling crept up her spine.

Listening as the men exchanged small talk, she took a chair as far away from their visitor as she politely could while Rob poured sherry from the decanter.

"I have had enough of the Cumberland winter. I find snow and cold very tiresome." Lord Sebergham took a long swallow of the wine. "I fear my blood became thin while I was in the Carribean. I am thinking of going to London early this year—not waiting for the season."

Iantha silently wished him a good journey. She could not like the man. His odor gave her an odd feeling of distress.

But Rob answered seriously. "I enjoy the winter myself. I missed it while I was in India. I believe Prince Vijaya finds it very uncomfortable, however."

"Ah, yes. Your perturbed Indian friend." One dark eyebrow rose slightly, and a suggestion of a smirk appeared on their guest's mouth. "I have not seen him except when I encountered you on the road. I trust he is well?"

"Oh, aye. He just doesn't get out much because of the cold."

At that moment Gailsgill appeared at the door to announce another visitor. "Mr. Broughton, my lady. Shall I bring tea?"

"Not for me." Sam sauntered into the drawing room

and stopped before Iantha's chair. "How are you, fair cousin?" He placed a polite kiss on her hand and turned back to the men. "Rob. Sebergham. Servant, gentlemen."

Iantha smiled. "Welcome, Sam." She found it hard not to like Rob's cousin, in spite of his constant harassment of her husband. She glanced at her butler. "I'll have some tea, please, Gailsgill."

Sam seated himself near Rob and Sebergham and joined the conversation. Iantha sipped her tea and listened quietly. Did men really find hunting and racing to be so interesting? Perhaps they discussed other things when women were not present. She had to admit, however, that those subjects were more entertaining than the gossip and fashions women liked. Her mind was wandering to her writing when Sebergham stood and took his leave.

Rob walked him to the door, and Sam, after helping himself to another glass of wine, moved to a chair closer to her own. He gave her a crooked grin. "Is my esteemed cousin making a good husband?"

Before she could decide how to answer, her esteemed husband returned. "Of course I am. What did you expect?"

Sam's mouth quirked. "Why not? You excel at everything else." He indicated their departed guest with a twist of his head. "What did Sebergham want?"

Rob shrugged. "That's more than I can say. Said he was bored."

"Can't believe he ever does anything without more design than that." Sam propped his feet on the stool and slouched in his chair. "Don't like the man above half myself."

"Any particular reason?" Rob pulled a footstool over for himself. Iantha longed to join them in their comfort, but remained primly erect. Ladies simply did not slouch with company in the drawing room.

"No, just always felt there was something havey-cavey about him. He is about our age, but I didn't know him well as a boy." Sam twirled his wineglass thoughtfully. "He grew up to be so wild that his father packed him off to South America about the time you went to India, but he has been back for several years. Came back when his father died. I see him in town from time to time." He grimaced. "He's the last of the Frasers, so naturally the barony came to the lucky rascal in spite of his misspent youth. It's quite a fine estate." He finished the sherry and set down his glass. "Though not as fine as the Eyrie."

"Have you come about the gunpowder mill?" Rob drained his glass and set it down.

"Yes, I'm here as your agent today. That's becoming an interesting investment. If your beautiful lady will excuse us...?" Both men stood.

"Certainly." Iantha set down her teacup. "I have work to do myself."

Rob bent to kiss her cheek. "Then I will see you later."

Iantha covered the damp spot on her face with one hand and watched his broad shoulders disappear through the door.

And something stirred in her.

She was so engrossed in her writing when Rob came into her bedchamber that she did not hear him until he came to a stop right behind her. Iantha jumped when he rested his hands on her shoulders and bent to drop a kiss into her hair. "Aah! I didn't hear you come in."

"Forgive me. I didn't mean to frighten you." He

peered over her shoulder. "Are you answering letters for *La Belle Assemblée?*"

Suddenly Iantha remembered what she had spread out on her desk. "Oh, no!" She hastily gathered the papers into a pile. "This is—"

A large hand came down on the heap, stopping her frantic activity. "Another guilty secret, my lady?"

Iantha searched his face. Yes, she saw a twinkle in the depths of his dark eyes. "Hardly, my lord."

Still leaning on the papers, he stroked her hair back from her face with the other hand, only his eyes belying his stern expression. "Then why this scramble to hide it?"

Iantha leaned back in her chair and crossed her arms over her breasts, favoring him with a reproving look. "You know it is nothing scandalous, my lord."

"True." He turned and sat on the edge of the desk. "So why won't you let me see it?"

"It—it is another of those things that men laugh at."

He shook his head admonishingly. "Did I laugh at your writing as Lady Wisdom?"

She thought about that for a heartbeat. "Only once."

He held up one finger. "Only in relief. I am interested in your talents, Iantha. Won't you tell me what you are writing?"

A heavy sigh emerged from her. She knew he would not look without permission, even though he easily could. But… "Oh, very well. You are bound to find out sooner or later." She indicated the papers with a gesture. "I am writing a novel, my lord."

"A novel?" His face lit with interest. "What kind of novel? Is it of an improving nature?"

Iantha chuckled and shook her head. "No, not at all. I detest *improving* books."

Rob laughed aloud. "As do I. So what then?"

"An adventure story. But I must confess that until I encountered you, I had not enough adventurous material. It is coming along very well now. I am including our adventure of yesterday."

Her husband grinned. "All of it?"

"Well, no." Hot blood flooded her face. "I cannot include the...the aftereffects. That would hardly be seemly."

Rob put his hands under her arms and lifted her to her feet. "But very adventurous."

He pulled her between his legs where he sat on the desk and wrapped his arms around her. For the next several moments further conversation became impossible.

When it became necessary for them to breathe, he held her close as he spoke. "I have been talking to Sam about yesterday's adventure. He is also very concerned about it."

"I, too." Iantha leaned back to look at Rob's face, and he released her and led her to the hearth chairs. "What is Sam's opinion?"

"He is as puzzled as I am. We discussed the possibility of a poacher, but I see no reason that a poacher would have for shooting *you*. I'm not severe with them, in any event. They no doubt need the occasional hare for the pot." He scowled. "I'm damned if I can get the least hint as to whom to pursue."

Iantha gazed out the window for a long moment. "I...I think I am remembering something else about that night."

"Indeed?" Rob leaned forward in his chair. "What?"

"A smell."

His brows drew together. "The scent associated with making love?"

"No, although I do find that a little disturbing. It *was* present...."

"I'm sorry." He reached out and took her hand. "I'm afraid there is nothing I can do about that."

"No. But perhaps I will grow accustomed to it. It is not unpleasant of itself." Iantha narrowed her eyes, concentrating, willing the other odor to return to her. "It came to me when Lord Sebergham was here. He had a scent rather like that which I remember. Some kind of wine or spirits and...tobacco, I think."

Rob nodded. "Absinthe. I smelled it on him, too, and I believe he smokes cigars."

"Absinthe? That's a strong liqueur, isn't it?"

"Aye, extremely strong, and flavored with wormwood, which some say brings on madness, though I can't say I've ever known anyone who went mad from drinking it. Still, I've never been willing to try it, not even in my worst time. Sebergham must be very bored indeed, to indulge in so risky a pastime."

Rob stroked her chin thoughtfully. "I wonder if I might discover where he was yesterday afternoon? I will make a point to ask around."

"Surely you don't think he shot at us? He came here today showing no signs of guilt at all." Iantha glanced at him.

"I am not sure that he would show it if he *were* guilty. He is too self contained."

"He seems very world weary. And so cold." Iantha shivered. "I cannot like him."

"He offers little to enjoy—unlike my scapegrace cousin, with whom I spent the balance of the afternoon." Rob chuckled and shook his head. "Sam always makes me laugh, even when the subject is serious."

Iantha smiled. She had been thinking the same thing.

"Yes, I like Sam very much. But I have wondered... Sometimes he speaks as though he were very envious of you."

"Sam?" Rob frowned. "He has little reason to be envious."

"I would not say that. You are much larger and much more handsome. He seems to covet your title and estate, also."

Rob looked startled, then smiled. "You think I am more handsome than Sam?"

Iantha felt herself flush. "Well...yes. I would say so."

He leaned across the space between them and kissed her gently on the lips. "Thank you, my lady. I'm very happy that you find me so. But however slender Sam may look, he is able to give a good account of himself in a set-to, as I can attest. As for the envy you perceive, he is just teasing me. He always has."

"Sometimes people say in jest what they truly think but would otherwise never say."

"That's true, but not Sam. He inherited a very pleasant estate from his father, and a nice house in London. And he has grown quite wealthy as my agent. We share our investments."

"A pleasant estate and a nice house hardly equal the history and grandeur of the Eyrie and the barony. And I would wager that you lent him money to invest."

Her husband gave her a puzzled glance. "Well, aye. But that was years ago. He has long since repaid me. Sam and I are almost like brothers. I missed him damnably while I was in India. Perhaps that is why Vijaya and I became such close friends—although Vijaya has no lack of siblings. Are you putting him into your novel?"

"Oh, certainly. He is such a colorful individual."

"He is that. And after whom is your hero modeled?"

Iantha ducked her head and looked at her hands. "That would be you, my lord."

Rob reached for her.

"It better be."

After several dreary days of being cooped up inside the castle, Iantha felt ready to scream. Rob had flatly forbidden riding out until they discovered the identity of the gunman, and she could feel her newly restored temper threatening to slip its leash at his authoritative stance. That would not be fair at all. He was only trying to protect her. She would be very foolish to defy him.

So, with paints in hand, she was heading to the battlements to find a new prospect to paint. Not wanting to go all the way back downstairs to the entry hall to enter the old castle, only to climb back up to the ramparts, she had taken the route through the floor on which her bedchamber was situated.

Or she thought she had.

After several minutes of wandering Iantha had not found the passage she sought. In fact, she seemed to have strayed into a completely unfamiliar wing. At last she saw a door she thought might be the object of her search.

She opened it and peeked in. "Oh, dear! Please excuse me. I have lost myself again."

A startled Vijaya glanced up from the scroll he was perusing. "Lady Duncan! Please come in."

"Oh, no. I didn't mean to intrude. I was looking for the way into the old section."

Vijaya got to his feet. "It is no intrusion. But I regret that I am not familiar with that particular door."

Iantha peered around the sitting room in astonishment. This seemed no chamber in an English castle, but rather an exotic scene transported from the Orient. She saw carved chairs and benches inlaid with ivory, and tall, massive chests with more carving and painted scenes. Bright silk panels decorated the walls, and a low table beneath one of these held several figurines.

"How remarkable! Did you bring all this from India?"

He gestured for her to enter. "Yes, of course. I thought it would help me not to long for my homeland."

Iantha stepped into the room. "This is so beautiful. Not at all like staid English furnishings." She turned back to her host. "Have you been very homesick?"

Vijaya sighed. "Only occasionally." He went to stand before the fire. "I find the constant cold very trying."

"May I look around?"

"Certainly." He swept a hand about the room. "I occupy this suite at the generosity of your husband, after all."

"Oh, you mustn't think of it in that manner. We are honored by your presence. But I do want to look at these lovely things." She stopped before a carved stone panel, squinting a bit at the figures on it. "What is—" She broke off and blood rushed to her face. The figures were handsome men and beautiful women, engaged in...in making love!

All with big, happy smiles on their faces.

Blood rushed into Iantha's face, and Vijaya discreetly set a screen in front of the panel. "That once adorned a temple now crumbling with age."

"You mean...does... That was on a *religious* building?" She could not keep the incredulity out of her voice.

He smiled slightly. "Yes, in India we do not view lovemaking as an embarrassment. We see it as an extension of the relations between the gods and goddesses. For us erotic art serves a noble purpose."

"I see." Iantha mulled over that extremely alien concept. "I have heard that you have goddesses—which seems very strange to me. We have only God—and He is represented as male."

"Most authorities are male."

She frowned. That was certainly the truth. Authorities that disapproved of everything women… Well, most of them did, she amended. She must remember to exclude her husband from that indictment.

But Vijaya was continuing. "We have many goddesses, including Shakti, the earth itself."

"Isn't Shakti the name of Rob's first wife?" A little pang of jealousy stabbed Iantha.

"Yes, she was named to honor the goddess." He looked at her kindly and, she thought, a bit sadly.

"Did you know her?"

"Of course. She was my sister—my favorite sister."

"Oh! I didn't know that. Then I am sorry for your loss."

He nodded. "Thank you."

And she was named for a goddess. The pang intruded again. Iantha turned away, surveying a row of figurines on the low marble table. "Do those represent deities?"

"Yes." He pointed to a crude figure with huge, staring black eyes. "This represents Lord Jagannath, Lord of the Universe. His eyes are watching over all of us."

"How interesting. That sounds very similar to what we are taught of God." She studied the figure pensively.

"Many similarities exist. And one must remember that India is a very large country and a very old civilization. It has seen many migrations of different populations. Every age and area had its deities. That is why the Hindu pantheon is so large. In my home area, which still has many primitive tribes, we have maintained Lord Jagannath—an ancient tribal god—as supreme overlord. He has a consort, of course.''

''Does he indeed?'' Iantha found herself fascinated by the idea of female deities—voluptuous female deities that smiled as they made love. ''And is she also respected, as he is? Or does—''

Vijaya nodded emphatically. ''She is revered, as are all our goddesses. They represent wisdom and nurturing, love and beauty—and sometimes destruction.''

''Oh, my. They have the power to destroy?''

He nodded solemnly.

That would require some additional consideration. After a moment's more thought, Iantha realized that she had been quite a while in a gentleman's private quarters. She really must leave. ''Thank you, your highness, for showing me your treasures. I would like to discuss your religion further with you sometime.''

''I would be honored.'' He bowed and closed the door behind her.

Iantha returned the way she had come, with much to consider.

Powerful female deities.

Who smiled as they made love.

That evening Iantha wore another new gown. Rose silk and silver ribbons fell in diaphanous folds from her shoulders to her feet. As she floated into the sitting room, Rob looked up from his reading and grinned. He set aside his scroll and held out his arms. She let him pull her between his knees and press a kiss between her breasts. His big hands slid down her sides, molding the gown to her body.

They might have done a great deal more, but Iantha wanted to discuss with her husband the new ideas she had garnered from her discussion with Vijaya earlier in the day. She kissed Rob's lips and pulled back.

Still grinning, he released her, and she sat beside him. "In the writings you study with Vijaya, do you read about the goddesses of India?"

Rob held up the parchment he had been studying. "Aye. Most of these are religious texts. We study the development of the theological concepts as well as the old languages."

"Then you know their female deities are very powerful." Iantha pulled her brows together in thought.

"They are that. In fact, Durga is the goddess of power." He set the parchment on the end table. "They are very interesting because the same goddess who represents motherly love may also serve as the destroyer. Of course, there are a great many versions of that." He gave her a teasing smile. "Which most men already know, of course."

"I don't see how you can say that." Iantha grimaced. "Here females have no power at all."

"I would not agree." Rob set her across his lap. "Even in England a woman can make a man as happy as a god or utterly destroy him."

"Only if he loves her very much."

"True. It is therefore prudent to love wisely." He nibbled at her ear.

Iantha pondered that for a moment. "Yes, I can see that from the letters I receive. Men can also destroy a woman—in so many ways."

"Also true. Human females in India fare no better—and often not as well. What has brought on this subject of conversation?" He untied the silver ribbon and combed his fingers through her shining hair, spreading it over the arm supporting her head.

"I stumbled into Vijaya's suite today. He invited me to look at the lovely things he has brought from India. I would like to paint them someday." She snuggled her head against his shoulder.

"Did you like his bed?"

"His bed!" Iantha struggled to sit up. "I did *not* see his bed!"

Laughing, Rob held her fast. "A pity. It is quite magnificent. I thought if you liked it, I would have a similar one that I have in storage brought up."

"You wretch! You are teasing me." She settled back against his shoulder.

"But I do have such a bed." He blew gently against the skin behind her ear.

Iantha shivered, and that certain warmth began to bloom throughout her body. "You know that is not what I meant. But I would like to see Vijaya's bed, if it is as magnificent as all that."

"Perhaps we can borrow it some evening." He untied the ribbon holding the gown together between her breasts.

Iantha drew in a hasty little breath, trying and failing to look severe. "Hardly. He would know what we were doing."

"I'm sure he would be happy for us." Rob dropped a kiss in the valley he had just revealed.

"I suppose so." She moved to look up into his face. "Do you know that they have carvings of…well, people making love…on their *temples?*"

Rob made an assenting sound as he kissed her throat.

"And they are all *smiling!*"

"As they should be." Her husband grinned down at her.

"And these powerful goddesses make love, also, with the gods."

"I have been trying to explain to you the power that females have over we poor males—mortal or immortal." His mouth started down in the direction of her nipples.

"But when we make love, I completely surrender to you."

At the seriousness of her tone, Rob raised his gaze to her face. "Shall I instead surrender to you this evening?"

Several heartbeats of silence ensued while Iantha considered the offer. At last she said, "I would not know what to do."

He leaned back against the sofa, his eyes twinkling. "Just tell me what you want me to do. I am yours to command."

There was another period of quiet.

Iantha sat up in his lap. "I have never seen you without your clothing. I don't know what... Well, I saw the carvings this afternoon, but..." Deciding to wield the power he offered her, she stopped stammering and took a deep breath. "I want to see you unclothed."

He cocked his head to one side, looking pleased. "I will be happy to oblige you. But I suspect this is going to call for a glass of brandy."

Iantha considered that. She was very close to losing her nerve. But when she drank brandy... "Yes, I think that would be a good idea. And I think we should go into my bedchamber."

He murmured agreement, and she stood. Rob poured the brandy and gave the glass to her. He gestured toward her chamber.

"After you, my powerful goddess."

Iantha nodded and swept regally through the door.

# Chapter Fifteen

Believing that her husband followed close behind her, Iantha was startled when she turned to find he was not there. "Rob?"

Setting her brandy on the bed table, she walked back toward the sitting room, only to collide with him in the doorway. He steadied her with one hand. "Speaking of Vijaya reminded me—he gave me this as a wedding gift. It may ameliorate certain difficulties."

"What is it?" Iantha examined the small marble bowl holding a lump of some brown material.

Rob set the bowl on the bed table. "Incense. One burns it to make the room fragrant." He dipped his head and sniffed. "Unless I am mistaken, this is patchouli." He grinned. "Very suitable for a wedding gift."

As Rob lit the incense from the fire with a twisted paper spill, Iantha eyed it curiously. "Why do you say that?"

He turned to her and wrapped his arms around her, nuzzling her hair. "Because it is said to kindle desire. But I am usurping your role." He released her and guided her to the edge of the bed. "You are to direct matters tonight."

He stepped back, and Iantha sat. Suddenly she flushed. "I...I am not sure—"

"Nay. That will not do." Rob folded his arms across his chest. "I await your commands."

Power.

Female power.

Iantha took a sip of brandy and lifted her chin. "Very well. Please remove your waistcoat and shirt."

Rob did as she asked, making a great show of slowly undoing the buttons before casting the waistcoat aside. At last he pulled the shirt over his head, and his own smoky scent mingled with the patchouli, waking a heat in Iantha's lower body.

Suddenly she realized her eyes were closed.

Resolutely she opened them and beheld her husband's broad chest with his bulky arms folded across it. Iantha drew in a long breath.

Beautiful.

Frightening.

Powerful.

So much strength. She would never manage to defend herself if he chose to use it against her—him or any other man. That she already knew.

To her sorrow.

But this was Rob. He had never used his strength that way. She could not even envision his doing so.

She took a larger swallow of the liquor and looked again. Dark hair covered the upper part of his chest and ran in a narrower strip across ridges of muscle into his britches. The heat in her made itself known again. She sighed.

He stood there silently, waiting.

Iantha reached for the brandy.

This time she took two swallows and gave him her

most imperious gaze. "Will you now please remove your britches?"

Rob grinned. "I can't do that with my boots on."

"Oh, bother!" How dare he be impertinent when she was giving him orders. In spite of herself, she smiled. "Then remove them."

He retreated to a chair and pulled off both boots and stockings.

"I said nothing about your stockings." She looked down her nose at him, doing her best to appear haughty.

"My humble apologies, my lady." His grin remained undaunted. "But any man looks perfectly ridiculous in stockings and no britches." He came back to stand in front of her. "Now—where were we?"

"I had ordered you to remove your nether garments." Even through the buckskin he wore, she could see a sizable bulge. Courage almost failed her, and she resorted to the brandy again.

Rob unbuttoned the flap and in one motion pushed britches and underwear to the floor. He then stood tall, watching her closely. Iantha covered her mouth with both hands at the sight of the erection springing from the thick hair that spread across his groin. Good heavens! He was so…so large. She drew in a deep breath, the incense filling her senses.

"Are you all right?" He looked concerned. "Shall I dress?"

"No… No. But please come and sit beside me."

"You are sure?" He did as she bade, and put an arm around her shoulders. "You look a bit shocked."

"I didn't quite know what to expect. It was dark before and…they all came out of the darkness…. In any case, I didn't look." She rested her head on his shoulder. "I don't feel very powerful presently."

He gave her a moment before saying, "Then we must remedy that. Tell me what you want now."

"I want you to kiss me. Just kiss me." He bent to her lips, and Iantha lifted her face. After an instant she realized that she could not feel his tongue. She opened her mouth, but he did not respond. Very well then. She ran her own tongue over his lips. And he ran his over hers, copying her.

Iantha opened wider, and he followed her lead, so she thrust her tongue into his mouth. At that point she suspected his restraint was failing, because he pulled her closer and met her thrust for thrust. For several minutes that seemed to suffice. And then Iantha begun to realize that there was a great deal more to kissing than she had suspected.

"You may touch my breast." The warmth of his hand closed around it, and she gasped. More. She needed more. Much more. "Please kiss it, also."

Without instruction Rob toppled her backward onto the bed, and his lips closed around her nipple. She arched against him, sighing. "The other one."

The heat of his mouth moved to the other nipple, and his hand came up to tease the one he had just left. Iantha moaned. He pressed his hard body against her hip. Her head began to spin as feeling pooled between her legs. She arched again, and his knee came across hers.

"I—I need more," she gasped.

"Tell me," he replied, implacable. He continued to devour her breasts.

"Touch me…there."

One hand cupped her between her legs, slowly moving. His mouth stayed at her breast. Iantha was moaning aloud now. She could hardly speak. "I…I want you… inside."

He slid one finger into her passage, taking her by surprise.

"Ah!" She pressed against his hand. It was not enough. "Not like that! I want *you* inside me."

Rob immediately rolled to his back and lifted her, setting her astride him. When she would have leaned forward over him, he held her upright. "Use your power, goddess."

At first Iantha could not fathom what he meant. Then his hands came up to her nipples, and he began to pulse under her. "Oh, dear heaven!" She tightened her legs against his torso. He groaned. She tightened again, and he bucked under her. She lifted herself slightly and slid back down. His breathing sounded hoarse, and he made a sound deep in his throat.

Suddenly she felt strong and abandoned.

Powerful.

She locked her fingers behind her neck and thrust her breasts forward. She lifted again. And again. He met her with stronger and stronger thrusts.

And her body began to convulse, writhing against him, out of her control. She could barely hear his voice over her own cries. Could not think. Could only feel.

She fell limply across him as his body stilled. His arms tightened around her. His breath sounded as if he had been running, and she felt as if she had been.

At length he whispered in her ear.

"How can you doubt your power, my silver goddess?"


"It appears that we are in for another storm." Rob ladled eggs onto his plate while Iantha poured coffee for both of them. As he came back to the table, he paused to drop a kiss on the top of her head.

Iantha smiled up at him. She really was very fortunate

in her husband. Last night's lovemaking had left her feeling more at ease with him than she had since they had met.

Comfortable.

She buttered a scone. "Yes, I heard the wind rising this morning while I dressed."

"This is certainly becoming a severe winter." Rob set his plate on the table and changed the subject. "Vijaya and I are planning to work in the library today. He said he would be honored if you wish to paint some of his furnishings and art." He winked at her. "I promise to keep him occupied if you want to look at his bed."

Iantha flushed. "I would not wish to intrude on his privacy," she said primly.

Her husband laughed aloud. "Then you have far less curiosity than any other woman I have ever known. He will not mind if you have a peek. He insists that he would like to see the results of your artistry."

Iantha grimaced, but then smiled. "I confess, I would like to see it."

"Then look. By the way, I believe I will send Feller to invite Sebergham to dinner." Rob glanced at her questioningly. "If you think you can tolerate his company. I want to be sure he has truly left Cumberland."

"Oh. I see." Iantha wrinkled her nose. "That is a good idea, although I had rather not. Perhaps he has already gone and will not be available."

Rob nodded. "Let us heartily hope so."

Breakfast eaten, Rob retired to the library, and Iantha went in search of her paints. She rummaged in a storage chest for her brighter colors. Her favorite pastels would not do for this project. Then she searched until she found the prince's suite, and knocked. Receiving no answer, she

opened the door and peeped in. As Rob had said, no one
was there.

Iantha set her paints down and gazed around the room.
Where should she start? It was all so exotic. She strolled
through the parlor, examining each beautiful ornament,
until she came to a silver screen. Peering behind it, she
found the door to Vijaya's bedchamber. One glance
through the opening settled the matter.

She stepped through the door.

The bed met and surpassed Rob's description. Tall and
wide, the headboard boasted both carving and silver
plate. Rich curtains in deep colors hung from the ceiling.
Iantha approached the bed and ran her hand over the silk
coverlet. Umm! So soft and smooth. Casting decorum to
the winds, she climbed up and sat in the middle of it.
She crossed her arms and legs and raised her chin. Proud.
Dignified. Like an Indian goddess.

Powerful.

And she knew what she would paint.

Several hours later she was startled by a tap on the
door of the suite. Glancing up from her work, she saw
Thursby holding out a slip of paper.

"I found this in the hall by your bedroom door, my
lady. I thought perhaps you would want it immediately."

"Oh. Thank you, Thursby, I appreciate your looking
for me." She smiled as she took the paper.

"Of course, my lady." The footman bowed and departed.

Iantha smiled again. Thursby seemed much more dignified in his livery than he had doing the sword dance.
He might make a good butler one day. She unfolded
the note.

My Dear Wife—
Meet me at the postern door of the old castle. There
is something I want to show you.
Duncan

Now what would Rob want to show her? A glance out
the window revealed snow blown by a high wind. The
storm must have wrought something interesting or beautiful.

She put away her colors. The painting was done, in
any event, and she felt very pleased with it. She carried
her paint case and the picture back to her room, careful
not to smudge the damp paints. Finding Camille nowhere
in sight, Iantha took her fur coat from the armoire and,
shrugging into it, went back the way she had come. Rob
had shown her the door into the old castle again, and this
time she had no trouble finding it.

Going through into the ancient building, she was
shocked by the cold the storm had brought with it. She
thrust her hands into her pockets and carefully descended
the worn stone steps. When she reached the lowest level,
she turned through the abandoned kitchen. Her footsteps
echoed off the massive stones of the arched roof. Skirting
the old well, she found, beside a giant fireplace set into
the wall, the crude wooden portal she sought.

"Rob?" Her voice skittered around the room, rico-
cheting in the narrow arrow ports, which let in the only
light. Where in the world was he? Seeing that the bar
was off, she cautiously opened the door and leaned her
head out. "Rob?"

Suddenly a gust of wind caught the panel and dragged
Iantha with it out into the snow. Oh, no! She wrestled
with the heavy door until a reverse in the gale tore it out
of her hands and slammed it shut.

"Rob? Are you here?" Only the wail of the storm answered her. Obviously he was not. He must have already come and, giving her up, gone back to the new section. The note may have lain on the floor for some time.

She tugged at the portal.

Nothing happened.

Annoyed, Iantha pulled harder. Still no result. What could be the matter with the dratted thing? It must have jammed. It felt as though someone had put the bar up.

A hard gust almost knocked her off her feet, and she clutched at the handle. She had to get back in before she froze. At the thought, she pulled her coat tighter around her and shivered. The cold bit right through it.

Well, she could not stay where she was. She would have to make her way around the castle to the front where the knocker was. She drew her hood firmly over her ears, and keeping as close to the wall as possible, edged her way along the narrow path that skirted it. The ground fell away sharply behind the building, and the stones underfoot were becoming coated with ice. She would have to be careful.

And as if thinking of the hazard brought it to life, her feet went out from under her, and she slid down the slope.

Rob was having difficulty keeping his mind on his studies. He could hardly believe that the woman he had known the night before was the same coolly polite, exceedingly distressed damsel he had brought out of the storm on that first fateful afternoon. How could he work when his hands still felt the tension in her tiny waist, when his body persisted in responding to the memory of her thighs against his flank, her passionate cries?

Sighing with satisfaction, he leaned back in his chair and stared into the fire. He could, at last, feel the icy knot of loneliness inside him slowly thawing. It occurred to him that he had not dreamed of Shakti in several days.

He could not say that about his sweet Laki. She visited his dreams frequently, and Rob wasn't sure that he even wanted to give that up. It was all he had left of her.

Across the desk Vijaya raised his head from the manuscript before him and cleared his throat. Rob glanced at him. The prince looked amused. No doubt he suspected the source of Rob's preoccupation.

His friend grinned and pointed to the parchment. "I find a very obscure passage here. Have you read of any references to—"

He broke off as a light tap on the door was followed by the entrance of Iantha's maid. Pulling himself from his reverie and Vijaya's question, Rob turned toward her. "Yes, Camille?"

She curtsied. "Excuse me for interrupting you, milord. Have you seen Lady Duncan recently?"

"Nay." Rob furrowed his brow, a faint disturbance growing in him. "The last I knew she was going to Prince Vijaya's quarters to paint. Have you looked there?"

"*Oui,* milord. She is not there." She held out a slip of paper. "I thought she was with you until I heard your voice in here a few minutes ago, so I went back for this. I found it on her dressing table an hour ago."

Rob took the note, serious alarm bursting through him when he saw the signature.

"I didn't write this!" He sprang to his feet. "Find Burnside and Feller and send them immediately to the old postern."

His heart sinking, Rob dashed out of the room, with Vijaya close on his heels.

How long had she been here? Iantha drew her coat closer around her and tried to hide from the wind behind the boulders that had her trapped. Somehow she had fallen between two huge, icy stones, both taller than she was. Her ankle had been jammed into the cleft between them near the bottom of the narrow space. She tugged at her foot for possibly the hundredth time since she had fallen. It remained stuck fast.

Oh, God! She was *so* cold.

She had tried shouting for help several times, but only the wind heard her. Where was Rob? Why had he sent her that note, then left the door unbarred, and not waited for her? Perhaps... Oh, no! When the possible explanation struck her, it took her breath away. Had he also fallen? If that were the case, it might be hours before anyone looked for them.

They might both die.

Fear flooded her, and another emotion she could not take time to examine. Iantha reached for control. Strange. She had not thought about needing control for some time. But she needed it now. By all means she must keep her head. She *had* to get out.

Rob might need her.

Perhaps if she could get her half boot off... But even if she could get her foot loose, she had no way to climb out of the slippery, narrow well formed by the boulders. She could not reach the top. She sagged back against the cold rock. Odd. She was beginning to feel warmer. And drowsy. And then she remembered. She had heard that those who froze to death experienced those things before they died. She jerked herself erect.

No! She had come too far to give up now.

And then faintly, on the wind, she heard something. Someone calling her name.

"Rob!" She pulled frantically at her foot. "Rob, I am here!" Oh, heaven. Please let him hear her. "Rob!" She heard his voice, nearer now. "Rob, be careful! I fell down here."

She heard a scrambling sound and looked up to see her husband peering down at her from the top of the boulder. "My foot is caught. I can't pull it out of the crack."

"Are you otherwise hurt?" Even over the wind she heard the concern in his voice.

"I d-don't think s-so." She could hardly get the words out been her chattering teeth. "But I am v-very c-cold."

"Thank God." He examined the crevice. "Don't worry. We will get you out." He turned and shouted back up the hill. "I have found her. Feller, fetch a rope." A faint response floated back on the gale.

Rob lay on his stomach and reached down. "Can you grasp my hands?"

Iantha stretched up as far as her arms would reach. Her numb fingers barely touched his. They would not close around them. He leaned farther. Her heart almost stopped. Heaven forbid that he should be injured on her account.

"Don't! You will fall, too!"

He nodded, looking back over his shoulder. "Feller should be back any moment."

As though summoned by the words, the groom appeared, sliding down the slope toward them and holding tightly to a rope fastened somewhere near the top. Behind him they could faintly discern Vijaya's bright clothes through the swirling snow. Relief coursed through Iantha, making her almost dizzy. Perhaps she and Rob would come out safe, after all. In vain she struggled to control her shivering.

The two men descended to Rob and knelt beside him, peering down into Iantha's prison.

"Steady the rope." Rob tied a loop around his waist and eased over the brink, down into the cleft. With feet and back braced on either side of the crack, he slid down to Iantha. "Are both feet stuck?"

"No, only the one. I was thinking of taking off my boot."

He paused for a heartbeat. "I don't like the idea. You have had too much exposure already." He removed the rope from his own body and looped it around hers. Looking up at Vijaya and Feller, he shouted, "Try an easy pull, but be careful—don't fall in."

The two men began to draw on the rope, and suddenly pain shot through Iantha's ankle. She cried out, Rob shouted and they promptly ceased their efforts. In spite of herself, hot tears of discouragement coursed down her cheeks, only to freeze in moments.

"Very well." Rob's voice remained calm. "See if you can take off the boot."

After some struggle, Iantha managed to bend over in the narrow space and fumble with cold fingers at the buttons of the half boot. When she made no progress, Rob, hanging from the rope by one arm, reached down with his knife. She did not even feel the cold steel as it cut the fastenings loose, but suddenly she could lift her foot.

"Can you grasp the rope?"

She flexed her stiff fingers. "I will try." With all her strength she forced her fingers to close. "I...I can't feel the rope."

"Then that won't do. Can you fasten your arms around my neck?"

Iantha nodded. "I believe I can do that." She clasped her arms around him, doing her best not to choke him, and clung to his wide back.

"Good. Hold tightly." He braced his feet on the stone, took a firm grip on the rope and began to climb.

For a moment Iantha thought they were saved, but then, with a teeth-rattling jar, they fell back.

"Damn! I can't get any purchase." Rob lifted his head and shouted, "Try pulling again."

"Nay, me lord. We can't get no foot grip, neither. Too much ice." To Iantha's ears the groom's voice sounded very far away. "We'll climb back up and try from there."

She could feel the swaying of the rope as, with some difficulty, the two men climbed back to the castle. Rob spoke encouragingly. "It won't be long now. Don't worry."

Iantha could only sniffle and nod. Then she heard a shout and felt herself going up. After several moments of agonizing anxiety, Rob got his feet on top of the boulder. Just as she tried to set her own feet on it, her arms began to slip. She cried out and commanded her limbs to obey her.

They refused.

She was certain that she would plunge backward again, but then Rob's powerful arm closed around her waist and his steady voice sounded in her ear. "I have you."

Later she could remember very little of their ascent. Suddenly they were out of the wind and a crowd of people were milling around them, myriad hands reaching for them. Not only Vijaya, shivering violently, and Feller were there, but Burnside and Thursby and Camille and…

She caught a glimpse of several other inhabitants of the castle before darkness claimed her.

Rob poured the can of hot water into the tub before the fire himself. He found himself unwilling to allow anyone else to come anywhere near his wife. Great heavens! He had almost lost her. He had insisted on stumbling up the stairs with her in his arms in spite of a wrenched shoulder and rope-burned hands, thrusting away the offers of assistance from the others.

He could still hear Iantha's startled scream when he had lowered her into the tepid water. Tears of pain ran down her cheeks as her fingers and toes regained feeling, but she kept her teeth firmly clamped together, allowing no further outcry. God grant that they were not frostbitten. Even after sensation returned, she continued to shiver. Gradually, one can at a time, Rob began to add hot water. He leaned around the screen to give the empty can to a weeping Camille and take another from her.

"Do your hands and feet still hurt?" When the maid left the room, Rob knelt by the tub and reached into the water for Iantha's hand. He turned it this way and that, examining it for damage.

She shook her head. "No. I can feel them now, but they're not painful. I am getting warmer, also." A shudder shook her small frame, belying her words. She caught his hand in hers and looked at the palm. "You are injured, too."

"Nothing to signify." Rob flexed his sore shoulder. It had been obliged to take their combined weight as they were pulled up the hill. He had needed the other arm to hold Iantha. "Burnside is probably lurking in my bedchamber with salve and bandages for this." He held up the scraped hand. "I'll let him deal with it when I have gotten you warm." He closed his fingers around her hand, his expression turning serious. "You frightened me into gray hair, goddess."

He dipped his head so that she could see his thick, dark locks. Iantha chuckled. "I don't see any damage yet. Do I understand that you did not write that note?"

He shook his head. "Could you not see that?"

Iantha pondered for a moment. "No. I cannot remember your ever addressing anything to me before. I have never seen your signature, only your notes on your studies, but they are... They are rather..."

"An undisciplined scrawl." Rob grinned. "No need to be diplomatic. I can't read them myself half the time." He thought for a moment. "You are correct. I don't recall any occasion when you would have seen my usual handwriting."

"I was a bit surprised that you signed it 'Duncan' rather than 'Rob,' but many lords always sign their title. It just didn't seem that you would use it with me."

He brushed the damp hair off her forehead. "Nay, I would not be that formal with you." Especially since the cold spot in his heart was finally beginning to thaw. "Ah, here is Camille with the warm bricks. She can hold the blanket while I lift you out. Don't put any weight on your ankle."

When Iantha was dry and clothed in a warm gown, and Camille had positioned several hot, wrapped bricks in the bed, Rob scooped his wife up and laid her tenderly between them.

Somehow that did not seem enough.

He dismissed the maid and began to undress. Moving all the bricks to her back, he lay down beside her and took her into his arms. Rob held her to his body, willing his own heat to flow into her. As she snuggled against him, the moment seemed deceptively peaceful.

Rob did not want to think about the traitor in his house.

He did not want to think about what had happened to Iantha.

Or what might have happened.

God! He had almost lost her.

# Chapter Sixteen

"If I knew that, do you think I would be sitting here drinking wine?" Rob snarled at his cousin. The day after Iantha's narrow escape the two of them were gathered in the drawing room with Vijaya and Iantha, her injured ankle propped daintily on a footstool and a cup of tea in her hand. Rob wished he felt as composed as she appeared.

Even the irreverent Sam looked serious, but he took the snarl in good grace. "But the note must have been written by someone in the house. Who else could have been here in the middle of that blizzard yesterday? I had the very devil of a time getting through today. If you hadn't sent Feller with that message, and the sun had not been out, I would never have tried it."

Rob rubbed a hand over his face. His shoulder ached. "I know, Sam. I appreciate your coming. Forgive my being surly. I have been so concerned for Iantha that I have not adequately investigated." In fact, he had not let her out of his sight for twenty-four hours. He was afraid to. "But it is high time I did so. I was hoping that you would have some ideas—and a clear head. I am so angry I cannot think of anything but murdering someone."

Sam's brows puckered in thought. "I suppose you talked to whomever gave her the note?"

"Thursby says he found it by my door." Iantha set her saucer aside and shifted her foot.

"And where were you?" Her cousin-in-law turned toward her.

"In Vijaya's rooms. I was painting some of his...uh, interesting furnishings."

She blushed, and in spite of his foul humor Rob wondered with some amusement what the subject of the painting, now discreetly tucked away in a portfolio, had been. His formerly frozen wife had indeed begun to bloom.

And now someone had tried to freeze her permanently.

His rage returned, and his fist came down on the arm of his chair with a loud thump. Everyone jumped and looked at him. "Damn them to hell! I will *not* let them take anyone else away from me!"

A respectful pause followed this outburst. Iantha made a small, concerned gesture, and his cousin and Vijaya sipped their drinks quietly, giving Rob time to recover. Finally he shrugged irritably and rubbed his shoulder.

Sam turned his gaze back to him. "Why was Thursby on that floor? Did he have some business there?"

"I don't know." Rob scowled. Damn. He was not being in the least effective. "But I shall bloody well find out." He sprang out of his chair and yanked the bell pull.

After a minute's wait, Thursby himself answered the bell. "Yes, my lord?"

Rob fixed him with a steely eye. "Thursby, when you found the note outside Lady Duncan's chamber, how did you happen to be on that floor?"

Thursby's face turned as red as his hair. He gazed at his shoes.

"Well?" Rob narrowed his eyes.

At length his henchman took a deep breath and looked him in the face. "I was hoping to see Camille."

"And did you see her?"

"Aye, me lord." He blushed again.

Rob pondered that for a moment. Apparently the maid had lowered her sights from master to man. Or was it men? If that were so, the woman might very easily create a problem with the staff. He really should discuss her with Iantha. Later. First things first.

"Before or after you found the note?" Sam interjected.

"Oh, after, sir." Thursby turned to look at him. "I didn't delay in my duty."

"Mmm." Sam's rejoinder was considerably less than believing.

"Truly, sir! I—"

Rob held up a restraining hand. "Never mind, Thursby. I trust you. You may go." The footman departed, and Rob sighed. "I can't imagine Thursby linked with skulduggery. I have found him to be a very good lad."

"Mmm," Sam said again.

Rob glared. "Very well, I will keep him in mind." He turned to Iantha. "I talked to Camille again earlier. She insists that she found the note on your dresser."

"I'm sure she did. I left it there when I went to meet you."

"Another burning question—" Sam paused to sip his sherry "—is who bolted the door? It might or might not have been the writer of the note."

"It was actually bolted?" Iantha turned a shocked face to Rob. "I thought it was only stuck."

Rob shook his head grimly. "The bar was in place

when Vijaya and I arrived. I did not want to tell you until you were more recovered.''

"Great heavens!" Iantha's hands flew to her cheeks. "That means someone locked me out." She looked around the group. "But surely not! Surely they did not see me go out.'' No one expressed agreement.

"They enticed you out," Rob reminded her grimly.

Iantha sank back in her chair. "Yes, I know that. Perhaps I do not want to believe it—not of anyone here."

"Nor do I." Rob rubbed at the pain in his forehead. "But it must be so. Since nothing untoward has happened in the house since Christmas, I thought—foolishly, it appears—that the killer left with the guests."

"Perhaps he did," Vijaya offered. "He may simply have a confederate."

"True. I should never have allowed myself to be lulled into a sense of security." Rob stared into the middle distance for a space of time, thinking. "Sam, how did you arrange for the staff to be employed?"

"For the senior staff I consulted the employment agency in London that I use for my own home. They have associates in Carlisle. Most of the junior servants came from the agency there. I shall write to them immediately to inquire further into the background of those we hired. It may take a while for them to assemble the information, however."

"Good. Do that." Rob pondered further. "And we need some more guards. Burnside and Feller are the only ones I trust at the moment, and I don't know that I would trust anyone new I might bring in."

"I'm sure my father could send someone. All his people have been with him for years," Iantha interjected.

"Aye. That would be an excellent solution. I'll send

Feller with a message at once.'' The weight on Rob's shoulders lightened infinitesimally.

''And I shall stay for a while.'' Sam set his empty glass aside with a significant glance at Rob.

''But Amelia—'' Iantha began.

Sam waved away the objection. ''I shall send for her when the roads—and the danger—are clear.'' He grinned at Iantha. ''Having no desire to sleep by myself.'' He directed his gaze at Rob again. ''You need another pair of eyes.''

Rob nodded gratefully. He did need that, as well as someone else he could trust. ''Aye, and possibly another strong arm. Thank you, Sam. I would appreciate having you here.''

At that moment Gailsgill came into the room. ''My lord, Feller picked up the post on his way back from fetching Mr. Broughton.''

Rob took the letter the butler held out to him. Bloody hell! He knew that handwriting. He tore the seal off with a curse. As he read the message, rage filled him until he could not speak. Without a word he held the paper out to Sam.

Sam read it aloud. '' 'Keep the bitch quiet.' ''

Without Sam's quips and stories, dinner would have been a dismal affair indeed. Happily Feller reported that Lord Sebergham had indeed gone to London, so they were not burdened with his unwelcomed presence as a guest. Rob was uncharacteristically quiet, and Iantha found herself struggling with the fear of knowing once again that someone near to her wished her harm. She had been feeling safe inside the castle, but now...

She picked at her curry, while Rob somberly sipped his wine. It was the betrayal, she thought. The knowing that one—oh, heaven, it could be more than one!—of the people they trusted in their home had deceived them.

And that was not all. Someone else had sent that letter, *before* this latest incident occurred—someone unseen and also unknown directing events from afar. Iantha laid down her fork and sighed. Would this nightmare never end?

Whoever it was must think that she might identify them. But did they not realize that if she could, she would have done so long ago? Perhaps it was as Rob had said—it gave them a sense of power to frighten and abuse her.

But she would defeat them. At last her fear had given way to anger, lending her a feeling of strength that she had lacked before. Somehow she and Rob would unmask the culprits, somehow bring them to justice. Neither of them could ever rest easy until they had accomplished that.

Iantha did not leave the men to their port at the end of the meal. Rob would not allow it. Instead they assembled in the drawing room once more, to meet Vijaya for tea. They ruthlessly avoided the subject of her recent misadventure, but she knew that Rob and Sam would find a way to discuss it without her hearing.

They made short work of the tea, and all of them dispersed to their beds. Rob did not go to his own room even to disrobe. He sat and visited with her while Camille brushed her hair and laid out her nightclothes. When the maid had unbuttoned her gown behind the screen, Iantha dismissed her and began to undress.

As she tossed her shift onto the top of the screen, Rob's voice interrupted her. "Wait. Don't put on your nightclothes yet."

She peeked around the edge to see her husband sitting naked on the bed, his clothes folded neatly on the hearth chair. Smiling, she limped across the room to him and stood in front of him, but he did not answer her smile.

"I want to be able to feel you—all of you." He pulled her across him onto the bed.

Iantha shifted to her back while Rob straightened himself. Before she realized what he was about, he rolled on top of her and caught both her hands over her head.

Iantha's breath stopped.

She felt her eyes snap open in shock. For a heartbeat she could think of nothing but his weight on top of her, the strong grip of his hands.

"Damn!" He hastily slid off of her onto one elbow. "Damn me. I'm an idiot. Forgive me, Iantha. I just wanted to experience every inch of you and—"

Her breath returned. "No… I mean, yes, of course. It is all right. I believe…I believe I might be able to tolerate you on me thus. I know it is *you* now. I was just taken by surprise."

He shook his head. "I don't want to bring back those memories, and I don't wish to be *tolerated*."

Iantha rested a hand on his shoulder and tugged. "Perhaps I can do better than that. Let us try." She smiled up at him. "I will call on my newly discovered power."

For a moment Rob's somber expression melted into a grin. Then, serious again, he carefully covered her with his body. He paused and looked questioningly down at her.

"It is all right. I like knowing it is you."

She felt his sigh of relief more than heard it. He clasped her hands again, fingers intertwined with hers, and gently stretched them over her head. She felt his arms along the length of hers, his body, his legs against hers.

He looked into her eyes. "I have been needing this. Your physical presence has become very important to me. I was so afraid that I would find you dead...." He pressed his forehead against hers. "This is very comforting."

They lay thus for a space, their breaths mingling.

Comforting. He found her comforting. Iantha had been so involved with taking comfort from him that she had given little thought for the needs of a still-grieving father. He always seemed so strong and cheerful.

She freed one hand and began to stroke his back. "Are you sad, Rob?"

This time his sigh was audible. "Yes, I think I am. I have been avoiding it by being furious. But yes, I am sad and afraid. I don't want to lose you. I don't want to lose anyone else."

"I'm sorry." Iantha felt a warm tear drop onto her cheek. "Do you miss them terribly?"

"Yes, especially Lakshmi. I can see now that I was close to Shakti only in a physical way, but my baby girl—" He broke off, and Iantha heard him swallow.

"What does *Lakshmi* mean?

"Lakshmi is the goddess of love and beauty."

Iantha stroked his hair. "So you lost two goddesses."

"But I have gained another." Rob lifted his head so that he could look into her face. He wiped his eyes and smiled a still-sad smile. "A lovely silver goddess."

"What can I do, Rob? How can I help you?" She laid her hand against his cheek.

"Hold me. Hold me and let me love you."

She wrapped her arms around him, and he kissed her gently. After several heartbeats she felt his shaft begin to harden against her. He deepened the kiss, and she lifted one hand to tangle in his hair. When she pressed her hips against him, he pulsed in response, and an answering heat grew in her.

Iantha opened and invited him in. He came into her with a sigh, all the while kissing her, gripping her hands. As the heat expanded to fill her whole body, he thrust faster, harder. When it burst into an all-consuming flame, she heard his cry answering her own.

They lay together for several minutes afterward, catching their breath. Rob at last moved off of her and pulled her against his side. He whispered into her hair.

"Thank you, my goddess. Thank you."

The banker might have been forgiven for feeling a bit unwelcome. When he appeared two days later, Iantha could not help viewing him with a certain suspicion—a suspicion she could also see in the eyes of Rob and Sam. After all, Welwyn had been one of the company at Christmas. Nonetheless, all of them greeted him politely when he followed Gailsgill into the drawing room.

Extending his hand, Rob hastened to meet his guest. "Welwyn, how have you been? What brings you to Cumberland in this snowy weather? Are you still researching gunpowder mills?"

"No, Lord Duncan, I am afraid I come on a much grimmer errand." Welwyn shook Rob's hand and Sam's, then pulled a large handkerchief from his pocket and wiped sweat from his plump, red face.

"Grim? How is this?" Rob exchanged glances with his cousin. He indicated a chair, and the banker sat.

"There has been a terrible occurrence." Though Iantha found the room cool, Welwyn continued to sweat profusely. "Young Wycomb has been killed."

All of them made appropriate sounds, but Iantha could not feel that the world had suffered a great loss. She had never liked Wycomb. He seemed sly. Besides, he had a strong body odor, as though always nervous. Perhaps that made her think of her attackers. Some of them had smelled that way. But that was hardly cause to wish him dead. She should have more sympathy.

Rob returned to his chair, and Sam followed his example. Rob's eyebrows were almost meeting in the middle. "That is indeed very bad. How did it happen?"

"That is the worst of it." The banker again wielded his handkerchief. "He and his best friend were found shot on a road outside of London. And the circumstances... I regret to have to introduce them." He glanced at Iantha. "Perhaps Lady Duncan would prefer to retire."

Rob looked sharply first at Welwyn, and then at Iantha, while Sam's eyebrows climbed almost to his hairline. "And why is that?" Rob asked, his expression dark. "How does this concern my wife?"

"I hope that it does not, but I am afraid, if my information is correct..." Welwyn cast another cautious glance in her direction.

Were they at last to obtain some information about her attackers? Iantha raised her chin. "If it concerns me, then I will stay."

The banker nodded and groped in his coat pocket, pulling out a small packet. "I hoped to have your evidence. I understand that those who perpetrated that foul deed against you wore masks? I regret to say Stephen and his friend were both masked."

Iantha nodded and held out her hand. "You want me to identify the masks."

"Iantha." Rob stood. "Let me."

She shook her head. "No. If this is an indication of who my enemies are, I want there to be no mistake. I will look."

Rob crossed the room to stand beside her while she

carefully peeled the paper away. Within it lay the crimson satin that she had expected. The two masks were identical—and certainly identical to those she had seen that bitter cold night six years ago. She looked down at them for a long moment.

And then tossed them disdainfully at Welwyn's feet.

The masks themselves had lost their power to hurt her. She had faced them in memory. Mask after mask.

She had conquered that fear.

"Yes, those are the same as the masks I saw that night." She looked at him calmly.

Rob sighed audibly. Relief at her composure, no doubt. He turned to the banker. "So Wycomb—and his friend, I suppose—were part of the gang?"

Welwyn nodded. "It appears so."

"Either that, or someone wishes it to appear so." Sam spoke thoughtfully from his chair near the fire.

"I'm afraid he was truly involved." The banker shook his head sadly. "I…I find I never really knew the man. Since his death I have examined his office and his records. I found a journal hidden in a secret space in his desk." He smiled sadly. "Young people forget that we were young once ourselves. I used that desk when I started with the firm."

"What did you find in the journal?" Rob asked.

"Espionage. Treason." Welwyn hung his head. "That I actually trusted someone like that…" He wiped his eyes.

"Had he done much damage?" Sam stood and poured a glass of sherry and handed it to the older man.

"That remains to be seen. Thank you." He took the wine and sipped. "I dare hope not. He seemed to have been gathering information on England's financial position. If Bonaparte had access to what was in that journal…'' The banker's pudgy frame shuddered. ''His Continental Plan might have brought us down. And of course, there was the information on gunpowder production.''

''So that was Wycomb's notion?'' Rob commenced to pour sherry for all of them.

''Yes, he brought the idea to me. Of course—'' the financier brightened a bit ''—it is still an excellent investment. We will need to use gunpowder soon, I have no doubt.'' He turned back to Iantha, somber once more. ''I feel I owe you an apology. I brought that young monster into your home—and into your father's home. Had I had any idea…''

''No apology is due from you, Mr. Welwyn.'' Iantha dredged up a smile. ''You were also his victim.''

''But now we are left with another mystery.'' Sam rose and began to pace the room. ''Who killed Wycomb, and why did they do it?''

Iantha nodded. ''And more important to me, why were they wearing those masks again?''

*She should be thoroughly terrified by now. He could not envision the fine slut withstanding both the shooting and being locked out in the storm. Her kind just did not have that kind of pluck.*

*Well and good. He wanted her to be exactly that way. It would make it easier to bend her to his will if she was already cowed. She had come away easy the last time. When he got his hands on her again, she would not escape with one lesson.*

*And it would be best if she saw him kill her husband. That would destroy hope.*

*He smiled at the thought and leaned back comfortably in his chair, picturing her on her knees in front of him.*

*Picturing her on her back.*

*On her belly.*
*Under his boot.*
*Waiting was the hard part.*
*But in the end, her terror would be well worth it.*

# Chapter Seventeen

Iantha did not wait for the visitors to be announced. At the sound of familiar voices, she flew down the stairs and into the entry hall while Gailsgill was still taking wraps.

"Mama, Papa!" She flung her arms around her mother. "Why didn't you tell me you were coming?"

After a startled moment her mother returned the embrace enthusiastically. "My dear, we all came on an impulse. I see I need not ask how you are. The roses are blooming in your cheeks."

Iantha's father stepped toward her, then hesitated. She turned to him and held out her arms. "Papa."

Lord Rosley cautiously wrapped his arms around his daughter. "How are you, minx?"

At the old endearment a lump rose in Iantha's eyes. "I am quite well, Papa."

Her father stepped back a bit and looked into her eyes, his own a bit moist. "After the last threatening episode, I feared I would find you pulled and wan."

"It was very disturbing, of course, but I have recovered. It has been a week, after all."

"I am happy to hear that, but look…" He turned to

another figure standing in the door. "We have brought you a surprise."

The newcomer, a tall young man with dark auburn hair, wearing a cavalry uniform, stepped forward. Iantha sprang at her oldest brother and threw herself into his arms. "John!"

He, too, paused for a heartbeat before enfolding her and resting his cheek on her hair. "Annie."

"Oh, it is so wonderful to see you!" The tears increased and slid down her cheeks. "It has been such a long time."

"True. I am sorry I was unable to come to your wedding. You do look well, better than—"

He was interrupted by the entry of another carriage load of guests. "Annie!"

Iantha bent to hug her younger sister. "Valeria! Oh, I have missed you!"

Valeria's arms locked around her waist. "And I have missed you." She lifted her head to gaze upward. "But, Annie, why are you crying? Are you well?"

Iantha wiped her eyes. "I am quite well, dear. I am just so happy to see all of you."

A moment of silence settled over the group. Well, no wonder in that. How long had it been since they had seen her weep? For that matter, how long had it been since she had cried from happiness? Iantha could not remember. Perhaps she had never done so. The swelling emotion in her heart did not even feel familiar. Perhaps one must suffer unhappiness before happiness could be fully appreciated. She sniffed and reached for her handkerchief. Suddenly she felt Rob's sturdy arm around her waist.

"Welcome, Lady Rosley...my lord." He bowed to the one and shook hands with the other.

"Thank you, Duncan." Lord Rosley indicated his tall companion. "Allow me to present my son, Major John Kethley."

"How do you do, Major. Welcome to the Eyrie." Rob clasped her brother's hand warmly.

John bowed. "Thank you, my lord. I have been eager to meet you since my sister wrote to me of her marriage."

Iantha thought an assessing glance passed between the two men. But then her attention was taken up by her two younger brothers, who were clamoring for her attention.

"Hello, Thomas! Nat, do give me a hug. I believe the two of you have grown by inches since I last saw you." Both boys hugged her at once.

"I *have* grown, Annie." Nathaniel stuck out one leg. "See, all my britches have become too short. I'll soon be as tall as Tom."

"No, you won't, sprout." Thomas rested his elbow on his brother's head. "I am growing faster than you are."

Some good-natured pushing and shoving immediately ensued.

"Ahem. Gentlemen!" The indulgent smile on Lord Rosley's face belied the sternness of his voice, but the rebuke served to restore order.

"Alas, they are both growing before my very eyes." Lady Rosley sighed. "I cannot keep them in clothes."

Rob laughed. "I seem to remember that Sam and I did the same thing." He gestured toward stairs leading to the drawing room. "But come, everyone. Let us make ourselves more comfortable."

As he led his guests up the steps, Rob marveled at the change in his wife. Weeping with joy! A thrill of happiness shot through his own heart. And embracing her father and brothers… The changes in her had penetrated deep, not only with respect to him, but to her family as well. His new goddess—his silver goddess—shone more brightly every day.

After a convivial dinner, they gathered in the drawing room. Iantha played Fox and Geese with first Nathaniel and then Valeria. Then she listened to the men discuss the Bonaparte situation while the two children played with one another. Nat's crow of victory put an end to these festivities, Lady Rosley declaring it to be bedtime for the youngsters. They departed, with only minor protests, under the escort of Valeria's governess.

When they had gone, Lord Rosley turned to Rob. "Have you discovered who perpetrated this latest outrage on my daughter?"

Rob shook his head. "I regret to say that I have not. Thank you for sending me Daniel. He has proved a very dependable lookout."

"Aye, he is a steady fellow. I have brought you Harry as well this trip. He should also prove useful. And I have brought you John."

"Oh, John, can you stay for a while?" Iantha's heart leapt at the thought of having her big brother, always her protector, with her.

He nodded. "Yes, I have requested an extended furlough." He turned to Rob. "If you think I may be of service, Lord Duncan, I would be honored to help you fight these bastards…uh, I beg pardon, Mama…these scoundrels who persist in tormenting Iantha."

"Thank you, Major. I would be extremely pleased to have your help." Rob nodded. "I seem to be making no headway at all in identifying them—except for Wycomb, of course. But the very fact that he is dead demonstrates that there are more of them."

"Has to be." Sam spoke up. "If he was into espionage, then he must have confederates—confederates who apparently no longer trusted him—unless, of course, he was found out."

"But what does his treason have to do with what happened to me six years ago?" Iantha searched the faces of the men. "Why were they wearing those masks?" No one produced an answer, but her mother shifted uncomfortably.

"I believe I will retire. I find I am more tired than I realized." She rose, and the men did likewise.

Poor Mama. Iantha knew she still could not bear to talk about the assault. "Of course, Mama. I'll walk you to your room."

"I'll join you, my dear." Lord Rosley took his wife's arm.

John nodded to Rob, Sam and Vijaya. "If you gentlemen will excuse me, I had little sleep last night. I arrived late at Hill House, and Tom had me out at the crack of dawn. Come, Thomas, you have been yawning, too, any time this past hour."

The major offered Iantha his arm. A murmur of goodnights followed them out of the room, Thomas on their heels. They climbed the stairs together, Iantha feeling closer to her family than she had in many years. She was so thrilled to have them in her home. She was so grateful to *have* a home of her own. A few months ago she would never have considered it possible.

As they strolled down the corridor toward their respective rooms, Camille stepped out of Iantha's bedchamber, nodded to Daniel on duty by the door and turned to close the door behind her.

As she looked up and saw the group approaching, she froze.

John also stopped in his tracks, bringing Iantha to a halt beside him. Thomas stepped back hastily to avoid treading on their heels.

For one short moment Iantha thought she saw a look of pure shock on her maid's face. Then Camille opened the door and retreated the way she had come.

Iantha opened her eyes and yawned. Rob had already risen. Even though she knew he would be within earshot, she missed his solid presence beside her. Near him she always felt safe. She stifled the small twinge of anxiety and buried her face in his pillow. It smelled like him—of smoke and soap and leather and—well, just Rob.

How important to her he had become! And not just because of the safety he represented. The physical closeness she had once so feared had now become, indeed, life's greatest adventure. But more than that she had come to value the touch of his hand, the shape of his shoulders, the thickness of his hair. The sound of his deep voice created a little tremor in her heart.

These reflections brought her up short for a moment. They sounded very much like symptoms of love! Could she, Iantha Elizabeth Kethley Armstrong, Lady Duncan, victim of rape and prisoner of her own fears, at last be falling in love?

Another of life's great adventures within her grasp.

If they could continue to preserve her life.

She shoved the thought aside and rolled over and tugged the bell pull, then relaxed against her pillow, for the moment warm and contented. What a joy to have her husband and her family around her. Even the threat hanging over her head could not dim her pleasure. Why had she shut herself away from them for so long? Never would she allow herself to do so again, no matter what happened.

To her surprise the door was opened not by Camille, but by the upstairs chambermaid bearing a tray with hot chocolate. "Good morning, my lady."

"Why, good morning, Ellen. Where is Camille?"

The girl flushed as she set her tray down and turned to help Iantha arrange her pillows. "I...we are not certain, my lady."

Iantha frowned. "What do you mean, Ellen? Is she not in her room?"

"No, ma'am, nor in the kitchen. Mrs. Lamonby sent Thursby to look for her, but he ain't found her. So I was asked to bring up your chocolate."

Iantha took the cup, but did not lean back into the pillows. She sat up straight, her brow puckered in thought. "She must be here somewhere. Did you check the sewing room?"

"Thursby says he did, my lady. Should I help you dress?"

"Yes, thank you." Iantha set the drink on her bed table and swung her feet to the floor. "I must discover what is afoot. It is not like her to be unavailable. The gray twill morning gown, I think, Ellen. Yes, that is the one."

While Ellen laid out her underclothes, Iantha gulped down the chocolate as rapidly as she could without burning her tongue, and looked in her bed table drawer for the pistol she always wore under her skirts.

It was not there.

Climbing out of bed, she checked thoroughly in the wardrobe, but the gun was not to be found there, either. How disturbing! She needed the sense of security that wearing it gave her. Without it she felt naked and vulnerable.

She dressed hurriedly and sat at the vanity long enough for Ellen to brush her hair back from face and secure it with silver combs. No sooner had that been accomplished than a light tap sounded on the door connecting her bed-chamber to her sitting room. She heard Rob's voice on the other side of the panel. "Iantha, are you dressed?"

"Yes, just a moment." Sending Ellen for coffee and scones, Iantha opened the door. "Rob, the strangest thing has happened. No one can find Camille... Oh, good morning, John. I did not know you were here."

"That is what we wish to discuss with you." Rob stepped back so that she could enter the sitting room. "John has brought me some interesting information."

"Oh?" Iantha seated herself on the sofa, and Rob took a chair near the hearth, where John stood warming himself. "What might that be?"

"John has encountered Camille before."

"Ah! I thought last night that there was something strange..."

"Yes, I recognized her in the hallway yesterday evening—and evidently she also recognized me. I imagine that is why she cannot be found this morning."

Iantha's eyes narrowed. "But why... What does that have to do with anything?"

"John met her in the company of Horace Raunds."

"Raunds? The younger diplomat—Lord Alton's son, who was here at Christmas? Now how would they know one another? I don't understand." Iantha watched her brother's face turn red and grimaced. "Oh, come now, John. I am no longer a schoolroom miss."

He smiled. "No, but I did not expect my very proper sister to be served by a member of the muslin company."

"The muslin... Oh, the demimonde." In spite of herself Iantha flushed. "I see."

"I doubt it. At least, I hope not." John laughed, then sobered. "But I *am* concerned. It was at a rather rowdy party I attended in London with some lads from my regiment about a year ago—mostly a soldiers' gathering, but there were a few people from the Home Office. Even though Camille arrived with Raunds, she spent a great deal of time flirting with the senior officers. In fact, she went aside with… Well, enough said about that."

"This sounds like quite an affair." Rob grinned at his brother-in-law.

John winked at him. "I came away immediately, of course."

Iantha leaned back against the sofa and pondered this revelation. She had never seen this side of her adored older brother. Did all men live lives separate and secret from their womenfolk? Her brow puckered in disapproval.

"Now, Annie. Come out of your high ropes." John became serious once more. "I really do *not* care much for that kind of carouse, and that one definitely did not keep the line. There was much drinking of absinthe and smoking…I don't know just what. Some intoxicant. I *did* gather up everyone I could command, and took us all away. Too much opportunity there for trouble—and far too much loose talk."

Ellen arrived with the coffee tray, and conversation ceased while Iantha poured for the three of them and John took a chair and a scone.

When they were all served, Rob nodded thoughtfully. "Did you know Stephen Wycomb?"

"Sharp-faced, dark-haired fellow? Sly looking?" John spoke around a mouthful of scone. "I met him. Didn't like him above half. If he was one of the devils who hurt Iantha, good riddance, I say!"

"No doubt about that." Rob sipped his coffee. "I was wondering—was he at that party?"

"I don't remember. Why? Oh, I see—the espionage." John rubbed his chin. "He may have been there. It would have been an excellent opportunity to glean some military intelligence."

"So it seems my new, skilled French maid may be a spy?" Iantha grimaced.

"I think that may be only one of many skills your *former* French maid can boast." John held out his cup for more coffee, his expression sardonic.

"I am inclined to agree with you about that." Rob held out his own cup in turn, and Iantha refilled it.

"But why was she here? And where is she now?" Iantha looked searchingly at her husband and her brother. "It is snowing a little, and it is very cold. Where could she go?"

"Where indeed?" Rob emptied his cup. "Does she have someone in the area who will take her in? I believe I shall send Feller out immediately. Perhaps she left tracks."

Iantha raised one eyebrow and the corner of her mouth quirked. "Tell him to be careful. She has my pistol."

In the end, Camille proved surprisingly easy to find. Feller appeared in the drawing room shortly after Iantha's parents and the younger contingent had left for Hill House. Another brewing storm had convinced Lord Rosley to take advantage of the lull to get his family home before it broke in earnest.

"Uh, me lord, could I have a word with you in private?" The groom cast an uncomfortable glance at Iantha.

Foreboding in his heart, Rob rose and walked into the corridor with his henchman. "What is it, Feller?"

"I found her, all right and tight, but I think you better come and see—and maybe Mr. Broughton or the major, too."

"She's dead?" Apparently his premonition of trouble was going to prove true.

"Aye, and not just dead." The expression on Feller's face told Rob more than he wished to know.

"Murdered?"

The groom nodded glumly. "Aye. You need to come look."

Rob returned to the drawing room. "Sam, you and I must go on an errand. John, would you stay with Iantha?"

"Of course." Her brother stretched long legs out in front of him. "We have to make up for a long absence."

"Vijaya, you'll be nearby?" Rob hardly awaited the nod he knew he would get before he turned to the door.

"Wait!" Iantha held up a hand. "Where are you going?"

"I'll tell you later." He threw the words over his shoulder.

He and Sam followed Feller down the stairs and through the old castle to the stable. The groom already had ordered their horses saddled, and they left the Eyrie at a fast trot, snow sprinkling around them.

When they had been on the road for a few minutes, Feller guided his mount up beside Rob's. "I just bethought meself of something, me lord."

Rob sent him a questioning glance.

"It's about the maid. I seen her a time or two in the stable at night, back in the stalls. I didn't think much of it—thought she was meeting one of the lads. She did have a bold eye.''

She certainly did that. Rob nodded in agreement.

''I thought it might be Thursby, but then I seen him in the house one of those nights. Now I'm wondering if it was someone from outside.''

Rob thought about that. He had no doubt that an outside force had been directing events in his home. He gritted his teeth. ''I'm afraid you may be right. At least that will not happen again.''

Half an hour's ride brought them to a hidden fold in the hills. The road wound through it in a series of turns. They had just come to the center of the dale when Rob saw one of his own horses tied to a tree, the saddle showing copious blood.

Feller gestured. ''She took the horse last night.''

Rob drew rein and looked down. A few feet off the road in the banked snow lay the remains of a woman. He dismounted and moved nearer. The shock of his first good look at her almost brought his luncheon back into his mouth.

''Bloody...!'' He turned away to recover himself.

''What?'' Sam swung down from his horse. ''What is the—Great God!''

Camille, bloody from head to toe, legs spread wide, lay on her back in the snow. Clearly the knife slash across her throat had been a mercy. The only part of her that the killer had not mutilated was her face.

''He wanted us to recognize her.'' Rob made himself glance at the corpse again. ''The bloody bastard!''

''Aye.'' Sam, his face pale, gave the body another quick look, then turned away. ''Why did he do that to her?''

"To frighten us." Rob's eyes narrowed in fury, and his hands shook. "This is another threat against Iantha."

"You're not going to tell her, are you?" Sam gazed closely at his cousin.

"What kind of idiot do you think I am?" Rob spat the words savagely. "And no one else will tell her, either." He glared at Sam and Feller.

"Nay, me lord." The groom held up a pacifying hand and shook his head. "I couldn't bring myself to tell *you,* much less Lady Duncan."

Sam shrugged. "I am not such an idiot, either."

"Sorry," Rob growled. No reason to take his rage out on them. After drawing several breaths to calm himself, he gazed around the clearing. "I don't think she was killed here. He brought her to this spot on our horse. I suppose he didn't want it traced to him." Rob turned to Feller. "Did you look for tracks?"

His henchman nodded. "Aye, that I did. He brought her down the road, I think, but it's too churned up to see nothing. And there's been some snow."

"Come. Help me with this." A feeling of urgency was growing in Rob's gut. This gory show definitely had a purpose. He pulled off his greatcoat and, with some help from the others, wrapped the stiff body in it. The struggle to get it tied onto the horse took all three of them.

When they were back on the homeward road, Rob glanced back at the pitiful bundle, his eyes narrowed in speculation. "Now who did she run to?"

Feller shook his head. "Don't know that, but whoever it was, she shouldn'ta done it."

As happy as she was to visit with her brother, Iantha could not keep her mind on the discussion. Surely the matter that took Rob off on the run must have concerned

Camille. While Vijaya, showing no sign of disquiet, calmly studied one of his old scrolls, John seemed to feel as restless as she did. He paced the room as they tried to maintain a desultory conversation.

Suddenly she heard a shout in the corridor, followed by the sounds of a scuffle. Casting his parchment aside, Vijaya came to his feet. John dashed for the door. Just as he reached it, she heard the crack of a shot, and he reeled back into the room.

Iantha shrieked. ''John!''

A burly man she had never seen before charged through the door.

Blood soaking through his sleeve, John stumbled to his feet and dived at the intruder. As he grappled with the man, two more strangers ran in. Both of them carried knives.

One of them advanced on Iantha. She backed away, putting a chair between them. The man sidled around the chair, and Iantha bolted toward another one. Why did Camille have to take her pistol? Iantha needed it now as she never had before. She snatched a vase off a table and heaved it at her attacker. He sidestepped and flashed a gap-toothed grin at her as it crashed to the floor. Inexorably, he moved toward her again.

Out of the corner of her eye she glimpsed the sparkle of jewels. Daring a quick peek as she moved toward the fireplace, she saw Vijaya, an impressively large jeweled knife in his hand, circling the third man. His opponent dwarfed the slender prince. John still struggled with the man who had shot him. Oh, God! Please don't let him be badly wounded, Iantha prayed.

Not on her account.

A sob rose in her throat, but she kept edging toward the fire, always keeping behind some piece of furniture.

After what seemed an eternity her hand closed over the handle of the poker. Her pursuer paused, a calculating gleam in his eye. She lifted her weapon threateningly. The man put his free hand up to ward off the blow.

Iantha could see clearly that if she swung at him, he would grab the poker and probably wrest it from her hands with ease. She drew it back, and he jumped for her. Bracing the shaft against the marble facing of the fireplace, she raised the point and prayed for incredible luck. For once, fortune favored her.

The man's weight carried him into the end of the poker, which caught him just under the ribs. He doubled over and staggered back, gasping for breath. Iantha raised the implement and brought it down on his head. He slumped face first to the floor.

Raising her weapon again with fierce exultation, she looked about for another opponent.

The man fighting with John had thrown him to the floor and was trying to get a grip on his throat. Iantha had started in that direction when her brother got his feet into his opponent's body and pitched him over his head. The man landed heavily, but rose to his knees and came up with a knife as John rolled to his feet. It seemed inevitable that he would thrust with the blade before John could rise.

At that moment there was another report of a gun. The knife sailed away as John's assailant flung out his arms and collapsed on his face. Iantha looked up to see Rob standing in the doorway, a smoking pistol in his hand. In a flash he was beside her. She let the heavy poker sag to the floor, but did not release it.

Sam made for the knife-wielding man confronting Vijaya, but stopped at Rob's warning shout. The brigand never let his gaze leave the prince, but continued to circle and feint. Vijaya did not respond, but turned slowly to keep his enemy in view. Suddenly the other man lunged, his blade aimed straight for Vijaya's heart.

The Indian moved in one fluid motion, stepping aside almost casually. The intruder did not make a sound. He simply crumpled to the floor, the hilt of Vijaya's knife protruding from the center of his chest.

Seeing that, Sam hurried to the man Iantha had clouted. Rolling him over, he felt for a pulse. He grinned at Rob. "He's alive, but don't ever let her hit *you*. This cove will be out for a while."

Rob tightened his hold around Iantha's waist. "I'll keep that in mind. What about the other two?"

A quick examination assured them that the other intruders had breathed their last. Rob rang the bell for a footman and hastened into the corridor, John and Iantha following closely.

They found Harry coming groggily to his knees, a large lump on his jaw. "I'm sorry, Lord Duncan. They jumped me from out of that parlor there. They were on me before I knew it. Never expected no one from there."

"At least you had time to shout a warning." John pulled the footman to his feet with his right arm. His left arm hung at his side, dripping blood. "They didn't take us completely unaware, although I rushed into that ball like the veriest cully."

"How bad is it?" Rob turned to his brother-in-law, only to be interrupted as Gailsgill, Thursby and two other footmen came pounding up the stairs.

"My lord! What's amiss? Was that shots?" The butler puffed to a stop.

"We have been invaded, Gailsgill. You and these lads see to Harry and truss up the survivor. Take that bastard below stairs and lock him up. I want to question him."

Rob took John's good arm. "And send someone with warm water and bandages to Major Kethley's bedchamber." Suddenly he became aware of Iantha, standing wide-eyed beside him. "Are you all right?"

"Yes. Yes, I believe so. John…?" Her face was as white as her brother's.

"It's nothing, Annie. Don't worry."

Rob was not so sure. "I'll take him up to his room and have a look."

"I'm coming, too," she stated.

One thing Rob had learned about his wife was that when she got that look on her face, there was no use in arguing. The two of them helped John up the stairs and into a chair in his chamber just as Rogers, his valet, hastened into the room. Together they eased his coat off, and Rob used his knife to cut away John's shirt. "Ah." He sighed in relief. "The ball just dug a furrow in your arm on its way past. This needs nothing but disinfecting and a bandage."

"Thank God." Iantha sighed and sank onto the footstool.

At that moment Mrs. Lamonby came in with the medical supplies. She advanced briskly on the patient and seized his arm in a competent grasp. John sucked in his breath sharply.

"Just some spirits to disinfect it," the housekeeper confirmed. "And then bed for you, Major."

Rebellion flared in John's eyes. "Now, ma'am, this is naught to fuss over. I won't be much use lolling in bed."

"No, sir, and you won't be much use out of your head with fever, either," his valet asserted, going to the bed to turn down the covers.

"You listen to me, John Kethley!" Iantha rose and stood over him with eyes snapping. "You will do exactly as you are told, or I will put you into that bed myself. Don't ever frighten me like that again!''

John tried to grin through the grimace occasioned by having brandy poured over the wound into a basin. "I am quivering in my boots, little sister."

Rob laughed. "Well, she will have my help. Tonight you stay in bed. Tomorrow, if you have no fever, I'll call off the watchdogs.''

Mrs. Lamonby expertly tied the bandage, and Rob made shooing gestures at her and Iantha. "Thank you, ladies. We'll get him into bed."

How fierce his formerly fragile wife had become!

And how precious.

For the moment he could not even think of what had almost befallen her.

*So she thought their long association would cause him to forgive her failure. Fool woman and her milksop scruples.*

*Damn all women and their cozening ways.*

*She came offering pleasure to distract him, and she had provided it in full measure.*

*A thin smile curled his lips.*

*Though not entirely in the way she expected.*

*And she had whetted his appetite for the other one.*

## Chapter Eighteen

Once he saw his brother-in-law ensconced in bed, Rob wasted no time in getting himself back to Iantha's side. He left John to his valet and almost ran down the stairs in search of her. Rob had been so occupied since the fight, that he had not had the opportunity to give himself the reassurance of holding her in his arms. He found her in the morning room, under the protection of Sam and Vijaya.

Ignoring their interested stares, he walked straight to where Iantha sat on a sofa, and pulled her to her feet. He wrapped his arms around her and held her so tightly she gasped. Loosening his hold slightly, he looked down into her upturned face. "You have not been harmed? Are you terrified?"

She shook her head. "No, I am quite unhurt. As for being afraid…" She thought for a moment, head tilted to one side. "Not in the way I was before. In fact, I found it a pleasure to be able to fight back. Did you find Camille?"

Rob clutched her to his chest again, an icy ball in his gut. The idea that she might suffer the same fate as her maid almost brought *him* to a state of terror. His voice was rough when he answered. "Yes, we found her."

"What—?" The question was muffled against his chest. Rob released her, and she tried again. "What happened to her?"

He brushed the hair back from her face, watching carefully for her reaction. "She is dead—murdered."

Both Iantha's hands came to her mouth. "Oh, no! No matter what she has done, I didn't wish that."

"Of course not. But I'm afraid she has done a great deal." He finally brought himself to release her, and sat on the sofa beside her.

"She certainly has." Sam stretched his legs out on the ottoman. "While you were tending John, Vijaya and I found horses sheltered in the old castle—good horses. Those brigands were well provided with a means of escape. And I had a little talk with our prisoner. Considering the humor you were in earlier, I thought I had better do it."

Rob tightened his lips. "You are probably correct. I would like too much to beat someone to a bloody pulp, which, aside from lowering myself to their level, would most likely not have gained any more information. Besides, I doubt they are the ones who killed Camille."

"No. According to what he told me—if it's true—they could not have done it. He did not prove very talkative, of course. He hasn't yet fully recovered his senses, but he was quick to tell me that he did not know his employer. He says a flash cove hired him in Carlisle. The worst of it is that they were in the house overnight. That is how they managed to work their way into that unused parlor without being detected. Says that they were let in and fed by a black-haired mort."

Rob glanced at Iantha to see if she understood the cant phrase. Obviously, she did.

She grew pale. "Camille."

Rob nodded glumly. "Aye. And I have little doubt that she is the party who enticed you out into the snow. Why she also arranged for your salvation remains a mystery. She even wept when we found you."

"Crocodile tears." Sam's lip curled in a sneer. "She was a sly piece. Perhaps whoever is directing these attacks on Iantha does not want her dead." His brow furrowed. "But I can't fathom what the devil their true intention is."

"Nor can I." Rob slipped an arm around Iantha's shoulders.

She stared solemnly at her hands resting in her lap. "I never knew betrayal was so painful."

The next morning John insisted on coming down to breakfast. "I am not going to be laid up by the merest scratch," he announced as he lifted the covers off the dishes and examined their contents. "My arm is only a bit stiff."

Rob's experience led him to believe that John's arm was considerably more stiff than he indicated, and that the wound probably hurt like the devil, but he decided not to interfere. After all, his brother-in-law was a man grown and a soldier.

"If you are feeling sufficiently fit to help keep watch, I believe I will ride to Carlisle and talk to the employment agency in person." Sam heaped a plate with roast beef and took a place at the table. "We need to know *now* where Camille came from—and why. Maybe that will tell us who else is involved."

"That will be a very uncomfortable ride." Rob looked

at his cousin over the top of his coffee cup. "You will freeze your..." He glanced at Iantha. "You will freeze, and the roads are bound to be bad."

"It isn't snowing this morning. I wouldn't try to get a carriage through the fells, but a horse should make it. I can stop for my carriage when I am down. There will be less snow at the lower levels." Sam gazed out the window for a moment. "Besides, it will give me a chance to look in on Amelia."

"Ah." Rob took a long swallow.

Iantha glanced up from idly crumbling a scone onto her plate. "I thought we had connected Camille to Horace Raunds."

John nodded. "He certainly brought her to that party, but that does not mean he is connected with the present skulduggery. I can't think why he would be. Doesn't seem that sort of fellow."

"Perhaps I can pursue that." Vijaya startled them all by walking into the breakfast parlor. Everyone laid down their cutlery and turned to look at him. "I had a letter from my elder brother recently. He is going to be in London for a few weeks, returning from the West Indies. He has traveled there on several occasions to research new methods of coffee planting for my father." The Indian took a chair and accepted coffee from Iantha. "I would like to see him, of course, but in addition to that perhaps he and I might learn something about young Raunds. People often ignore foreigners when they are talking. Perhaps they believe we do not understand them. Of course, if you need me more here..."

Rob had to chuckle at the thought that a linguist of Vijaya's stature might be believed not to speak English, but the proposal gave him pause. Could he protect Iantha with both Vijaya and Sam away and John with a bad arm? In the long run he must have the information they might garner. He would never be able to keep her safe until all of her enemies were made known.

A hard decision.

He turned to his brother-in-law. "What do you say, John? Can the two of us hold the castle?"

John grinned. "You mean the two of us, five footmen, several grooms and a pair of valets?"

A crack of laughter answered him. "When you put it that way, I believe we could hold off Bonaparte." Rob turned to his cousin and his friend. "Very well. The information you bring back might be just what we need to put an end to this nightmare. Go, but be careful."

"Certainly." Vijaya stood. "I will take a horse to the nearest posting inn. Perhaps when I am out of the fells, the road will be open to a coach."

"If you don't die of the cold." Iantha looked stricken.

He smiled. "But it is warmer in London, is it not?"

"Oh, yes. You will find it warmer. And I will give you a letter for my sister, Lady Rochland. I will ask her to include you in some entertainments where you might be able to eavesdrop." She held out a hand to him. "Thank you so much, your highness."

He clasped her fingers briefly. "It is my honor to serve you, my lady."

*A good enough plan,* Rob thought.

So why couldn't he shake off his uneasiness?

At bedtime his misgivings still dogged him. Rob tried to tell himself that his discomfit lingered from the previous day, but he could not believe that his enemy had given up on getting his bloodstained hands on Iantha. Although a thorough search of the whole stronghold revealed no further intruders, he knew he must not let his vigilance slip for a minute.

He sent Ellen away and unbuttoned Iantha's dinner gown himself. Having got that far, he slid his hands inside the dress and cupped her breasts, resting his chin on the top of her head. Their image in the dressing mirror looked back at him, his broad shoulders outlining her delicate ones. "My lady, do you know how important you have become to me?"

She turned in his arms, letting the gown slide down to her elbows. "Truly?"

"Aye, truly." He brushed her hair away from her upturned face and then let his hands rest on her slender waist. "I look forward to seeing you every time we are apart—even for a brief time. I enjoy your conversation and your talents. You have a very quick mind, goddess. You are a real companion to me—one I never expected to find. And…"

"And?" Iantha smiled into his eyes.

"I sometimes feel it should not be as important to me as it is, but our lovemaking… I don't know quite how to say it, but it comforts me in a way that nothing else does. I *feel* then that I am no longer alone. I've heard Sam say something similar. Perhaps it is true for most men."

"Yet you risked never having that comfort when you married me." She gazed steadily into his eyes.

"Aye, and I feared at times I had asked too much of you. But I could not believe that a woman with your fire—even though you had kept it so carefully banked for years—would not eventually let it blaze."

"I doubt that I ever would have been able to do that without your help and your patience. I don't know how you saw that in me. I have never understood why you took the risk."

"For all the reasons I gave at the time." Rob smiled. "And a few more. The truth is, I was openmouthed at your beauty the whole two days you were here. I wanted nothing more than to see all of you—to hold you close in my arms." He lowered his hands and pulled her hips against him, grinning at her. "I am also a bit of a cockscomb. I never believed you could withstand my siege forever."

"And I am so grateful that I did not. Mama told me that lovemaking could be wonderful, and you have shown me the truth of that." Iantha placed a hand on each side of his face, her own solemn. "You are a remarkable man, Robert Armstrong. And very important to me, also. I fear for your safety as much as my own. I couldn't bear for anything to happen to you."

"I will not allow it—I must be here to enjoy you." He turned his head to kiss the inside of her wrist. "And I have proved to be very durable. Sometime you must ask Vijaya about the tiger." Suddenly Rob grinned again and, turning his back to her, pulled his shirt over his head. "You see those scars on my shoulder? If I had not already shot it once, it would have bitten through my neck. Of course, it might still have done so if Vijaya had not walked calmly up to it and cut its throat."

She ran a hand gently over the scars, then reached around his waist and held him close, her breath warm against his skin and her soft hands stroking his belly. His body stirred. "Thank God for Vijaya! He is such a contradiction, is he not? So quiet and scholarly, but he killed that man yesterday as though it were easily done."

"And the tiger, fortunately for me." Rob turned to face her again, holding her against his hips again. Just being near her, feeling her hands on him, lightened his mood. "Are you going to show me whatever it was that you painted in his room?"

Her face turned scarlet, and Rob laughed aloud, stroking her fiery cheek. "Now I certainly want to see it."

"Right now?"

"I am sure I do. I can see that it will fit well with my present frame of mind." He released her and stepped back expectantly. Iantha lowered her arms, and her dress fell to the floor. She clutched at it and missed. It pooled around her feet.

"I don't know...." Her blush now covered her throat and breasts. "I can't think why I painted such a thing."

"You have no choice. My curiosity is now rampant. Along with other things." Rob put his hands on his hips. "You may as well fetch it, or I shall give you no peace."

"Very well. I do rather like it."

Iantha crossed the room to her desk as Rob watched. He loved the way her shift clung to her swaying hips. His erection grew rapidly. She drew a paper from a portfolio and came back to him, the painting at her side. Rob crossed his arms over his chest and waited. At last, hesitantly, she held up the picture.

Rob's shaft came immediately to full attention.

She had painted a scene fit for the *Kama Sutra*—a scene of a couple making love on a huge carved bed. The woman, triumphantly astride the man, wore the elaborate silver headdress of a goddess. The muscular man's hair was a dark brown, his face partially hidden.

But the face of the goddess was definitely his wife's.

After a moment of dumb astonishment, Rob lifted the painting out of her hands and placed it on the nearest chair. His arms closed around her, and he clamped her body tight against his. "I am not perfectly sure, but I believe that is a very beautiful painting. I will examine it further later.''

For the first time in making love to Iantha, Rob felt no need to hold himself back. Fiercely he took her mouth with his, his tongue entering her deeply in an echo of the entry that must be only moments away. With one hand still holding her to him, he tugged her shift over her head and began to fumble with the buttons of his britches. He made little headway, but could not bring himself to let her go.

And then he felt her hands dealing with the buttons.

And her gentle fingers on his straining shaft.

She had never before touched him.

Rob groaned and fell backward onto the bed, pulling her down with him. He never knew how he got the britches off. Her touch blinded him to everything but his need for her. Some part of him wanted to see her above him, as she had painted herself. But sheer, primitive, masculine need demanded that he achieve his own triumph.

He covered her with his body and joined it with hers. She lifted her hips to welcome him. Her sheath tightened around him. Over his ragged breathing he heard her moaning. She grew tighter and writhed against him, banishing all thought.

But he heard her joyous, ecstatic cry.

And followed it with his own.

They made love twice more before exhaustion claimed them, the next times more slowly and with tender murmurs. As he drifted off to sleep, replete and content, Rob knew that if he dreamed erotically again, his silver goddess would be included in that dream.

And another thought struck him.

Might he dream of both of them?

And in an instant he knew that he did not want that.

He would always want his silver goddess alone with him.

Shining, pure and perfect.

More than a week passed with no further alarms. In spite of the anxiety that never completely left her, Iantha thought that, in some ways, she had never known a happier time. Neither she nor Rob uttered the word *love,* but she could feel it growing between them. They could not be near one another without touching. They made love every night and slept in each other's arms. When Rob's business took him from her side for even a short while, she found herself listening for his footfalls. And when he stepped into a room, his eyes found hers in the next instant, and her heart leapt in her breast.

Only to plummet when she recalled her danger.

She could not ignore the fact that someone kept watch in her vicinity every minute. Burnside or Thursby, Harry or Daniel, Feller and one his lads from the stable were to be found in the corridor every time she walked through a door.

In addition to that, in spite of his bravado, John's arm continued to pain him. One day it would appear to be healing, and the next the wound would open again. He doggedly ignored it, except to allow Rogers to dress it with an herbal salve that Rob had brought from India.

"It worked well for me on several occasions," Rob assured Iantha, "including the tiger episode."

But she could not help worrying. Infection had brought more than one strong soldier low. She could not bear the thought of losing her big brother, especially when he had been injured protecting her. It hardly surprised her that her feelings went from euphoric to panicky in a moment.

Near the end of the second week neither Sam nor Vijaya had returned, but a letter arrived from London, addressed in the prince's graceful script. Gailsgill brought it to Rob as Iantha struggled to learn to read an old manuscript in the library. Rob hastily opened it.

"Thank God. I hope he has found something pertinent." He spread out the folded paper, revealing a page covered in beautiful symbols. "Hmm. He has written in Sanskrit. He must desire secrecy." Rob read silently, then looked up at Iantha. "Well, this is an interesting development." He began to translate aloud.

My dear friend—
An event of interest has occurred. Lord Alton has been murdered in his bed. Unfortunately, this incident happened not long after I arrived in London, and was perpetrated with a blade. As before, there are those who would like to lay his untimely departure at my door. I have found it expedient to become unavailable for a period. Do not be concerned. They will not find me.

On the subject of primary interest to you, I have discovered nothing about the younger Raunds—now known as Lord Alton, I suppose. However, I have stumbled onto another bit of disturbing information. My elder brother tells me that on his first trip to Demerara—some eight years ago—he encountered Lord Sebergham who, as you know, had been sent there by his father. Sebergham had so dissipated himself that he died, apparently of overconsumption of alcoholic beverages.

Of particular interest is the fact that the baron also

had an English friend, a man of low birth named
Higgans, who worked on the coffee plantation as an
overseer. My brother describes him as dark-haired
with startlingly blue eyes, not unlike the former
baron. This description appears to me to fit your
neighbor, the man you know as Carl Fraser, Baron
Sebergham, and that man does not appear to be in
London.

   I recommend that you become very cautious of
him.
Vijaya


Looking thunderstruck, Rob dropped the letter onto the
desk. "Egad! What a tale. I believe I shall make it my
business to call at Sebergham's home immediately."

"But Feller said Sebergham's butler told him that his
lordship *was* in London."

"Perhaps he has been there. If he is our man, Lord
Alton's death may be his work. I want to be sure, however, that he is not in this area now. It sounds as though
he may be in hiding."

Iantha jumped to her feet. "But you might be hurt!"
She ran to him, flung herself into his lap and clutched at
his coat. "Oh, Rob, please don't go. I couldn't bear it if
something happened to you."

The warmth of his strong arms enclosed her. "Nothing
will happen to me." His lips brushed her temple. "As I
told you, I am extremely durable. I will be careful, and
I will not go alone."

A sob escaped Iantha. She couldn't bear it. She just
couldn't!

Rob let her cry until she hiccuped to a stop. He then
tipped her chin up to look at him. "I must investigate,
Iantha. You know that I must."

Fishing in her pocket for her handkerchief, Iantha nodded. She blew her nose and wiped her eyes. "I know. Just promise me that you will take the greatest care."

"Of course. Come now, that's my strong lady." He kissed her lightly on the cheek.

Iantha did not feel very strong. "You will be *very* careful?"

"I have told you I will." Rob pulled her against his hard-muscled chest. "I must return to make love to you, my goddess."

# Chapter Nineteen

The rest of the afternoon took on a nightmarish quality for Iantha. She sat in the morning room with John, neither of them wanting to stay in the large drawing room alone. They remembered the last time they had done so all too well. With Camille dead, Iantha could not imagine anyone else in the house opening the door to assassins, but then…

She had never suspected Camille.

Iantha found herself jumping at every little sound. Visions of Rob dying at Sebergham's hand tormented her, and she could not talk herself out of them. She tried sketching in her notebook, but as before when she felt disturbed, the images she produced were gloomy and stiff. She began to draw Baron Sebergham with a knife in his heart.

John calmly read from a novel—which he assured her was not in the least of an improving nature. Grinning, he offered to read her the passages about ghosts, but Iantha was in no frame of mind for that sort of brotherly humor. And she recognized it as a cover for his own anxiety.

When Rob had been gone for almost two hours, she put her notebook aside and simply waited, pacing about and from time to time staring out the windows. It was on one of her circuits that her gaze fell on John's arm. She hurried to him and examined his sleeve. "Oh, John! You are bleeding again. It has soaked all the way through your coat."

"Drat!" John laid his book aside and peered at the blood. "That must have happened when I stretched just now. I thought it stung a bit."

"Why didn't you have Mrs. Lamonby stitch it in the first place?" Iantha frowned disapprovingly.

"Because I did not want to be stitched." He scowled back at her.

"Well, it would have gotten well sooner in the long run. You'd best go and let Rogers put a fresh bandage on it."

John examined the bloody sleeve again. "It can wait until Rob returns." A drop of blood falling to the floor put the lie to this optimistic view.

"You are bleeding on the carpet. Do go at once." Iantha tugged him to his feet by his good arm and pro- pelled him toward the door with a hand on his back.

He dug in his heels. "I am not going to leave you alone."

"I am not alone. Feller is right beside the door. We will walk upstairs with you. I want to go to my room for a while in any event. Rob will surely be back soon." Iantha offered up a silent prayer that it be true.

Hearing the argument, Feller put his head into the room, considering John with a practiced eye. "Lady Dun- can has the right of it, Major. You won't do her no good if you're weak as a cat from losing blood. We'll ring for Dan to help keep watch when we get upstairs."

Thus bullied on all sides, John capitulated, and the three of them went up, John to his bedchamber and Iantha to hers. Feller took up his post outside her door. She pulled the bell rope for Daniel and went to resume her vigil at the window.

Suddenly she heard Feller's voice. "Here now! What are *you* doing up here, mates?"

Iantha hastened to the door and opened it. She beheld two men in coal-stained clothes, their faces black. The coal men on this floor? Their only job was to deliver coal for the kitchen. As she tried to make sense of the situation, one of them lunged at Feller.

Iantha pushed the door shut and fumbled with the key. Before she could turn it, the door burst inward, throwing her back into the room. The second man followed her in, a wicked blade in one hand. A beard covered his cheeks and chin, and coal dust liberally coated his face, but Iantha knew him in an instant.

She could not mistake those piercing blue eyes.

She made a dash for the poker. Before she could reach it, the man's fingers closed in her hair, pulling her head back and jerking her up against him. The knife pressed against her throat, and a trickle of blood slid down her neck. Iantha grew still.

"Very good, my haughty lady. I see you remember your last lesson. That is excellent. It will help you learn the next, more advanced one to my satisfaction. I have just the place for a schoolroom—a secluded spot, hidden away." He nudged her with a knee in her back and started steering her toward the door with his body.

Stunned with horror for a moment, Iantha moved forward mechanically. Dear heaven! Were all of her worst nightmares to become manifest? He really was here! He really did intend to do to her what he had done before!

And more.

His threats had been horribly real. For several heartbeats fear filled her mind, leaving no chink for rational thought. Then gradually it began to clear. The situation would *not* be as before. She would not allow it. She was no longer a terrified eighteen-year-old.

She had claimed her power.

But her tormentor did not know that. He trusted too much in his own power. That would make him careless. Sooner or later he would make some small mistake.

And she would be ready.

Higgans forced her out into the hall in time to see Feller deliver a crushing right to his opponent's jaw. The man went down like a felled tree. Feller whirled to face her and her captor. He saw the knife at her throat and froze. John and his valet were racing down the hall toward them—John with a pistol in his hand—but they also came to an immediate halt.

"Very good, gentlemen," the imposter baron purred. "I see that you appreciate the situation. If you will be so good as to clear the way, I will not need to cut Lady Duncan's throat." All the men stepped back, but continued to look alert. "No, no. That will not do. All of you—into that room to my right. Close the door and toss out the key."

Her protectors hesitated, glaring defiantly at Higgans. He yanked on her hair and pressed harder on the knife. The rivulet of blood increased. Iantha winced, but did not cry out.

John snarled. "If you hurt her again, I will cut you limb from limb."

"You will be welcome to try—after I cut *her* to bits." He shifted the knife slightly. "Before you can move, I could give you her ear." He shifted again, bringing the point against her cheek. "Or take out an eye." The knife moved back to her throat. "And still kill her if you come at me. Get in the room. And take the man behind me with you.''

He turned his back to the wall, and Iantha saw Daniel creeping toward them up the main staircase. When the young man realized he had been seen he turned and bolted back down the stairs.

Higgans laughed and called after him, ''Tell Lord Duncan when he arrives that we will await him in the old castle.''

Seeing that the footman would bring reinforcements, John, Rogers and Feller reluctantly entered the room and tossed out the key. An ironlike arm closed around Iantha's waist from behind, and with a lightning swoop, Higgans scooped up the key and turned it in the lock. Iantha tried to wrench away. Before she could twist free, the knife pricked her cheek.

''Don't try that again, slut, or I will take your eye now. Or perhaps both of them. Difficult to paint with no eyes.'' He turned so that he could drag her backward down the corridor.

Iantha let him do it. She would wait for a better opportunity. Higgans seemed to believe that Rob was on his way home. Rob would come after them, she knew without a doubt. She must stand ready to help him in whatever way presented itself. She closed her eyes and reached for her control, shoving her fear into a far corner of her mind.

Higgans pulled her through the door into the old castle and locked it behind him. He towed her unwilling body up the stairs toward the battlements. At a landing halfway up the circular steps he stopped. ''This will do. He will have to come up to me. I will be able to kill him easily.'' He bent his lips to her ear and blew his breath into it. ''I want you to see that. I will use your little pistol.'' Laughing quietly, he shifted the knife to the hand with which he held her, and pressed it to her breast. "You will be silent, of course."

Iantha judged it better not to answer. She ducked her head and did her best to appear submissive.

"Ah. Already silent. Excellent. Of course, if you do not remain so, you will pay dearly for it later. I may drop you partway down as we descend the rope." Iantha tensed, and Higgans chuckled. "You did not think I would be foolish enough to attempt to go out the door, did you? They will search for us, of course, but not in the right place. I am no longer Lord Sebergham, nor even plain Tom Higgans. I have a new life—one you shall share—for a while."

At that moment the sound of the lower door opening floated up to them, followed by stealthy footsteps. "Fools," he snarled in her ear. "They should know every murmur echoes in a place like this." He pulled her small pistol from his pocket with his free hand and aimed it down the stairwell. "If you make a sound, this blade will be in your heart with your next breath."

Before she had opportunity to think, she heard familiar footfalls climbing the stairs. Rob! Iantha knew it was he. She could feel his presence. Her captor was staring intently down the stairs, the pistol steady.

This was the moment.

She grasped the hand holding the knife and pushed with all her might. Higgans's preoccupation with Rob allowed her to move it away a few inches. She screamed.

"Rob! Rob, be careful. He is here."

Rob came charging up the stairs. Iantha struck at the pistol just as the report sounded. Rob stumbled and ducked back around the curve of the stair.

Higgans grabbed her arm and flung her behind him. "You will account for that later, bitch. Never doubt it."

Rob reappeared with a pistol in his hand. Higgans, realizing his mistake, reached for Iantha to shield himself.

But she was already running.

She could not let him get his hands on her again! She turned and bolted up toward the ramparts. He pursued her, dodging around the spiral to avoid Rob's shot. It ricocheted off the stone wall, as Rob followed it.

Iantha burst through the door onto the battlements with Higgans on her heels. Rob fired again, and the false baron ducked to the side of the door, throwing out an arm in an attempt to recapture her.

She refused to let that happen.

Higgans backed toward her, his eye on Rob, who had emerged from the stairwell. Desperation put wings to Iantha's feet. She ran in the only direction open to her, around the ramparts and up the dizzying stairs to the tallest tower. From the corner of her eye, she saw the cliff falling away on both sides of the castle. Endless, empty space seemed to open around her. Iantha ignored it. Halfway up she turned to look back.

Rob and her pursuer faced one another, each in a fighting stance. Oh, God! Rob's leg was bleeding. As she watched, he tossed the empty pistol away and drew the knife from his boot. "This is better, Sebergham—or whoever you are. A blade is much more *personal,* and my quarrel with you is very personal indeed."

The false baron did not answer. He backed slowly toward Iantha's perch, his gaze never leaving his adversary. Iantha knew that he was making for her. She could see that Rob and his knife stood between Higgans and his escape rope, and John and Feller with their contingent had appeared in the doorway. Clearly his only hope of getting away was with her as a hostage.

She moved a few steps higher. Higgans inched toward her, then suddenly whirled and darted toward the stairs. Rob gave chase, and Iantha fled up to the tower. Higgans halted midway up and spun again to assess the threat. Rob put his foot on the bottom stair. Very slowly he moved up another step. And another. Very carefully. Higgans turned back to Iantha and started confidently upward.

And suddenly Iantha remembered.

Rob had no head for heights.

And he was hurt. Dear heaven! He would fall. He certainly could not fight his enemy on the stairs, yet he moved inexorably toward him, determination in every line of his body. In panic she glanced around for a weapon. Her gaze fell on several small pieces of stone, broken by frost from the old fort. Iantha seized the nearest one and drew back her arm.

Not for nothing was she the sister of three brothers. The missile flew with satisfying accuracy. It whistled by Higgans's ear, and he dropped into a deeper crouch, eyeing her warily. Rob advanced another step. So did Higgans. Iantha picked up another stone. This one clipped the stair on which her pursuer stood, and bounced down toward Rob. Higgans began to hurry, determined to reach her before Rob got to him.

Iantha grasped another chunk of stone. She could not miss this time. Control! She must call on all she possessed to steady her aim. And suddenly rage burst through both her fear and her control.

She was powerful!

Female!

Destroyer!

She launched the rock straight and true.

It struck Higgans directly in the center of the forehead. He dropped his blade and flailed his arms for balance. Iantha threw again. Her tormentor wavered, lost his footing and went over the side of the castle. His startled cry trailed away down the cliff. The sickening sound of impact drifted up to her.

She had but one thought as she ran lightly down the steps.

*Take that, damn you!*

They had again taken possession of the drawing room, and all seemed normal once more. Rob could only pray that the nightmare had truly ended. Yet an uncomfortable remembrance of the men Higgans had commanded nagged him. Were there more of them somewhere? Must he continue to look over his shoulder for the rest of their days?

At the moment, however, the only thing to which he could give his attention was the warmth of his wife's body held tightly to his side where they sat on the sofa. Since their tearful reunion on the battlements the day before, all he could think about were the jumbled words of love and relief that had passed between them, the feeling of her in his arms, and the fact that he had not lost her.

He feared the image of Higgans pursuing her up those dangerous stairs while he fought his own lightheadedness would visit his dreams for years to come. Had he had no other choice, he would have dragged the man who had dared to hurt her so badly over the precipice with him.

Thank God for his very determined stone-throwing goddess!

These thoughts were interrupted by Gailsgill bringing

the post. Rob shifted his bandaged leg to a more comfortable position and glanced at the letters.

"Hmm. This one is franked by Lord Alton. It must be a reply to the letter of condolence I wrote to Horace after his father was killed." He opened it and began to read, only to stop with an exclamation.

"What now?" John muttered irritably. They had bound his arm to his side to prevent his moving it and tearing the wound open again, and he complained bitterly about being restricted.

Rob hastily scanned the letter. "Egad! Now here is an astonishing turn of events. This is from Horace Raunds—a confession of sorts. Listen…

"Duncan—

"I find that I shall have no peace until I write to beg you—and especially Lady Duncan—for your forgiveness. Yes, I was one of the fools who allowed Sebergham to seduce me into that horrible assault on an innocent young girl. How could I ever have done that? Perhaps we never really know ourselves.

"All I can tell you is that during that time I was angry at my father, angry at our royal family, angry at the world. Sebergham made a point of gathering others like me and entertaining us with wild revels, plying us with absinthe and providing other drugs that attack the intellect—drugs he had found in South America. I can hardly remember the night of the attack on Lady Duncan.

"But Sebergham would not allow me to forget. He began to blackmail me and some of the others. I had access to secrets important to the safety of our country. He was in Bonaparte's pay, and he wanted them. I could never admit to my father what I had done, so I complied, and in so doing became not only a rapist, but a traitor. Needless to say, I soon came to despise myself, but I could see no way out of the coil.

"But now my father is dead, and I have become the lowest creature in nature. No, I did not sink to the point of patricide. Father caught me with certain documents and would have exposed us all, but Sebergham killed him in his bed. Perhaps that was a mercy to my proud father.

"Before I kill myself, I have undertaken to remove the remaining members of the ring that would bring England low. I cannot find Sebergham, but if I do while I still have breath, he will breathe no more. When you receive this, you will know who your enemy is and that I am dead by my own hand. The attached list contains the names of those threats to you that I have removed. It is all I can do for you now.

"HR"

Silence settled over the room. After several heartbeats Rob laid the letter aside and looked into the stunned faces around him. He pulled Iantha closer and spoke with a sigh.

"May God have mercy on his soul."

# *Epilogue*

*Cumberland, England, Spring of 1808*

"It is true, Mama." Iantha clasped both her mother's hands and smiled into her tearful face. "I am to have a child."

"Oh, my dear." Lady Rosley sniffed and freed a hand to search for her handkerchief. "I have prayed and prayed for this. You love children so. I could not bear it that you might never have any of your own."

"I know, Mama. A year ago neither of us would have ever thought it possible because of my…*situation*. But I am so happy now." Iantha wiped at her own eyes.

"Lord Duncan is indeed a remarkable man. Have you come to love him?"

"Oh, yes. In truth, I believe I loved him from the beginning. I was so paralyzed with fear and anger, though, that I could not let myself recognize that. I was afraid of…well, you know. But you were correct. It is very pleasurable and comforting."

Her mother gave Iantha a close look. "And he returns your love?"

"I believe that he does." Iantha nodded. "He tells me he does, and acts as though he does. He would have given his own life to save mine."

"Perhaps you will repay him with another little daughter to take the place of the one he lost."

"No." Iantha stared into the fire. "I cannot do that. No one will ever replace Laki for him—and that is as it should be. He still dreams about her, and I feel sure he always will." Iantha smiled and turned to her mother again. "But he has such a great heart. I have no doubts that whatever child I bear him, he will love it with all of that heart. And I will love it with all of mine. Never again will I let anything cause me to lock my love away. I will give it freely—to you and Papa and my brothers and sisters. To my own children."

Iantha turned and smiled as the door opened.

"And most of all to Rob."

\* \* \* \* \*

# *Author's Note*

The reader may be curious about the experience that Iantha had in Chapter Eleven in which she relived her dreadful assault. Psychotherapists would call what happened a regression or a rage reduction. It is sometimes useful in therapy for rape and other traumas to induce such a regression deliberately. But it can happen spontaneously as it did in Iantha's case.

Such an experience is, in fact, very frightening. Sometimes the person remembers the regression. Some people do not. The person often fears that they have lost their mind, but they have only experienced one of nature's most amazing opportunities to deal with the past. When they are properly comforted, they later find themselves amazingly free and able to get on with their lives. They may not recover completely as rapidly as Iantha did, because all episodes in a novel are symbolic of the story.

But they do recover.

Also, people suffering from the effects of trauma, or any other strong emotions, often do fear that if they let their feelings go, they will go crazy or harm themselves or others. It is important to protect them from that and to reassure them that they are normal.

Iantha was very fortunate to have Rob at her side, and that Rob was the man he was.

But, of course, we knew that.

# FALL IN LOVE WITH THESE HANDSOME HEROES FROM HARLEQUIN HISTORICALS

On sale September 2004

## THE PROPOSITION
### by Kate Bridges

Sergeant Major Travis Reid
Honorable Mountie of the Northwest

## WHIRLWIND WEDDING
### by Debra Cowan

Jericho Blue
Texas Ranger out for outlaws

On sale October 2004

## ONE STARRY CHRISTMAS
### by Carolyn Davidson/Carol Finch/Carolyn Banning

Three heart-stopping heroes
for your Christmas stocking!

## THE ONE MONTH MARRIAGE
### by Judith Stacy

Brandon Sayer
Businessman with a mission